Send My Roots Rain

Send My Roots Rain

Ibis Gómez-Vega

aunt lute books

SAN FRANCISCO

Copyright © 1991 by Ibis Gómez-Vega

First Edition
10-9-8-7-6-5-4-3-2-1

Aunt Lute Foundation Books
P.O. Box 410687
San Francisco, CA 94141

Cover and Text Design: Pamela Wilson Design Studio

Cover Art: *Recuerdos de México* by Alexandria Levin, San Francisco

Typesetting: Debra DeBondt

Production: Jayna Brown
            Martha Davis
            Eileen Anderson
            Lisa Kahaleole Chang Hall
            Gina Kaufer
            Kathleen Wilkinson

This is a work of fiction. In no way does it intend to represent any real person, living or dead, or any real incidents.

Printed in the U.S.A. on acid-free paper

Library of Congress Cataloging-in-Publication Data

Gómez-Vega, Ibis, 1952–
     Send my roots rain / by Ibis Gómez-Vega. — 1st ed.
          p.   cm.
     ISBN 1-879960-04-4 (trade paper : acid-free) : $9.95 —
   ISBN 1-879960-05-2 (lib. bdg. : acid-free) : $19.95
       I. Title
   PS3557.04618S46   1991
   813'.54—dc20   91-37831
                                                              CIP

ACKNOWLEDGEMENTS

Many people deserve my gratitude, but I would particularly like to thank:

Tomas Vallejos, for encouraging me to enter the aunt lute/Spinsters fiction contest and laying bets on my chances.
I'll never stop mourning you.

Roberta Frances Weldon, for your patience and generosity in reading the manuscript more often than you had time to and always finding something good to say about it.

Joan Pinkvoss, the book's editor at aunt lute, for never forgetting that the writer's voice counted when she made sensitive corrections to make the novel better, which is what we both wanted.
It made me a better writer.

June Bourgeois, for patiently sitting through the many early rewrites and encouraging the process.

Small, for the vote of confidence.

Benji and *Alley Cat*, for keeping me happy.

1

Mescalero Apaches lived here not many years ago. For all I knew some still did, but it must have been the mountains and not the desert that kept them here. From where I was on Highway 54, trying to find 180, the visual spectacle of the Guadalupe Mountains overwhelmed me. Had I been Apache I would have stayed too, and I would have fought as they had for every inch of soil under their feet. The view alone was worth the fight, worth the deaths, but the desert at the foot of these mountains was another matter. It filled me with dread. The Apaches may have called this desert home once, but I could only call it hell. It tapped within me a subconscious fear for which I had no explanation, other than the fact that it was hot and empty.

Mumbling that it would have been nice if that damned Pozo Seco place hadn't been in the desert, I rolled up my window. As I veered right into a country road that led to Pozo Seco, I had visions of snakes and other hostile creatures, including very un-desertlike lions, chasing me in flight. I considered getting out of the car to stretch my legs and breathe some fresh air, but I couldn't be sure that the brown fuzz of hair by the side of the road wasn't a tarantula, so I continued. When I turned a corner and found myself staring at a Spanish town, I screeched the VW to a halt.

"Oh shit," I said aloud. "I ended up on the wrong side of the border!"

I got out of the car reluctantly and walked towards an open space that looked like a plaza. The heat had become unbearable, so I returned to the car and drove up to the plaza where a little girl was riding her bike. Wishing I hadn't taken the turn off 180, I stepped out of the car to examine my map, which seemed to argue somehow against my being lost. I had drawn a red line over the roads to follow. As far as I could tell I had reached the end of the line, but the heat in the air made it difficult for me to concentrate.

The little girl, who seemed about seven or eight, was now staring at me. Considering the way I felt, I must have looked awful. She walked towards me with a confident smile on her face that told me she held the key to my bewilderment in the palm of her hand. An impish look of self-satisfaction that became her, like innocence, shone from her face. I was in trouble, and she was coming to rescue me.

"Hi!" she said.

"Well, hello!" I grinned back. "Where's everybody?"

"Sleeping," she told me. "Who are you?"

"I'm a painter," I said, not thinking that she may have wanted my name. "And you?"

"Zemi," she said.

"Zemi?" I repeated, trying to imitate the sounds. "That's pretty."

"I know," she answered smugly, staring at me. I realized how hungry I was and that I couldn't stand up much longer.

"How come you're not in school?" I asked, hoping to end the meeting. I had to find a restaurant and get something to eat.

"I was sick. So I couldn't go." She spoke quickly but clearly, annoyed at having to produce an explanation for a stranger.

"Oh," I said. My head was throbbing with pain, and I knew it was from hunger. "I should've stopped on the way," I mumbled. She echoed my "oh" and held the note for what seemed to me an interminable length of time. I stared at her, puzzled.

"Are you okay now?" I asked.

"Sure," she assured me, shrugging her shoulders.

"Some illnesses are like that. They hit you one second, and then they go away. Just like that," I said as I snapped my fingers. She nodded. "I've had them myself," I told her.

"You have?" she demanded, incredulously. I nodded convincingly, but the space before my eyes turned red, then green, and my body temperature rose like a whip lashing from within me.

"You don't look too good right now," she told me.

"I forgot to eat," I told her. Then I groped my way back into the car to look for a newspaper. The name of the person I was supposed to see was jotted in the margin, but by now I couldn't see very well. Drained of energy by my journey to this dry hole, I leaned back in my front seat and sipped from a warm Coke. Slowly, the red faded and ordinary colors returned. The kid was saying something, but I couldn't hear her until she leaned into the car through the open window. I thought she would be curious about the canvases, paint cans, boxes and other items piled up in the back seat, but she ignored them.

"You lost or something?" she demanded.

"Nah," I assured her.

"You look lost," she told me.

"I can't find the address I need," I told her as I showed her the paper. She watched me rumple pages as I rubbed my eyes. "I should've stopped for that burger," I mumbled again.

"What?" she shouted, almost in my ear, as she leaned into the car.

"I'm hungry," I said, "but I have to find this priest."

"Father Arroyo?" she asked, surprised.

"Yes! That's him!" I exclaimed, more excited than the information merited. "Do you know him?"

"Sure!" she said, and ran off across the plaza.

"Hey!" I screamed, panic-stricken. "Where are you going?"

"To tell my mom about you," she yelled back as she ran, and with her went my chances of finding the priest.

On the other side of the plaza was an inn, and I thought I might be able to walk there for lunch. In a haze, I took a few steps forward. I felt as if I were walking on air. A hot desert wind slapped my face with a vengeance. The sand got in my mouth and wound its way through my hair like airy snakes. I felt the heat in the air, the stifling breath of the sand, drawing the life out of me because I had dared come this far into its essence. The air turned red, and I fell.

My clothes, drenched in sweat, clung to me as if a new layer of skin were tightening in on me. Then suddenly the heat was scented, and I felt the cool touch of water on my lids. Someone was breathing beside me. I opened my eyes and the sky hung above me, off-green, closing in. The green switched to blue by a trick of the shadows that floated in and out of my field of vision, but the blue was sharp, painful. I closed my eyes to shut out the colors, but red remained. When I ventured to look again, I noticed multi-colored specks of dust flying in all directions through the vaguely purple air.

Someone came from my left and lifted my body. He was a large, faceless mass. I closed my eyes again, but the rising feeling stayed with me as I floated in his arms through space. To rise from the sand and feel the earth pull you back to its breast, that must be life. I wanted to stay down and never rise again, but the arms that drew me from the sand carried me away, with no regard for the body that yearned to cease motion and settle somewhere.

The arms laid me down, on a bed perhaps. Voices drifted in and out of my mind, and some words lingered, but I couldn't focus on them. The dream had begun, and I was falling off the edge as I always had, in a long, drawn-out fall. My body, perilously close to the mountainside as it fell, felt nothing other than the pull of the earth from the bottom. It was my way out, this fall, from the things that chased me even in my sleep. If, as I fell, I looked to the edge of the mountain, I could see them with their round faces poised, eyes focused on me. They followed me down with their eyes, I believed to make sure that I would stay where they put me, somewhere in mid-air about to hit bottom, but I never did. I lingered forever in the air, forever jumping to my death away from them. And so it was today.

Zemi ran towards the house screaming for her mother. Maria heard her even before she reached the house and met her at the door.

"Zemi, what's wrong?" she asked.

"Come quick!" Zemi yelled. "She's dead!"

"Mi hija, who's dead?"

"Hurry up! You gotta help her!"

"Where are we going?" complained Maria as she followed her daughter.

"To the plaza!" screamed Zemi, who was running in front of her mother. "She died smack in the middle of it. There! You see?" She pointed to the body lying in the sand.

"What happened to her?" asked Maria as she reached the body.

"I don't know!" Zemi said, her eyes round with fear. "She just died."

Maria felt the woman's pulse and found her heartbeat.

"No, mi hija," she told Zemi, who seemed unconvinced. "She's not dead. Why don't you run and get the Padre, and tell him to bring some water."

Zemi ran towards the house as if something very frightening were chasing her while Maria knelt beside the woman and fanned fresh air with her hands towards her face.

It's just the hot, stale air, Maria thought as she tried as best she could to revive her, yet it didn't seem to work. She undid most of the buttons on the woman's blouse. Who wears a long sleeve shirt into a desert? she wondered, annoyed, as she rolled up the sleeves. She didn't notice that Cora was watching her from the street corner as she leaned her body over the woman to keep the sun away from her face. The sight of Father Arroyo rushing towards her made her feel relieved. He carried a small pot of water and Zemi, who walked rapidly beside him, carried a mug. She had watched Father Arroyo fill the pot of water and had taken her own mug and filled it with water too.

"How is she?" the priest demanded as he took control of the situation.

"Unconscious and feverish," Maria answered. "Her pulse is weak."

She took the water brought by the priest and moistened the woman's forehead, but the woman didn't react. Zemi offered her mug to Maria, who took it and let a few drops of water fall on the woman's lips and into her mouth.

"I bet that feels good," she said to Zemi, who was now convinced that she had done the right thing. Maria hugged her to her as Zemi moved closer.

"Let's carry her in," she told the priest. He agreed.

"I wonder who she is," he said.

"A painter," Zemi informed him.

"Well!" he exclaimed, pleased. "It's about time!" He lifted her from the ground with some effort, but he was careful not to show it. Maria and Zemi walked beside him and once or twice Maria thought she saw the woman's eyes open and close.

"Take her to my room," she said when they reached the house. Worried that he might drop the body, the priest followed as he waited for Maria to remove the bedspread. Then he laid the woman on the bed.

"Now what?" asked Zemi, who was obviously shaken over the painter's fate.

"Now we try to keep her cool, I guess," her mother answered.

"The doctor is out of the question," observed the priest. "She'll be conscious by the time he gets here."

"We should call Miriam," Maria suggested, "and ask her what to do."

Father Arroyo was visibly offended. "How would she know what to do?"

"From doing it all her life," Maria answered calmly, as she wiped the woman's face. "And besides, she's all we've got. Do you know how to revive her?"

"She's only fainted," he argued. "Give her time, and she'll come back around." Then he left the room.

Stubborn as a mule, Maria said to herself.

"You want more water?" asked Zemi, eager to help her mother. Maria nodded and Zemi ran to the kitchen. She returned dragging a heavier bucket than she could carry. Maria, seeing her solicitous daughter struggling with her load, rose to meet her.

"Is this enough?" Zemi asked, trying not to show the signs of what her effort was costing her.

"Sí, mi hija. Gracias."

"You're gonna call Miriam?"

"I don't know," Maria admitted. "But I want to."

"I can go get her!" Zemi was excited.

"Let's wait a while," Maria suggested. "I'll wash her face and the back of her neck. Like Miriam does. What do you think?"

"Then you can be a curandera too," Zemi said proudly, watching her mother's hands as she wrung out the cloth.

"You think I could be that?" Maria asked, pleased to see the love her daughter had for Miriam.

"Sure!" Zemi assured her, and she asked again if she should go get Miriam.

"Let me try this first. Okay?" Zemi nodded as she shrugged her shoulders, and Maria wet the woman's forehead until the water fell on the pillow. Zemi saw the wet spots forming on the pillow case and began to wave her fan ferociously.

"Mom!" Zemi yelled. Maria was startled.

"What?"

"She's awake." The painter was opening her eyes slowly, as if she didn't want anyone to catch her in the act.

"Don't scream so loudly," Maria told Zemi.

Zemi, as always when cautioned by her mother, shrank a little. Maria saw it and drew her to her.

"She'd still be out if it hadn't been for you," she whispered in Zemi's ear.

"She's gonna be okay, right?" demanded Zemi.

"I think so," Maria assured her, and the painter turned in bed. An extended hand searched for the pillow beneath her head and hid itself there.

"She's going to sleep!" Zemi whispered loudly. Maria nodded, smiling. "Let's wake her."

"Let's not," said Maria.

"You think she's tired and that's why she passed out?"

"Could be," Maria answered.

"I get tired, but I never pass out like that."

"But you've got lots of energy," Maria told her as she tried to tickle her and keep her quiet at the same time. The she leaned over her child, who was eagerly jumping up and down to be picked up, and carried her to the living room.

"Where are we going?"

"You're going to Father Arroyo's room to borrow his pajamas."

"How come?" Zemi asked, puzzled, but not for long. "You're going to take off her clothes?"

"I have to," her mother answered her. "Hers are full of sand."

"Is she gonna get in trouble for getting sand in your bed?"

"You go get me the pajamas," Maria said.

"The ones he doesn't like?" Maria nodded, and Zemi ran into Father Arroyo's room.

On the bed, the painter had turned again. Maria removed her tennis shoes and socks and placed them neatly on the floor. She rolled the woman over, face up, and noticed the sand in her hair. She pulled out the shirt tail ends from the blue jeans. Removing the jeans embarrassed her. She felt a flash of something, some kind of emotion, rush though her body, and she had to stand back to recover and reason through her embarrassment. Was she doing something wrong? There was a soft knock and Zemi's head showed through the edge of the door. "Mom?" she said, holding up the pajamas.

"Come in, mi hija, we have to put those on."

"He didn't like giving them up," whispered Zemi, a little embarrassed at seeing the woman's body.

"But he doesn't like them," Maria complained.

"I know he said so," said Zemi. "But you know how he is."

Yes, she knew. He still didn't know how to share his things, and having Zemi point that out to her made Maria think that perhaps her daughter had grown beyond her years.

"Take them back to him, then," she said, and got up to find her own.

"But what's she going to wear?"

"She'll wear mine," Maria told her as she opened a drawer and took out her own, worn thin from use, from a drawer.

"But Mom," complained Zemi, "she's taller than you are! Those won't fit her!"

"She's not much taller," Maria argued as she slipped the painter's leg into the pants leg. "Besides," she added with a wink, "she's lying down." Zemi looked at her as if that made any difference. "Go take those back to him," Maria told her. "Tell him we don't need them after all."

"Okay," Zemi said, resigned. She didn't like seeing her mother's pajamas on somebody else.

"And remember to say thank you."

"Claro, mamá," answered Zemi.

"Thanks," Maria said, smiling. She found herself looking at the woman's breasts and then quickly buttoned the pajama top that was, as Zemi predicted, too short for her.

Standing in the kitchen, Maria wondered who the stranger lying in her bed was. Strangers came and went through Pozo Seco, but this was the first time she'd had to pick one up and bring her back to life.

"¡Oye! ¡Maria!" a voice called from the living room and startled her into attention.

"Not so loud, Cora," she called out in a loud whisper as she signaled her friend to come into the kitchen.

"He's here?" Cora demanded, disappointed.

"No," Maria said soothingly.

"What's going on, then?"

"That woman is sleeping."

"Everybody's talking about her!" exclaimed Cora.

"Already?" Maria asked, surprised. "How did they find out?"

"How do they always find out?" Cora practically screamed in her eagerness to get to the bottom of the story. "The bums at Gloria's bar saw the whole thing."

"But nobody went out to help her."

"So? What else is new? They don't help nobody but themselves," philosophized Cora, whose opinions on men and their goodness or lack of it differed sharply from Maria's. "Don't argue with me," she added before Maria could disagree.

"Okay." Maria smiled. She knew Cora was eager to get back to the story.

"So, what happened?" Cora asked in her most conspiratorial voice. Maria told Cora what had happened.

"So, you called a doctor? What's wrong with her?"

"No," said Maria, the edge of her lips curving up in disapproval.

"No...what?"

"I didn't call a doctor."

"Did you at least call Miriam?"

"Cora, you know I can't do that." Maria waved the question away. "You should know what would happen if Miriam came here, to his house."

"But this is an emergency! That woman could be dying!"

"She's not dying," Maria added calmly.

"Who died and made you doctor?" Cora demanded. She knew what to say to handle Maria. "Would you be responsible if she dies here?"

"She's not dying, I tell you!" exclaimed Maria, but she was not entirely convinced. "She was just unconscious, and now she's sleeping."

"Aha!" said Cora, with a sound that meant, "sure, she is." She cocked her head to look at her friend with that sideways look of hers that meant defiance. Then she leaned her body on the kitchen table.

"I guess I should at least call Miriam," said Maria, knowing that Cora had something up her sleeve. "You know where she is now?" she asked humbly, as a way of giving in to her friend's higher authority without having to admit it.

"Outside," Cora informed her.

"¡Jesús!" exclaimed Maria.

"No he's not, but she is, and aren't you lucky?"

"You had this planned!" accused Maria loudly as Cora headed for the door in search of Miriam.

"Be quiet!" Cora whispered. "There are sick people in this house."

"Not as sick as you're going to be," Maria said as she watched her friend step outside the house. It was just like Cora to make her do what she didn't dare do. Cora didn't understand that she depended on this housekeeping job to put food on the table for her daughter.

"So where is she?" Maria demanded, as Cora came back inside alone.

"She was out front," Cora informed her, "but now she's not. Maybe she's in the courtyard."

Cora opened the back door and walked outside. Moments later, she returned with a woman whose bent body was almost entirely hidden under a poncho.

"She's traveling escondida," explained Cora to ease the tension, for neither Miriam nor Maria felt right about her being there.

"I'm glad you came," Maria said as she embraced Miriam. She felt bony, but light, like a bag of twigs.

"It's the years," said Miriam gently, for she could read the sadness in her young friend's eyes. "They pass." Maria nodded. Although she saw Miriam almost every day, her frailness had never seemed so evident. It made Maria wonder about the time left and about how she had allowed the priest's obduracy to keep her from loving this friend openly. Her eyes clouded with tears.

"We do what we have to do," Miriam told her, as if Maria had voiced her thoughts, and as she smiled her wrinkles stretched into a wide circle around her face.

"Go see the woman before the priest gets back," urged Cora with her characteristic directness.

"Yes, let's," agreed Miriam. "He shouldn't find me here."

"I don't know what he'd do if he did," Maria said, and she led Miriam slowly out of the kitchen.

"He probably wouldn't do a thing," Cora reasoned, "but it'll let him know you've got a mind of your own."

"Coralia," Miriam said. "Only a fool would argue otherwise, and the good Padre is no fool."

Cora laughed at Miriam's remark, but Maria wondered if Miriam had learned that Father Arroyo was more dangerous than he seemed.

In Maria's bed the woman lay still, her light hair tousled on the pillow.

"She's so güera," Cora noted.

"Compared to us," Maria answered.

"She's very weak," Miriam told them, "but she's conscious."

Maria didn't answer. She wanted to explain what had happened earlier, how she had given the woman water and kept her cool with it until she gave a sign of life, but she thought that somehow Miriam knew. Nobody had to tell her much of anything. She could see it all written on their faces, or maybe she just sensed it.

Miriam was now sitting at the edge of the bed, the woman's hands in her own, rubbing them carefully as if feeling for signs of life.

"Is something wrong?" asked Maria, concerned, for Miriam was now rocking back and forth as if she were in a trance, and Cora had grown much too quiet for her comfort.

"She's very troubled," Miriam said, her eyes still closed.

"How do you mean?" Maria asked in a whisper.

"There are some things she has to find out," Miriam answered, "but you can help her with that."

"What kind of trouble can she have?"

"Coralia," Miriam admonished her, "you should listen. Troubles aren't all the same."

"I should have her troubles," Cora said, annoyed.

"Would you let her finish?" demanded Maria, and Cora withdrew into a corner against the farthest wall. The sight of her friends, overly concerned about the "güera", made her jealous.

"How can I help her?" Maria asked Miriam, aware of the full import of her words.

"Give it time," the woman said cryptically, smiling warmly at the woman whose fate she could see.

"But is she all right now?" said Cora. She had little patience for Miriam's mystic lapses.

"Of course she is! All you have to do is feed her."

"You mean," Maria said, "she's hungry." Miriam nodded as she laughed.

"Well!" exclaimed Cora, annoyed. "If she's too dumb to eat...."

"I'll feed her," Maria told Miriam.

"I know you will," Miriam answered as she rose to leave.

"¡Ay, Jesús!" complained Cora as Miriam hugged Maria.

"Don't be too harsh a judge, Coralia," said Miriam, hugging Cora to her and feeling her cringe at the show of emotion.

"You guys are always hugging," Cora complained. "Pretty soon you'll be hugging that güera."

"Miriam is my family," Maria explained, ignoring Cora's comment, "and she is right. You shouldn't judge people until you know what they've been through."

"And even then," Miriam added in agreement.

"A lot she's been through," Cora argued, thinking about the woman who was whiter than the priest and had a car of her own.

"You never know," Miriam said, as she led her out of the room with her arms wrapped around her waist.

"Thank you for coming," said Maria, who followed behind them. She would have liked to visit longer with Miriam, but it wasn't possible. Not here.

"De nada, mi hija," said Miriam, "but come over tomorrow, after she's awake."

"One of these days," said Maria, "I'll have a place of my own, and you'll be able to come whenever you want."

"That'll be the day!" exclaimed Cora, her one last jab at Maria, who never complained.

"Coralia!" Miriam chided.

"I'm just kidding her." Cora reached the door ahead of Miriam and looked out as far as she could in search of the priest. "The coast is clear," she said.

"No need to be ashamed," Miriam said to Maria. "This is his house. I understand."

"I don't," said Maria, "but when I have my own place, someday."

"I'll come," Miriam, who knew better than Maria what someday would bring, promised her.

2 I awoke at what must have been dawn. Through an open window I felt the soft blue hue of the morning light gently falling on my lids. Before me, a half-dressed woman slept in an armchair. The light behind her framed her body in colors, and my eyes teared as I tried to focus them on her.

This must be heaven, I thought, and I would've given anything to paint someone like her, under such light. Her body was strikingly real in the subdued light of this southern daybreak, and yet it seemed more like an apparition than something solid that I could paint. In a room where the light filtered through the cracks, she sat in varied shades of brown and her long, curly hair fell over her bare shoulder and robe in large waves.

"Wow!" I said, and as I shifted in bed trying to alter slightly the angle of my perspective, I knocked the bed off its slats.

As soon as the bed crashed, the house came to life. The woman before me was startled to her feet, and she opened the windows. A brown child in a long nightshirt rushed into the room. She jumped into bed with me, and as soon as she could the woman grabbed her by an ankle.

"Did you do this?" she demanded of the child in mock ferocity, a smile dancing on her face. The little girl giggled and pointed at me.

"She did!" she accused, and the woman gave me an inquiring look. I nodded apologetically, not knowing what to do.

"I was trying to get up," I said. "It just crashed." The woman laughed and waved at me not to worry.

"It happens all the time," she said, and I felt relieved. "I hope you're not hurt."

"No. I don't think so."

The kid had settled next to me on the mattress. The woman picked her up from the bed and straddled her on her hip. "I'll send your clothes with Zemi so you can dress for breakfast," she said. Then she left the room with the little girl wrapped around her. I burrowed my head in the pillow on the collapsed bed and wondered where I was and why I was there. It took me a while to remember the little girl as the one I had met earlier. I assumed that the woman who had slept in the armchair across from me was her mother.

"I must've passed out," I said aloud. I saw the child's face sneak up to the crack of the slatted door.

"Come in," I said. She hesitated. The door gave, and the light rushed in. The child walked coyly, almost reluctantly, her head tilted gracefully over her shoulders. Her right hand was playing with a lock of her hair as she approached the bed.

"Mom said I shouldn't bother you," she told me.

"You're not bothering me," I assured her.

"That's what she said, though."

"Okay," I agreed. "How did I get here?"

"You died," she explained. "But then you came back."

"How?"

"With a glass of water," she explained. "And also, we fanned you."

"Fanning always does the trick," I told her. "Thanks."

"It's okay, I guess."

"You picked me up?" I asked. She shook her long brown hair as she opened her eyes wide and grinned. With raised eyebrows, I speculated further into the matter. "Your mom?" I asked, pointing to the empty armchair. She nodded.

"Is this her bed?"

"Claro," she said, "and mine too, sometimes."

"So I broke your bed!" I cried as I stretched out to tickle her. She slipped away. "I'm sorry I broke it."

"But you didn't," she told me. "I did!"

"You?" I feigned amazement. She nodded, obviously pleased.

"When I was little," she admitted as she illustrated the story with her hands. "I was jumping up and down one day," she explained, "and it just went down. I fell on the floor and everything, and got a bump on my head. Here!" she said, pointing to her forehead. "Let me see yours."

"I didn't get a bump," I said.

"How come?"

"I wasn't jumping. I was just trying to get up when the whole thing collapsed." She laughed.

"So you want to get up now?" she asked.

"Sure," I said, and she gave me her hand. I pretended to use her strength in rising. She smiled wickedly at me, and a rush of warmth rose from the pit of my stomach into my head. I wondered if I was going to pass out again.

"Whose pajamas are these?" I asked, looking down.

"My mom's," she said, pointing to the sleeves.

"I know," I nodded. "They're kind of small."

"This one's big," she informed me as she handed me a robe. I put it on. "Whose is this one?"

"Father Arroyo's," she said.

"Hey!" I exclaimed. "That's the guy I'm supposed to see."

"I know," she said. "He's waiting for you."

"He's here now?" I asked.

"He lives here," she informed me as if I should have known. "Come on!" She took me by the hand and led me through the living room into the dining room where the green-eyed woman waited, the morning sunlight shining through the ringlet curls of her hair with such brilliance that I blinked.

"Good morning," she said. "Feeling better?"

"I'm having problems with the light."

"Should we close the windows?" a mellow voice came from behind me.

"No," I answered as the woman rose to close them. "I'll get used to it."

"It's Carol," a slender, tall man dressed in black said. "Isn't it?"

"Carole," I corrected him by saying my name in the proper three syllables as I shook his hand. "You must be Father Arroyo."

"I am," he said. "I'm the one you came to find."

"Looks like you found me first," I said.

"Actually, Zemi gets all the credit. She was the one who found you. We just brought you home."

"And she's also the one who fanned me," I added. The woman laughed.

"Zemi worked very hard to help you," she told me. "I'm her mother," she said, "Maria Soledad."

"Mucho gusto," I said. We shook hands the way I remember seeing my mother greet strangers, the ones she didn't hug. Ordinarily, I would've just said hi, but this woman shook hands.

"Are you feeling better?" she asked.

"Much better," I told her. "And I'm sorry you had to sleep in that chair because of me."

"It's all right. We were worried about you. I mean, you passed out."

"I was just drained. I drove myself hard to get to this place," I said, remembering what suddenly prompted my decision to make the trip.

"Nothing is easy," said the priest. I had been staring at Maria so intently that I had completely forgotten about him. He was saying something about how we have to try as hard as we can to get to where we want to be. I nodded agreement, but I questioned his words. What would a cloistered man know about life or the hardness of it? Had someone ever made his life a living hell for following his instincts, being who he was? Probably not, but he was staring at me as if he had read my mind. A quick, ill-conceived apology sprang to my lips, but stuck in my throat. Maybe he just didn't like my frown.

I mumbled something dumb about how true his words were and smiled at Maria. He clapped his hands as a signal to Zemi and said, "Let's eat!" Zemi ran towards him with her arms extended. He picked her up from the floor and, in one great swirling motion through the air, swung her to the table. Maria was not amused.

"Zemi," she said. "You're getting too big for that."

"I can still lift her," Father Arroyo explained.

"Until your back goes," Maria argued.

"Don't remind me," he said, laughing. I followed, amazed at the obvious familiarity that existed between them.

"Zemi said you lived here," I said as a question.

"It's his house!" piped in Zemi.

"I'm the housekeeper," Maria explained with a frown.

"We're one big happy family," he added.

"I see," I said, and decided at that very minute that I should leave. I had heard all about Spanish priests who use young women as servants. They are a pathetic breed of men who hide behind their positions in the church to impress and use women. My father, the most anti-Catholic Catholic I knew, never got tired of talking about them. His own father had told him some of those tales, and once he even let it slip that one of his aunts may have fallen for a priest and borne him a child. "What possessed those women?" he wanted to know. I didn't want to know what had possessed them, and now that I was in the middle of what seemed to be a living version of one of my father's stories, I didn't want to stay and be a party to it.

When I finished breakfast I thanked Maria.

"De nada," she said, with a wave of her hand. She was standing behind a chair, rearranging it at the table. She gave it a shove with her wide hip when the chair wouldn't move where she wanted it.

"I'll pay for the bed," I said, assuming, as I always did, responsibility for breaking what was already broken.

"That's not necessary," she said as the priest looked puzzled.

"Are you leaving?" he asked.

"But you just got here!" said Zemi, looking at me accusingly. Her newest playmate had just betrayed her.

"It's better for me if I leave," I explained.

"Not at all," said the priest. "Not with all the work you have to do."

"Work?" I asked. The damned priest was getting on my nerves. I had no work whatsoever to do, and I meant to keep it that way.

"Aren't you the painter who answered my ad in the paper?" he demanded.

"Yes," I agreed, noncommittal. Answering the ad was not a contract. It had just amounted to a long drive.

"There you have it," he announced.

"What do I have?" I said when he approached me with extended arms in what looked like what was going to be an embrace. He took me by the elbow and walked me to the back door.

"You have possibilities here," he assured me, almost conspiratorially.

"Possibilities?"

"An artist today should consider herself lucky to get a commission like this."

"Well," I said. Maybe.

"How many artists get commissioned these days to paint churches?" he demanded.

"I don't know," I admitted.

"Call your classmates," he told me. "Ask them."

"Okay."

"Not one," he informed me. "Not a single one of them could get this commission," he added. "You name any church. The walls were done centuries ago."

"I guess, but...."

"But it's the chance of a lifetime!" he exclaimed as he walked me into a courtyard where birds drank from a fountain. They flew off, in waves of colors, and perched on trees whose branches covered the yard with shade.

"But I really don't think I'm the one to do it," I insisted.

"The fact that you're here," he assured me, "makes you the right one." Then he added in his priestly voice, "You were sent to us, and we shouldn't question a higher authority."

"Higher than what?" I inquired, but I was actually thinking about his simplistic reasoning, his blind belief that things are sent and we are not to question them. My father called it "the party line." Father Arroyo's face grew solemn with the realization that I was probably not a believer.

"Higher than us, of course," he said.

"I see," I said, not willing to argue the point of His existence with someone who was obviously partial. "I can't paint church walls," I told him.

"But why else did you come?"

"I thought I could, but I've changed my mind."

"You haven't even tried," he argued.

"Look, if you saw my work, you'd be the first one to agree that I'm not the right person for painting church walls."

"Fair enough!" he exclaimed, to my surprise. I had the feeling I had said the wrong thing. "I'll look at your work," he added.

"It's in the car," I said, annoyed. The damned priest had tricked me.

"Let's get it." I could tell that he was in the mood to like whatever junk I showed him, but I decided to let my artwork speak for itself. The chance was slim that he would still offer me the job after he had looked at my work.

You're not fit to paint churches! he would scream, and I would then be sent off packing, back to where I had come from, which was just fine with me. I had only answered the ad on a whim. And now I was sorry I had. Why did I think I would be able to do the work he wanted?

"Okay," I said, and I walked back to the house. Maria had already cleared the table, but she was still there talking to Zemi. I was embarrassed to think that she and the priest could be lovers.

"So?" Zemi asked. "You're gonna stay?"

"For a while," I told her. "I have to show the priest a few things."

"Like what?" she asked.

"Like some of the paintings you saw in the back of the car."

"And then what?"

"Then, we'll see."

"Don't you like it here?" Zemi demanded.

"Zemi!" Maria said, laughing. "Leave her alone."

"I'm just curious," Zemi explained.

"Thanks for helping me," I said.

"I'll get your clothes," Maria told me as she left the room. It had not occurred to me that she must have been the one who undressed me. Not only did she save my life but she gave me a bath too. Damn! "They were full of sand," she explained as she handed me the clothes. My face was burning. I knew it had changed colors. I thanked her for what I hoped would be the last time and walked away.

She's embarrassed, thought Maria as she dried the dishes and placed them on the kitchen counter.

"What?" asked Zemi.

"Nada, mi hija," Maria answered. "I was just talking to myself."

"But what did you say? Was it about Carole?"

"Kind of," said Maria.

"Isn't she neat?" squealed Zemi, excited.

"She's nice," Maria agreed.

"Yeah!" Zemi spoke with her best proprietary tone.

"You're the one who found her," Maria added. Reliving the seriousness of her accomplishment, Zemi beamed. "But you've got to let her make up her mind about staying here."

"Why?"

"Because she's the only one who knows what's best for her. And if she doesn't want to stay, she shouldn't have to."

"But she just got here."

"I know, mi hija, but let her make up her own mind. Okay?"

"Okay," Zemi said, reluctantly. "Even if she goes away?"

"I'm afraid so. Why don't you go check on how she's doing," Maria suggested, and Zemi rushed out of the kitchen in search of Carole. Alone, Maria sat down to think about the conversation at breakfast. Something about it had disturbed her, but she had not realized until this moment what it was. In her mind, she could still see the look on Carole's face when she learned that Maria was the housekeeper.

"The nerve of that woman!" Maria exclaimed, and then she quickly looked around to see if anyone had heard. She could also hear the sound of her own voice, stating at breakfast that she was the housekeeper. Carole had blushed and looked from Maria to the priest, as if in her mind the two had become a couple, however illicit or ill-matched.

She doesn't know the first thing about me, and she's made all kinds of assumptions, Maria thought.

Through the years, she had always refused to explain herself to people. Father Arroyo did not know who Zemi's father was, and he had not asked. When he had offered her the housekeeping job, he had done it to get her out from under Miriam's influence. Miriam was the one who had taken her in when she first arrived. No one else in Pozo Seco knew very much about Maria, which is how she wanted things to remain, and now this woman thought she had learned some dirty secret.

"The nerve!" she said again.

I had arrived in Pozo Seco during Lent, which was news to me, since I never observed Catholic holidays. The priest, however, reminded me. It fit in with his notion that I had been sent to him by God. Personally I would have considered myself lucky to be in on the traditional carnival just before Lent, but by the time I arrived in Pozo Seco all good Catholics were doing penance.

My lack of observance should have made it obvious to the priest that I wasn't right for the job; still, he insisted on looking at my pictures. It annoyed me, but I pulled them from the car, making a performance out of the act, handling each canvas as if it were a sacred object.

My work was limited. Even I had to admit it. I had a collection of watercolors I had done at full speed during a particularly creative week when I had a crush on someone who didn't want me. Those studies were still-lifes, and the feelings behind them were just as still. There was nothing there.

The oil portraits of famous people were pretty interesting, and the priest stared at them the longest. He was, of course, looking for someone who could paint people on his church walls, and these were pictures of people. I couldn't tell if he noticed what my rude roommate had once called my subjects' most significant characteristic. According to her my Kennedy, King, Marilyn, Chopin, Picasso, Bette Midler, and James Dean looked stiff and bored, much like my collection of building sketches done during an "I Love New York" tour.

The towering buildings were drawn, in different hues and directions, crowding people out of the streets. The famous faces were drawn staring fixedly ahead. Neither the buildings nor the people had much life in them, which was not too terrible a thing to be said of buildings. However, the people seemed even emptier than the buildings, and nothing I could do could make them seem less so.

"Interesting," the priest commented. I could see myself packing and heading out for California.

When he picked up the last group of canvases, I had to explain that they weren't finished, but the priest liked them best. They were my feeble attempts to deal with my lions. There were lions in motion, chasing their prey or being chased, and there were lions stretched the full length of their bodies in the shade of a tree. There were lions that seemed to be smiling, looking over a cliff, and there were lions waiting, maybe to be slaughtered and hung on my father's wall.

"These are very real," the priest said.

"They're not even finished," I argued.

"Maybe," he said, as he slapped something off his neck, "but there's something there. As if you really cared about them."

"I don't," I informed him. I couldn't tell him I was drawing my nightmares on the canvas. The priest was quiet. He was still looking at the lions. "Look," I told him. "I'm not what you need. I can put the image on the canvas, but it doesn't look real." I should've told him that it didn't move the soul, which is what he needed. Nothing I could paint would lead his flock to religious contemplation.

"It looks real enough to me," the priest answered, "especially these."

"You want lions on your walls?" I demanded. He thought about it.

"There's the lion and the lamb," he suggested.

"I don't do lambs," I told him. "You need someone religious."

"Why don't you stay with us a few days and think about it," the priest said.

"But you need someone who can do people well," I argued.

"People?" he wondered aloud.

"Saints!" I explained. "Don't you want saints on your walls?"

"Yes," he agreed. "The Stations of the Cross, the Madonna and Child," he explained. "You know, the usual."

"The usual," I repeated. The priest actually wanted me for the job.

"This really is the chance of a lifetime," he reminded me.

"So you've told me," I said.

"This could be the monument where you leave your mark," he insisted.

"Men leave marks," I said. He opened his mouth as if he were about to say something, but he refrained. He stared at me instead. I had actually had this conversation once at school. Someone in class had been talking about monuments being the mark of a man's genius, and I had asked him to explain the phrase, but there was no need. He had meant exactly what he said. Men leave marks. They put up buildings, monuments, paint murals. Women admire both the buildings and the men.

"Think about it," the priest said again. I nodded.

"Okay," I said. I agreed to think. The priest, trying to get me settled as quickly as possible, took me to a restaurant, although it was too early for lunch. He told me about how small the town was and how the people had been looking forward to their church walls. I nodded and smiled a lot. I met the restaurant's owner, Gloria Peñaranda, a woman who smoked cigars and spat on the floor. She also owned the rooms upstairs, which she rented. The priest asked about one for me.

"You might as well stay," he insisted.

"Sure, sweetheart, stay," Gloria added.

"Stay," said a man slumped over his beer. A chorus of encouraging "stays" emerged from the bar. The priest pulled a handkerchief from his pocket and wiped the sweat off his brow. I had to laugh. There was no getting out of here. He would come up with an answer to whatever objection I could think of, and if I tried to sneak out of town in my loaded VW he would probably chase me and bring me back. I had visions of the man, sweat over the thin hair on his upper lip, kicking a burro into motion.

"Don't worry about them," he told me as he noticed my smile.

"It's not them I'm worried about," I said. He grinned. He knew he had me, more or less. And so it happened that, in an informal interview conducted in Señora Peñaranda's Cocinita, the only restaurant in town, I let the priest talk me into painting his walls. I had no reason not to stay, since I had no other prospect of a job and no place to go, but it also seemed somehow logical that I should end up here and here leave my mark.

"The only problem is," the priest informed me, "that you won't be painting just yet."

"What do you mean?" The man had just hired me to do a job, and now he was telling me that I wouldn't be doing it yet.

"It's the church," he told me.

"What about it?" I asked. I was beginning to worry now.

"It burned," he explained. He was suddenly looking at the ground as if he were confessing something awful. "We had to tear it down."

"What!"

"The foundation is still there," he said, eager to dispel any uncertainty. Señora Peñaranda laughed loudly from a corner of the room.

"She obviously knows something I don't know," I told the priest.

"There's nothing to know," he said. "There was a fire, and the church burned down."

"Why didn't you rebuild?"

"I could have, but I wanted to wait for something special so we could build to specifications."

"You couldn't get anybody to do it for you."

"If that's what you want to think," he said.

"Hey, Padre!" yelled Gloria Peñaranda from the opposite side of the room. She was a tall, large woman who seemed to move about in a cloud of smoke. "Is that the girl you found?" The priest acknowledged her question with a nod and a smile, but he didn't answer.

"By now," he explained, "everyone's heard about you."

"That's what I love about a small town," I said sarcastically.

"It's like a big family," he said, missing my point. He suggested that we take a look at the site.

He led me out of the restaurant through a side door, and I immediately discerned the rubble that must have once been the church. He noticed my reaction, and his eyebrows shot up in concern. Then he told me about the Catholic Church and what it meant to him, what it did for the people in a place like Pozo Seco. I told him that I was less than impressed with the position of women in his church.

"This won't be easy," he said as he shook his head and stared at the ground.

"Are you from here?" I asked.

"No," he answered. "Priests are seldom sent home."

"How long have you been here?" I asked.

"Seven years," he said.

"And you haven't had a church in all those years?"

"I had one at first," he said, cautiously, "but then I lost it."

"How long ago?"

"About five years," he said. But he said no more about the burning. Since then, he told me, he had preached in the open square and anywhere he could find a group of the faithful, but he wanted more than anything to have his church back.

"The church gives the community a core," he told me, "a center of unity." I yawned. He must have interpreted my yawn as lack of interest, for he looked fixedly at the ground before him and grew silent. Eventually, he added, "It is important for the community to be united."

He searched through the rubble as if he were in fact looking for something. "There are forces in this town, as in most towns, that seek to divide. The church is the one place where those forces have no power, where people can be united."

As long as you buy the party line, I thought. If he found out about me he'd be the first to run me out of his community. But instead of arguing I simply nodded absentmindedly.

"I must be crazier than I thought," I said, and Father Arroyo examined me carefully, trying to figure out what connection my words had with his own. "How in the world am I supposed to help you with this?" I added.

"Don't worry about the work. When the people find out you're here, they will come. We'll have plenty of help."

"We'd better have," I said, tartly, annoyed at letting him talk me into staying, at listening to his nonsense about leaving a mark. How do you leave a mark when you can't even begin to do the work? Did he expect God to help? "We'll need a hand from the devil himself if we're going to pull this off."

His face grew solemn. I watched him balance himself from one foot to the other as his hands dug deeper, fisted, into his pockets. He said nothing. He gazed, lost in thought, from the rubble on the ground to a house that was barely visible in the afternoon haze far away in the desert. I took his measure and braced myself for whatever it was I had gotten myself into.

When Father Arroyo got home that day, Maria went out to greet him.

"Did she take the job?" she asked, excited.

"I'm not sure. I think she did."

"What do you mean, 'you think'?"

"She's not happy about it," he said, rehashing in his head his conversation with Carole. He could still hear the woman questioning God's will. "And I'm not either."

"Why? What happened?"

"She's scared of the work, and she's not a believer."

"But that doesn't mean she won't do it," Maria countered. "Does it?"

"It doesn't mean she will, either," he snapped as he walked by her into the house. He looked defeated, very much the same way he looked when he had to deal with Miriam.

"No," Maria agreed as an afterthought and left him to himself. She wanted to ask about the woman, but she knew that the priest was in no mood for questions.

He probably had a theological argument with her already, she thought, and it pleased her to think that Carole could stand her ground in an argument with Father Arroyo.

"She has no religion?" she asked as the priest walked across the room into the kitchen.

"That's what it looks like," he replied. "She's one of those feminists with an ax to grind, but no knowledge whatsoever of what she's talking about. I don't think she even knows about the Stations of the Cross."

"Maybe she's not a Catholic."

"And maybe I'd better forget the whole thing."

"And who would build the church?" she asked. He didn't answer. Since the church had burned down, he'd not been able to rally the community behind him in the rebuilding effort. His connection to Luz and her death in the fire had created a fear, an almost palpable fear. No one ever mentioned it, but its influence had kept the people from rebuilding the church when Father Arroyo asked them time and time again. They had come to believe that only an outsider, someone ignorant of the event, could lead them through the task.

It's just your bad luck that it should be a woman, Maria thought, and a Godless feminist to boot!

"Did you say something?" Father Arroyo asked.

"No," Maria said, startled. "I mean, yes. Who's going to build the church if she goes away?"

"Maybe I will," he answered. "It's my church."

Wishing she could show him the arrogance of his words, Maria nodded and left the room. She had never argued with him about religion or anything else. He would have reminded her that it was not her place to tell him what to think about the scriptures, and her efforts would have been wasted because he did not believe he had anything to learn from ordinary people like her.

In the kitchen, she started a pot of coffee. She knew Father Arroyo would retire to his room to work on Sunday's sermon, and she wanted to be ready with his coffee before he called for it. More than anything, she wanted to think. She wondered what the conversation between the priest and Carole had been about, and she wondered why she cared.

She intrigues me, she admitted to herself, and I haven't been intrigued in a long time.

"Damn!" she exclaimed as the coffee she was pouring spilled.

"What are you cursing about?" asked Cora from behind her.

"Damn it, Cora! You startled me."

"So who startled you the first time?" Cora demanded, "because you were cursing when I came in, sweetie."

"I spilled coffee," Maria explained, vexed by her friend's appearance at a time when she wanted to think, not talk.

"He's here?" Cora asked.

"In his room," Maria answered. "Let me take him some coffee, and he'll leave us alone."

Cora served herself a cup as Maria left the room. She wished she had noticed the priest's presence before coming in the house, but she didn't want to leave.

There'd be a scene, she thought, and she shook her head in dismay over Maria's lot. Why doesn't she just get a real job?

"Well, that's done," Maria said as she reentered the kitchen. "He's busy writing," she explained, "so I'm sure he won't bother us."

"Good," said Cora, who had risen to serve Maria a cup of coffee. "You know where I'm coming from?"

"No, but you're going to tell me. Right?"

"Gloria's bar," Cora informed her, mysteriously.

"At this hour?"

"Get over it! You're such a prude."

"Ah, yes."

"Don't you get it?" Cora asked as she rearranged her position on the chair and sat staring out the window into the patio. Maria looked puzzled. "I saw the whole thing."

"What whole thing? Would you get to the point?" she demanded. "I still have to drop by Miriam's before dinner."

"This is gratitude," complained Cora. She had always resented, and always managed to forget that Maria, unlike her, had work to do and that,

when she visited her friend in the middle of the day, she would actually be
disturbing her.

"I'm sorry," said Maria, although she wasn't. She looked at Cora seriously in an attempt to get to the point. She lifted the bulk of her hair and
pinned it into a bun.

"Buns make you look old."

"I am old," Maria argued, "and I'm getting older by the second waiting
for you to say something."

"The güera took the job," Cora beamed conspiratorially. "I saw the
whole thing."

"At the bar?" Maria asked.

"What's the big deal?"

"Arroyo wouldn't go to that place!"

"Oh, that's right. He's holier than..."

"He's a priest, Cora."

"He was at the restaurant. Okay. I was at the bar."

"Oh."

"You'd think we were talking about God!"

"He doesn't go to bars," Maria explained.

"He doesn't know what he's missing," Cora told her. "I've always
thought that guy was too good to be true."

"Anyway," Maria said. "He told me already."

"Did he tell you she was staying at the inn?" Cora asked. Maria shook
her head. "She's got the room next to mine."

"She'll never sleep again," Maria joked.

"You're going to pay for that, Maria Soledad. I know a few things about
you."

"Go ahead," Maria urged her. "Tell! I want a reputation."

"Yeah? The good Padre would put you 'de patitas en la calle'." *With your
feet out on the street.*

"And who would cook for him?"

"¡Pues, la güera!" Cora exclaimed, laughing.

"The good Padre is really worried about Carole," Maria confided. "That's
her name."

"Why?" Cora asked.

"She's not religious," Maria said.

"¡Ay! He's got himself some trouble there!"

"That's the way he sees it."

"But she don't need no religion," Cora asserted. "She's a white girl with
an education and a car."

"What are you saying?"

"Religion's for people who don't have nothing else," Cora explained.

"And tell me, Karl," Maria said, "how did you reach that conclusion?"

"What did you call me?"

"I called you Karl," Maria answered, "because you're sounding more and more like a Marxist every day."

"So is that good or bad?"

"If you knew how to read," Maria added, "you could decide for yourself."

"Thank you, maestra," Cora replied. "How come no matter what I talk about, you always bring up that I'm ignorant?"

"You're not ignorant," Maria said. She knew how sensitive Cora was about her lack of education, but she was now determined to do anything, even embarrass her into learning to read.

"I just don't know a whole hell of a lot," Cora admitted.

"You know more than you think," Maria told her, "but you have to learn to read if you want to know more."

"I'm too old for that," Cora said, and Maria stopped arguing. She knew how it would end. Instead she changed the subject.

"Father Arroyo is worried because she's not religious and she's probably too radical for him."

"How do you mean?" Cora asked, trying not to sound interested.

"She's a feminist," Maria answered, "and he's not too impressed with that."

Cora wondered what a feminist was, but she didn't dare ask. However, if the priest didn't like feminists, they couldn't be all that bad. Maybe she was one and she didn't even know it. She might have to revise her opinion of that woman after all.

"Don't feminists burn their bras?" Cora asked abruptly.

Maria laughed.

"Sometime I'll read you something my mother wrote about being a feminist."

"Was your mother a feminist?"

"Yes," Maria answered and pushed her friend out of the house into the patio. "Get out of here." Cora left wondering what it would be like to have a feminist mother and know about that Karl guy.

"We're leaving now?" Zemi asked for the third time.

"Yes," Maria answered. "Get the bike."

Before Maria had finished speaking, Zemi was riding her bicycle out of the house through the back door. She rode ahead of her mother as fast as she could, but she turned and rode back again before she got too far. They traveled everywhere like that, Zemi riding in looping circles and Maria walking, but no place was as important to them as Miriam's house was. Zemi liked the way Miriam allowed her the run of the house, and she looked forward to the cookies Miriam would give her. Her mother always complained about her appetite, but Miriam said something about "comer por haber comido," which made no sense at all.

"Watch out!" Maria warned her. "Here comes Celia's dog." Zemi slowed her bicycle to a halt and got off to walk beside Maria. The dog barked at the bicycle and sniffed the air near the girl.

"What does 'comer por haber comido' mean?" Zemi asked her mother.

"It just means 'to eat is to have eaten'," Maria explained. "I always tell you not to eat the cookies so you won't spoil your appetite. Miriam thinks it doesn't make any difference, but she doesn't realize that cookies are not the same as green beans."

"They taste better," Zemi argued.

"But they don't do as much for your health," Maria explained.

"How come Celia's dog doesn't like me?" Zemi wondered.

"You're bigger than he is, and so is your bike. He's probably scared of you."

"But I like him."

"Maybe you should save one of Miriam's cookies and bring it to him," Maria suggested.

"Dogs eat cookies?" Zemi asked.

"This one might," Maria answered. "He looks pretty hungry."

Tired of barking, the dog turned around in a circle three times and sat against a wall. Zemi, realizing that it was safe to ride again, got back on her bike. She rode ahead of Maria as fast as she could and turned back again. Maria watched her. It used to be that Zemi worried about these trips. She knew that she couldn't tell anyone about visiting Miriam's house. Her mother had warned her to keep it a secret because of Father Arroyo. Zemi couldn't understand how he felt, since Miriam was so nice to everyone, but she understood that it made her mother cry to argue with the Padre about Miriam.

The first time she saw her mother in tears was after Father Arroyo called Miriam a "bruja." Her mother had stopped arguing then, walked into her room, and sat down to cry. Zemi curled up in her arms and watched the tears roll down her mother's cheeks. She hadn't known what to say, but it worried her that her mother would listen to the priest and stop visiting Miriam.

Miriam was not a bruja. Everybody knew that brujas were ugly and mean, and Miriam wasn't those things. Zemi had plenty of story books with brujas in them, which is how come she knew. She had explained the difference between Miriam and the brujas to her mother, and she had shown her the pictures. It made her mother stop crying. The problem was that Father Arroyo had a lot of books too, but he couldn't tell the difference between a real bruja and someone like Miriam who just happened to have strange-looking hair. Zemi told her mother how Miriam's hair was why the priest called her a bruja, so Zemi gave Miriam a hair brush on her birthday.

She also gave the priest one of her favorite books. It had a bruja in it who gave a poisoned apple to a girl. Miriam would never do that, and Zemi thought it would help him decide once and for all that Miriam wasn't a bruja.

But Miriam didn't use the brush to brush her hair. She used it on Rafi, her cat, instead. It didn't help because his hair stood on end just like Miriam's. And Father Arroyo never said anything about reading the book. He and Maria hardly ever mentioned Miriam. What happened since then was that the visits became a big secret that nobody mentioned but everybody knew about. There was no way to hide going to Miriam's house. It stood all by itself in the desert, and everybody who saw them walking knew where they were going.

Today's visit to Miriam's was unscheduled, in the middle of the day. Zemi thought that, perhaps, if Miriam wasn't expecting her, there would be no cookies for her, but a glance back at her mother told her that today cookies weren't important. Her mother was thinking about something serious, and she walked as fast as she could to get to Miriam's quickly. She had that same look she had when she was angry. It made Zemi wonder if something was wrong.

The room over Gloria Peñaranda's Cocinita was so large that my claustrophobia hardly noticed it was only one room. It also had enough windows to satisfy my craving for light. From side to side across three walls, the world outside was projected through my windows, and the light filtered through so seductively that I found myself taken from the start by the space, the windows, and the light.

I took the room and immediately began a love affair with the view. From the western window, a rather quaint and safe desert landscape spread itself before me. From both the eastern and southern windows, the sleepy town and its inhabitants composed my canvas. The priest's house, particularly, stood out among the others because the flowers in the garden added life to the colorless surroundings.

The window sills in my room were also part of the charm. They were wide and comforting, like the ones my mother used to tell me about. She used to tell me that in Spain, when she was young, the best part of her day was spent sitting by her window. She would watch the people go by and talk to the ones she knew, and the young men who admired her used to leave flowers and notes tied to the bars where they knew she would find them. It made her happy, she told me, to sit by her window because in the old days in Spain, young women weren't allowed out of their houses unescorted by a chaperone.

At the mention of the chaperone, I and any one of my brothers or sisters who were listening would laugh and carry on about mother's upbringing. She would laugh too, and we would consider ourselves lucky that mother didn't raise us the way that she had been raised. Our mother trusted us to do the right thing at all times, even when we had no adult supervision, and I for one tried to live up to her trust. She claimed that she had raised us the way she had because in America she had to work too hard to keep track of her children, but I knew the real reason. When mother left Spain behind she was also leaving the stifling role of the Spanish woman and the rules that bound her. She came to America not just to work but to be free.

I sat on my window sill and stared out. It made me feel connected to her spirit in some way, as if she were behind me, her hand on my shoulder as she used to be when she talked to me. At this very moment I watched as Zemi, ahead of her mother, rode her little bike in a great big hurry towards the solitary house that stood out in the desert. Mother would have created some kind of story about them. That's what she was like. One could hardly tell with her where reality ended and fantasy began. I however was simply content to watch, uninvolved, as people went about their lives.

My eyes filled with tears and I whispered, "Rest in peace, mama." Wishing that I could pray for her as I had at her funeral, I looked for a candle and made a mental note to unpack that box first.

"Spirits need light," she used to say, as she lit candles for the dead whom she had loved and for victims of the same war that she had barely escaped. Since her death, my sisters and I kept candles burning for her. We wanted her to be in a good place, so we sent with our offering whatever light we could give her. The fact of the matter, though, was that she had been our light, and not having her with us left us in darkness.

"¡La puta de tu madre!" *Your mother, the whore,* an angry voice yelled and a door slammed. It made me snap back to reality. The screaming woman was probably the one who lived at the other end of the hall with a man and several children. When I came up the stairs carrying boxes, I'd seen the half-dressed kids hanging on to her dress as she yelled at another one trailing behind her. She nodded hello when she saw me, without missing a beat amidst the harangue. I thought then they were too far away to be heard. Wrong.

The woman in the room next to mine was the one who worried me. When I walked by her door, I heard a lot of moaning and groaning.

"It's 3:15!" I said to the señora who showed me to the room.

"So what?" she answered.

"I need a quiet place to live," I told her.

"But this is the only inn," she informed me, a wide grin breaking on her lips.

"I see," I said.

"You'll take it?" she demanded. I nodded. She left me to myself with the woman's noises.

The señora herself lived directly across the hall from me, at the other end of the house. Her room must have had windows like mine, but I couldn't imagine her looking out of them, admiring the desert. I could not picture her anywhere but here, renting rooms to strangers and running the cocina with an ill-tempered cook.

Zemi jumped up, and the old woman caught her and held her sideways, under her arm, like a loaf of bread. Maria tried to keep Miriam from exerting herself and Zemi from asking for more.

"You'll hurt yourself," Maria said, but Miriam ignored her, laughing that throaty laugh of hers, and bent to lift the child again.

"Zemi! You're too big for her."

"¡Ay, mamá!" Zemi loved the woman whose hair smelled like smoke from a fire, and she loved the attention that she got from her.

"That's enough!" said Maria, this time seriously, and Zemi knew to stay on the ground.

"You got cookies?" she asked of Miriam.

"What do you think?" Miriam countered. Zemi ran to where she knew the cookies would be. When she returned with her hands full of cookies, Maria gave her a glass of milk and sent her outside to play. Rafi, Miriam's cat, followed her.

"Don't give Rafi any milk," Miriam said. Maria helped Zemi to settle outside before she went back in.

"I know why you came," Miriam told her.

"I'm glad one of us does. I just knew I had to come."

"What's worrying you? That woman at your house?"

"She's not there anymore," Maria told her. "She's at the inn."

"Yes," Miriam nodded. "She would be."

Maria poured herself a glass of juice and offered another one to Miriam. "So you came to pour juice?" Miriam asked, accepting the glass.

"No," Maria sighed and looked out the window to check on Zemi.

"She's not going anywhere," Miriam told her. She patted a spot on the sofa and waited for Maria to sit down. Dejected, Maria sat beside her.

"What's wrong?"

"I don't know," Maria answered. She meant it.

"Is it the woman?" Maria nodded.

"All I did was wash her and dress her and feed her. Things anyone would do."

"And what of that?"

"Nothing!" Maria exclaimed. "I shouldn't have come."

"Nothing could mean anything," Miriam said, philosophically.

"It means," Maria explained, "I think she got the wrong idea." Miriam listened but made no comment. "About what I do there."

"¿Cree que eres su amante?" *She thinks you're his mistress?*

"I think so," Maria admitted, reluctantly. "But I don't know. At first I thought I had offended her because I washed her clothes."

"And did you?"

"I don't know," Maria answered. She was losing her patience. "She gave me this look."

"But you can't read her looks yet," Miriam warned.

"But I can see," Maria argued.

"And what did you see?" Miriam asked. "You have to know people pretty well before the looks they give you make sense."

"That's not always true," Maria insisted. "I was pretty sure about that look, I know it meant disapproval."

"Why didn't you ask her to explain?"

"You think she'd tell me?"

"Maybe," Miriam said, smiling. Maria's brow wrinkled in a frown.

"I don't think I want to know."

"Well, that's different."

Maria got up to check on Zemi. The child had Rafi sitting in the basket and was giving him a bike ride.

"Rafi's going for a ride," she said. It made her forget what had been on her mind, the thought of Carole's naked body in her bed. A woman's naked body, however, had never disturbed her before, and it worried her that this one had.

"She came for the church, didn't she?" asked Miriam, amused by the consternation in Maria's eyes.

"Yes!" Maria answered, a little too eagerly. "To paint it."

"Then he's going to build it up again."

"I think so."

"He's talked about it for long enough."

"He's serious about it this time."

"Then I suppose," Miriam said softly, "someone should write to her." Of course, Maria thought, Miriam would think of Maria. Miriam examined her as if she had said something wrong.

"I'll write to her," Maria told her. Thinking of their severed friendship, her eyes filled with tears. "What should I say?"

"Tell her the truth," Miriam whispered roughly, for her voice was not meant for whispering. "And tell her to come. It's time for her to come and put this thing to rest."

"Okay," Maria said, "but I'll do it in your name."

Miriam seemed hurt.

"She won't listen to me," Maria argued. "You know she won't. She's been jealous of me for years."

"What are you talking about!"

"You know perfectly well what I'm talking about," Maria insisted. "One of the reasons why I took the job at Arroyo's house was Maria."

"That can't be."

"But it is. She was jealous of me from the day you picked me up until the day she left, and she probably still is."

"Jealous of what?" Miriam demanded.

"Of your love for me."

"But you're like a daughter."

"I told her that," Maria said, "but you should have been the one to tell her. That's why, this time, when I write the letter, I'll write it in your name." Miriam nodded agreement. "This kind of request should come from you. She's your friend."

"And yours too," Miriam insisted.

"I know it, and nothing will ever change that."

"Looks like something has."

"It hasn't, but she was your friend long before I knew her. It should come from you, this letter."

"It should. Write to her in my name. Write it nice for me."

"I will," said Maria, aware that Miriam's mind was now crowded with memories of her friend, and her own problem worried her no longer.

"Take your daughter home," Miriam told her in her most serious mock-scolding tone as she took Maria's hand.

"Stop reading my palm. You should sit down every once in a while and read your own."

"Stop worrying about things," Miriam told her. "And what's that cat doing on that bicycle?" she exclaimed when she saw Zemi riding Rafi around.

"It's a brave new world out there. You have to take the cat by the tail."

"What in the world does that mean?" Miriam laughed as Maria grabbed Rafi and deposited him on the porch. She would have laughed harder if she thought Maria hadn't been trying to tell her something.

"Well, Rafi," she said as Zemi and Maria left, "it's your tail."

I slept for most of the day after unloading my car and dumping my things on the floor. I didn't want to face having to put my life in order all over again. I thought I'd be done with that by this stage of my life, and it always depressed me to find out I wasn't. Unpacking my things would bring the truth closer to home, so I threw them on the floor and left them where they fell. And I would've left them in the car if I hadn't been afraid that one of the local characters would steal some piece of my life from me.

A look at my watch told me it was time to go downstairs for dinner. The restaurant had its hours, and you couldn't get a thing after it closed, or at least that was what Gloria Peñaranda said when I took the room. Keeping that in mind, I took a shower, dressed, and went down to find a table reasonably far away from the crowd at the Cocina. When I walked in, Señora Peñaranda was at the bar, smoking a cigar and mumbling to herself because she had to leave it behind to wait on tables. That I chose the farthest table in the room did not ingratiate me to my hostess, who aimed a sizable body towards the spot where I was sitting and came wafting through the smoke to take my order.

"You like this table?" she said tartly, the scent of her body a mixture of cologne, sweat, and cigar smoke.

"Actually, I do," I said, trying not to breathe while making sure I conveyed that I wasn't about to move.

"What's your pleasure?" she asked.

"The specialty, I guess," I said, not knowing what it was. I just wanted to send off the smell of her.

"Hm!" she exhaled. I surreptitiously covered my nose. Then she turned around and yelled, "¡Un especial!" and walked back to her cigar. Her posterior was huge, the largest I had ever seen, and her legs rustled as she walked on stiletto high heels. How did she keep her balance? I could hardly walk in flats, and I had nothing to carry back there.

The men at the bar whispered something to her and nodded in my direction as soon as she sat down. She was explaining something when a woman in the kitchen stuck her head out the door.

"Pá quién es el especial?" *Who's the special for?*

"Pues pá la güera," *For the white woman*, Señora Peñaranda informed her with a nod in my direction. The woman took a furtive look at me and slipped back into the kitchen. The men at the bar laughed. I wondered if I should have ordered something else.

At the bar, Gloria Peñaranda assumed her position again. Perched on a stool, she listened to a man who drank and spoke at intervals. After a while, a look of calculated disdain appeared on her face, but it had no effect on the confessant. He continued to talk, even as she rose to carry my dinner to my table. I was grateful in a way to hear him talking, for it kept her from sitting at my table while I ate. I was still too moved by memories of my mother, and I wanted to be alone.

I went to visit Maria after dinner. The flowers in her garden made me feel homesick, and I wanted to smell them. When I arrived, she was cooking dinner so I stood around watching and handed her plates and things. We talked about poetry and gardening, and I had a lot of fun dodging as she whirled about in her kitchen getting dinner ready, but Zemi insisted that we play hide and seek.

"You go hide," I told her, for although I liked the child, I didn't feel like playing. The intricacies of the game had returned quickly enough to my wicked mind. While Zemi hid, I slipped back into the kitchen to hide with Maria and left the poor child wondering why a grown woman of twenty and some years couldn't find a little girl hiding almost in plain view. She figured out before too long that there was something wrong with our game and, after a long wait, gave up.

"What are you doing here?" she demanded, her hands on her little hips, accentuating her annoyance.

"I'm too tired to play," I claimed. She frowned. "Don't forget. You had to pick me up off the street just yesterday."

"You're still tired!" she exclaimed. I nodded.

"Why don't you sit with us?" Maria suggested. "Carole was telling me about her mother's garden."

"Yours reminds me of it," I told Zemi, who wasn't interested.

"I wanna play," Zemi said and looked accusingly at me.

"We can play later," Maria assured her as she smoothed out the child's hair. She had become more ill at ease since she sat down at the table with me. I didn't know what to make of her discomfort, but I also could find no polite way to leave. I guessed she'd figured out I was gay. Some straight women sense it. And here I thought I was behaving rather well.

"I saw you walking towards the desert today," I told her.

"You did?" Her eyes opened wide, she looked alarmed. I nodded.

"My room is the one in the corner. It's got three walls of windows. One of them faces the desert."

Maria rose to stir something in a pot and exploded into a flurry of activity.

"Did you visit that house way out there?"

She stopped. "Yes," she answered, looking at Zemi, who was staring at her mother with her mouth hanging open.

"Mom!"

"Who lives out there? Your family?"

"More or less. That's Miriam's house."

"Miriam?"

"You're not supposed to tell," Zemi reminded her.

"It's okay, mi hija."

"Is she the lady who wears a poncho?"

"Yes, that's the one." Maria's voice was a bit too intense. "You know her?"

"Oh, I don't, but she walked by while I was talking to Father Arroyo today, and he said something about her. I didn't understand it, though."

"What did he say?"

"He just mentioned her name and said 'solavaya' or something like that when she passed by. You know what it means?"

"It's superstition. It means 'go alone'."

"Oh! That's right! Sola vaya." The words, separated, had acquired meaning.

"It's what people used to say when they thought they'd seen a witch," she explained.

"Or a Jew," I added.

"Right. It's an extremely sophisticated way for the pious to protect themselves from evil."

"You sound like my mother. She was a Spanish Jew, and words like 'sola vaya' infuriated her. She used to tell me all kinds of stories about being a Jew in Spain."

"I'm sure it wasn't pleasant. Where is she now?"

"Gone." I shouldn't have brought up the subject. Talking about her could make me cry, and I didn't want to cry now.

"I'm sorry," Maria said.

"Why does Father Arroyo say 'sola vaya' when Miriam walks by him?"

"She's different, and much too uncontrollable for him."

"Good reasons for a woman to burn at the stake in the Middle Ages."

"They still are. Anyway, that's her home out there. She says 'in the desert, people are free like lions'."

"You mean there are lions out there?" I asked.

"No," Maria laughed. "Not in a desert. That's a line she learned from a poem I used to read her."

"Are you afraid of lions?" Zemi asked. She had been listening quietly to our conversation and watching my every move.

"I sure am," I told her. "Aren't you?"

"I'm not afraid of anything."

"Lucky you. I wouldn't want to run into a lion for anything in the world."

"I'm afraid of lions," Maria said to Zemi, "and I wish a certain person here wouldn't go into that desert looking for any."

"She won't," Zemi pouted.

"I won't either," I added, to make her feel better. She gave me a smile that told me we were still friends.

"Nobody who has any sense will," said Maria. And she meant it. Zemi's face flashed a combination smile and raised eyebrow expression that I had already seen on Maria. I smiled back.

"Well, I guess I should leave," I said.

Maria seemed disappointed. "Aren't you staying for dinner?"

"No, I'm sorry. I ate at La Cocinita."

"Why?" Zemi yelled as though this were another form of not playing with her.

"I was hungry," I told her. "And that's also where I live now, so I'm supposed to eat there."

"You can eat here. Mom'll let you."

"You can," Maria assured me. "In fact, I was sort of expecting you."

"Ask me for some other time," I said, and now I was consciously flirting, openly staring at the woman, admiring her curly long hair and her almond-shaped green eyes.

"Ojos brujos," I whispered, and I felt the heat rising, making my face turn red. She heard me.

"Did your mother tell you stories about green-eyed women?"

"No," I lied. She had. They're supposed to be the product of a mixed union.

"It's too bad," she said.

"All the witches have green eyes," Zemi said.

"You're making that up," I said.

"I'm not." She was following me to the door and occasionally trying to trip me.

"Zemi," Maria warned. The kid and I were giggling on our way to the door because I couldn't hold her back far enough to get away from her agile legs as they got in my way.

"Let me go, legs! I still have to unpack."

"No, you don't!"

"Yes, I do. I took everything out of the car and dropped it on the floor. It's still there."

"Really?"

"It's a mess."

"I'll help you. Can I, Mom?"

"Help me what?"

"Unpack," Zemi explained. "Can I, mom?"

"After dinner," Maria told her. She looked at me. "If it's all right with you?"

"It'll be a big help," I said, hoping that Maria would come over with her daughter.

"Awright!" Zemi yelled. The kid got happy about the simplest things.

"See you later," I told her and left her leaning against Maria, who stood there grinning, holding Zemi's face with both hands.

What had really been on my mind tonight at Maria Soledad's place was the nature of her relationship with the priest. She didn't look as if she were anyone's mistress, but the full gist of my father's words had never stayed with me. He was a man who believed that priests were no better than most ordinary men. He was, in fact, given to assuring people that priests, because they believed themselves to be so damned holy, were actually worse than your average sinner.

There was a logic to what my father said about priests. Why would anyone think that he could be God's instrument on earth? It seemed presumptuous to me then, and it did more so now. Father Arroyo couldn't deny that he lived under the same roof with a woman whose child seemed to have no father. I couldn't help but think that my father, in his own crude way, wasn't far from the truth in his evaluation of the priests, but thinking evil of Father Arroyo meant thinking evil of Maria, which didn't seem right.

A knock on the door called me back to the present.

"Hi!" said Zemi. "I came!"

"Hey!" I said, and looked beyond her in search of Maria. "Where's your mom?"

"Home," she said curtly, as if it were understood.

"Oh." I tried to hide my disappointment.

"You want me to leave?"

"No!" I exclaimed, but I did.

"I just came to help you."

"Well, I'm glad." I closed the door behind her.

"Wow!" she said, "what a mess!"

"I told you."

"If my mother sees this..."

"She doesn't like mess?" I inquired innocently.

"She hates it!"

"Well, I'm glad she didn't come then." Zemi laughed.

I put her to work on organizing my dresser. I did the hard work. I hung pictures up on my one wall, put away or destroyed the empty boxes, organized my clothes in the closet, and asked difficult questions.

"Where do you come from, you and your mom?"

"Brazil, I think. You know where that is?"

"Sure, I have a map."

"Me too," she said. "My mom's from there, but I don't think I am."

"Where do you think you're from?"

"Here, I guess," she answered, unconcerned. "What about you?"

"I'm from up north."

"What's that?"

"You know, New York." She seemed unconvinced. "Isn't New York on your map?"

"Yeah. But you speak Spanish."

"Some of us do, you know," I said. "Besides, my mom was from Spain, remember."

"So that's how come. My mom already knew."

"She did?"

"She told Cora about your accent. You know, the way you sound."

"Yeah, I know that. Who's this Cora?"

"A friend of my mom's. She came to see you when you were still fainted."

"Why would she do that?"

"I don't know. And Miriam came too."

"I hope you charged admission."

"No," she said, surprised. "You can't charge Miriam. She cures people."

"She's a doctor?"

"I guess," she said. "But don't tell Father Arroyo nothing about it, okay?"

"About Miriam?"

"Yeah. He doesn't like her."

"Why not?"

"I don't know," she said. "He calls her a witch. You know, like when he said sola vaya."

"Yeah." I was beginning to understand.

"And he doesn't want me and mom to see her a lot. It's her house in the desert, you know," she said. "We're not supposed to go there either."

"But you went today."

"But it's a secret," she added mysteriously. "Nobody's supposed to know."

"Oh, I see! That's why you were so surprised when your mom told me. And now that I know, you're worried that I'm going to tell on you. Is that it?"

"I'm not worried," she said, defiantly. "But I think, maybe, my mom is."

"Well, tell her I won't tell," I said.

"You won't?"

"Not a soul!" I promised her. "Hey! How're you doing with that dresser?"

"Almost finished. You don't have a whole lot of stuff either."

"No, I don't," I said. "Who else doesn't have a whole lot of stuff?"

"Oh," she said, as if she had said the wrong thing. "My mom. She used to, but now nothing fits."

"I don't believe it."

"It's what she says. You know, because she's got hips."

"Does she want things?" I asked, smiling at the memory of Maria's generous hips and wondering how Zemi, who was so young, knew so much about people.

"She never says nothing. You know."

"Yeah, I know."

When we finished unpacking, we played guessing games. She beat me.

"What now?" she asked when she got tired.

"Now you go home and I go to bed, but thanks for helping me."

"Ah, sure."

"Look! There goes Father Arroyo."

"Wow!" she exclaimed. "You can see the whole town from here."

"And the desert too."

"Both deserts," she pointed out. I looked puzzled. "Miriam's desert and that other one."

"What's the difference? They look the same to me."

"Miriam's desert is okay, but that one is really scary."

"Why?"

"Because!" she answered as if I were some kind of idiot. "It's big! It's got hills and mountains. If you get lost in there, it's bye bye you."

"I'll be sure to stay away from that one," I said as I walked her to the door.

"Stay away from both," she commanded me, fully aware of the authority that she had over me with her superior knowledge of the desert.

"I will," I said, and she ran down the hall. Moments later, from my window, I saw her run to her mother's arms. She whispered something in her mother's ear and looked my way to wave goodnight. I waved right back and turned off the lights so that I could stand in the dark and look at Maria. She had put Zemi down and was leaning against the doorframe, waiting. But for whom?

That she had been in and out of the desert that day worried me. Did she know the way? Miriam's house wasn't too far in, but it was far enough to make me wonder whether Maria felt any fear as she ventured in. I would have been scared. The promise of peace with which the desert draws you is deceiving. It makes you believe in the calm, like a mirage. I knew from listening to Mother tell me about it. The desert makes you give up your sanity the moment you slip into the sand, looking for peace. Peace isn't there.

When I crossed the Sierra Diablo Mountains on my way to Pozo Seco, not just out of curiosity but because I had to; I couldn't forget the history behind them. It had been a violent one. The desert that spread on the other side of Miriam's house, towards the Guadalupe Mountains, blended somehow with the Sierra Diablo sands through Salt Flats where nothing lived. How could a person who got lost in that desert make it out alive? I shuddered just thinking about it, and I closed my eyes to rest. Maria was safely at home. The desert was around her, and she must have learned by now to live with its threatening presence. Now I had to.

5

Cora fears the encroachment of the morning sun, for he comes with the light when she no longer wants him. She has grown to like his wife. But he comes and comes every morning with the sun. When the music dies at the bar, he enters her realm, incensed by rejections. She no longer fights.

He comes from somewhere south of the border. She doesn't know the place. It has an Indian name with rolling consonants that fill her mouth with water. At first, she said the name with ease, her mouth filled with the sound, like having mango juice spill from the mouth while she sucked at the core. But now she never says it.

"Things change," she said, examining herself in the quiet of her room. Her hands covered her face as if to block out his image. The thought of his wife remained.

I wonder how old she is, she thought, remembering her embarrassment the last time they met. Like always, the woman was surrounded by her pack of wild children, her loose clothes looking much too old for her.

"So what?" she demanded of her mirror. "She looks like all the others, the wives of all those men." She wasn't one of them, and until now the thought had not occurred to her that they hurt. This woman did. Cora could tell.

"So why do they let themselves get so used? I'd never do that to myself. No way!" But the fact remained that she was going nowhere fast, and she knew it. Her clothes were as worn out as theirs.

"Mierda," she said as she checked the street through the open window. She had to get out of there before he came, before the painter left.

"Who the hell gets up at this hour?" she asked of her mirror. "Even the chickens are still in bed."

She traced the outline of her lips with a pencil and put her lipstick on. The kiss she threw at the mirror was for herself.

"That's all the painting *you'll* ever do," she said, and shadowed her eyes in two shades of blue.

From her wardrobe she took a skirt and a long-sleeved blouse. Her thick mantilla hung from a nail on the door. She put it on as well. It would be cool outside until midday, and she wanted to give herself enough time to observe without having to worry about the weather.

"Some women have all the luck, that's all there is to it." She heard the painter's door close softly outside while she was stepping into her shoes. A rush of heat ran through her.

"What's the matter with me!" she exclaimed, but she knew. It was time. The painter was on her way to the site of the church, and Cora was ready to follow her.

I saw her every day when I walked to the site of the church. She never spoke to me beyond a greeting, but she followed me to breakfast downstairs at the Cocinita at such an early hour that, at first, Gloria Peñaranda questioned her about it.

"What're you doing up at this hour?" she yelled at her in that familiar tone i'd heard her use with Cora. It sounded possessive, strident, as if she could tell Cora what to do, when to get up.

"Couldn't sleep," answered Cora.

"I bet!" snapped Gloria. Cora ignored her and ordered her breakfast, embarrassed to admit that she had been found out. What difference should it make that she chose to get up early? I smiled from my table to let her know that it didn't matter. That she was curious about me, I could understand. I too had many questions that needed to be answered, so today, because she was embarrassed, I signaled to her to come over to my table.

"Would you care to join me?" I asked, knowing that she did. She came over.

"I hope you didn't think nothing of my getting up like this," she said. "Gloria just don't know I come up for air early somedays."

"You do?" I said.

"Sure." She sat down.

"I hate to get up early," I said. She smiled. "I had a friend back home who got up at 4:30 every day."

"No matter what?"

"No matter what. Every day, at 4:30 a.m. she was up and about doing things around the house. It was very annoying."

"Where was home?"

"Back East," I said, not wanting to give too much away. To say I had left Brooklyn was somehow too hard right now.

"How did you know to come here?"

"I saw the ad in the paper—the one asking for a painter. So I came."

"You're a painter?"

"I think I am. What about you?"

"No," she shook her head.

"I mean, what do you do?"

She fixed me with her eyes. "I do things around the town. Like if somebody needs something, I do it." I nodded several times, pretending approval. I should have known better than to ask that question. "You're gonna work with Arroyo?"

I was still not used to the Spanish sound of his name.

"Sí, él. I guess I have to, since he's the one who knows what he wants." She laughed as if I had said something funny.

"He seems to be very popular around here," I said, but our breakfast came, and Gloria Peñaranda came with it. Her presence threw a blanket of silence over my companion. I wanted to find out whatever I could about the priest and the people in this town, but most of all I wanted to be told that Maria Soledad was a servant in his house and nothing more. She was beginning to worry me. The things I had and had not said were rattling inside my head.

Cora and I finished breakfast without speaking. I could tell she was as curious about me as I was about her. When I finished, I thanked her and rose to walk away.

"See you tomorrow," I said.

"Sure," she answered, and I walked outside, turning my back to an orange dawn breaking over the mesquite trees.

At the church site the workers had already started. Some picked up where they'd left off the previous day, but others looked as if they had not gone home at all. The priest, all in black, was pulling his own weight. I had thought that he was the kind of man who would stand around giving orders all day, protected as he was by his authority, but he wasn't. He worked alongside the crew, as if he were one of them, the only difference between them being the clothes they wore.

Of course, the men at the site knew it wasn't the only difference. He fulfilled his role as priest even as he bent to pick up the broken blocks of plaster or the piles of stone. His every move was made to prove a point, as if he were aware that he was being watched by someone other than God.

"So you're real good friends now."

"Can it, Gloria," snapped Cora. "Don't want none of your crap."

"What you want with that güera anyway?"

"Don't want nothing, I tell you! So take your fat ass out of here and leave me alone."

"Hey! Leave my ass out of this!" yelled Gloria. "It never bothered you before, my ass." Cora shifted in her chair as if to turn her back on Gloria, who had sat beside her and was leaning forward.

"All I wanna know is how come, all of a sudden, you're up at 5:30 in the morning and it ain't even daylight!"

"I couldn't sleep, Gloria," said Cora, sadly. "That's all."

"You coming down with something?"

"No," Cora assured her but thought about it a long time. "It's just my life coming down on me."

"That don't make no sense to me. Not from you."

Cora thought for a moment about what to do before she got up to leave.

"Yeah," whispered Cora. "Not from me."

"Ah, come on!" said Gloria. "You can't leave now."

"I need some air, okay?"

"Talk to me some more," pleaded Gloria. "Coralia!" she called out to the woman's back.

"Damn it!" she said aloud. "I hate talking to myself."

Cora ended up at Maria's doorstep, almost unconsciously. She had gone out for a breath of fresh air, expecting to find the townspeople still in bed, but she found instead men walking towards the church everywhere she went. Some recognized her and simply looked at her, their eyes hungry even at this hour, but others whistled and called out her name, making lewd remarks about what they would do to her if only they didn't have to work today.

On any other day, she would have joked away the coarser comments that the lewdest of them made. It was part of the job, as she saw it: cutting through the bravado performance and getting on with the act. Today, however, wasn't one of those days. She was losing the energy it took to listen to their stories and make it all seem right no matter how she felt.

She had spent the night awake, thinking about life, her life, and about how tired and lonely she was. Her time seemed mostly wasted, spent on merely getting by, surviving. By the time she was twenty-eight, Maria's mother had been arrested twice for doing political things and Maria had finished four years of college. She, on the other hand, had nothing to show for her many bruises, and they were beginning to hurt.

"What's wrong?" asked Maria. She had seen Cora walk by through an open window and rushed out to meet her, and bring her into the living room.

"I don't know," Cora stopped to answer. "I've been talking to myself."

"Why?" Cora looked away from Maria, but shook her head no. "You can talk to me," Maria insisted.

"I can't run to someone every time I have a problem."

"Says who?"

"Me! I like to do for myself, you know."

"I know, but sometimes...." She didn't bother to finish the thought. Arguing with Cora about self-sufficiency was of no use. "Well, you're here now," she added. "So tell me what's wrong."

Cora sat silently looking at her hands, tears rolling slowly down her cheeks.

"It's her birthday again, isn't it? I should've known," whispered Maria.

"I know what you're going to say," Cora exclaimed, her anger rising in her again.

"No, you don't."

"I hear it every year!" Cora practically shouted. "You think I should send for her! You think I'm a fool to let her stay there!"

"I wasn't going to say that."

"Cut it out, Maria," snapped Cora. "I know you. Every year I go through the same shit. I toss and turn in bed for weeks before the day, and I come here to tell you that I'm tossing and turning, and what do you say to that? Send for her! It's what you always say."

"Okay, that's true. I say that, but that's only because this is the time of the year when I see what you feel. Don't you think about her the rest of the year?"

"Of course I think about her!" Cora yelled. "What do you think I am?"

"A very sad woman," Maria answered. "Listen, Coralia, I love you like a sister, but I hate what you're doing."

"I'm doing what I have to do," Cora snapped.

"How can you live your life not knowing how Clarita is?" Maria asked. "You don't even know if she has enough to eat."

"I send her money," Cora reminded her.

"You send your mother money."

"For her!"

"Is this the same mother who threw you out in the streets?"

"I never should've told you that," Cora groaned.

"The same mother who beat you until you came back with money?" Maria continued.

"So I'm sending her money," Cora said, defeated.

"And how long do you think it will take before she sends Clarita out?" Maria asked.

"My daughter is going to school!" Cora yelled, her eyes so full of rage that Maria was almost afraid to continue.

"How do you know that, Cora? Do you wake her up and feed her in the mornings, send her off to school? Do you help her with her homework?"

"I'm sure I can do that," Cora said.

"You could raise your child, Cora, if you just gave yourself half a chance."

"I'm a whore."

"And your mother is a cruel, callous woman. And she's going to do to Clarita what she did to you."

"I never should've told you that! Never!" Cora cried out, rising to leave.

"Don't you dare walk out of this house!" screamed Maria, grabbing Cora by the waist and wrestling her back into her chair. "Every time we get into a fight, you walk out on me. Well, not anymore! You're going to hear me out this time even if I have to sit on you."

"¡Jesús! I've heard enough already!" said Cora, still flushed with anger.

"When I'm finished! That's when you've heard enough!" Maria yelled with such firmness that she surprised herself. She had a sudden memory of her mother in just such a pose. She straightened out from her fighting stance and settled herself.

Cora, also surprised, stopped fighting. "Well, get it over with. I have things to do."

"I know," said Maria, "the town's full of men."

"That does it!" Cora burst out, springing from the chair, but the look on Maria's face stopped her short. "If you don't cut it out," she warned her, her index finger ominously rising and falling in front of her.

"Okay. That was unfair. I take it back." Cora sat back, the heat on her face rising at the ease with which Maria could apologize. That was one of the things that disturbed her the most about Maria. She didn't think anything of lowering herself, of saying she was sorry or admitting she was wrong. It comes with her upbringing, Cora thought. If she was raised like I was, she wouldn't ever say that.

"What kind of a life do you think she has without you?" said Maria, a bit calmer.

"A better one than I can give her," Cora shot back.

"Don't you think she wonders about you?"

"And if she lived with me, she wouldn't have to wonder, would she?"

"You can change, Coralia," said Maria, gently. "You can get a job that pays steady wages."

"Like yours?" Cora added, her eyes cold with rage.

"Now *you're* being unfair," Maria said, but she knew that Cora wouldn't admit it or apologize. She would shift in her chair and alter the expression on her face, but no word of apology would ever cross her lips.

"What could I do?" demanded Cora, still on the defensive. "I've got no education, like you have. Hell, you can pick up and leave any time you want. You can always find a job. Not me."

"You don't need an education to do the work I do." Maria ignored the invitation to argue Cora's favorite theme: everybody else is better off than I am.

"I don't wanna do somebody else's shit work! And that's all I'm good for."

"I don't think of my work as shit work."

"But you're so accustomed to sacrifice," added Cora softly in her most sarcastic tone.

"You know, Cora, you don't fight fair."

"You want fair? I'll give you fair. You think it's fair the way I've turned out? You think I look in the mirror and like what I see? Look at me, damn it!"

"I'm looking, Cora. I don't have any problems with what I see."

"I do. I had a lot of things I was gonna do."

"What's keeping you?"

"You don't understand. You just don't understand." Cora leaned back, looked away from Maria, and whispered, "I don't even have dreams anymore."

"You had them once. They're probably still in there somewhere."

"Don't you understand? People like me don't get to have dreams."

"Everybody dreams, Cora, but some of us do something about it."

"Here comes the lecture," Cora warned.

"The real difference between people lies in whether or not we do something to get what we want, instead of just sitting around and feeling sorry for ourselves."

"Yeah," Cora snapped, and Maria immediately regretted the part about her feeling sorry for herself. "And that really galls me."

"What galls you?" said Maria, but what she was actually thinking was, "what doesn't gall you?"

"That güera!"

"Carole, her name is Carole, Cora."

"She came in here ready to conquer the world," Cora said. "She can do what she wants and not worry about a thing, but I can't even work to keep my baby."

"That's just your anger talking," Maria argued.

"Of course it's my anger talking!" Cora yelled. "Today's her birthday, and all I can do is think about her. It hurts, damn it. It hurts," she said more quietly.

"Send for her."

"You're a big help, Maria. It's no wonder I come to you."

"I don't want to be any help. I won't ever tell you you're doing the right thing on this. You're not."

"How do I do the right thing? How do I support her?"

"You'll think of something," Maria said.

"It must be nice to think that way," said Cora, rising to leave.

"What way?"

"You know, the way you think that things, somehow, are gonna work themselves out."

"They do."

Cora stood silently, her eyes fixed on the door. She had told herself for years that all the problems in her life were just a preparation for the day when life would be what she wanted it to be. It was her way of dealing, her way of staying alive in spite of the knowledge, which occasionally hit her like a blow to the face, that she was going nowhere and that life as she knew it would not change.

"You know what you're really good at?" Maria added after thinking about it for a while. Cora's eyebrows shot up in expectation. "Colors," Maria informed her.

"So?" Cora demanded.

"So, maybe you can help Carole when she starts on the walls," Maria suggested. Cora got up to leave. "Wait a minute," Maria said.

"What for? I'm going to bed, Maria, I'm exhausted."

"Didn't you do all those pictures of Clarita? You can draw!"

"I don't have no schooling." Cora was immediately defensive.

"She can teach you." Maria was getting excited about the idea. "I don't know that she'll be able to pay you, but you'll learn something."

"You have to know how to read and write to do something like that," Cora argued.

"I'll teach you. This'll finally give you a reason to learn."

"I'm too old to learn," Cora argued, somewhat less vehemently than she had before.

"But learning what you need will open doors for you, Cora. Think of Clarita. You want her to grow up the way you did?" And for the first time, a sign of recognition flashed on Cora's face. She bit her lip.

"She's all I think about." Cora sat back down again as if her body were a great load to her, and buried her face in her hands.

"Cora, you have no way of knowing if she goes to school or not. Your mother never sent you; why should she send her?"

"I told you," Cora insisted. "I'm sending her money."

"Use it to raise her here, or she'll be following in your footsteps before too long."

Maria waited for a reply but nothing came. Cora stood up without a goodbye and slowly walked away, her head down. Maria hated to see Cora so defeated and hurt, and yet she wouldn't go after her to comfort her, or lie and tell her it was okay to look the other way. Cora was her friend, so she let her go off alone, to think and maybe gather the courage to act.

The priest was usually at the site when I got there and today, as usual, newly arrived workers were gathered around him waiting for directions. He made them wait for me. For some reason he had decided that I was in charge of the project. I suspected from the way he talked to the men while nodding in my direction that he didn't think they would do for him what they would do for me.

He's using me to bolster his image, I thought. I didn't bother to point it out to him.

Between the two of us, we had decided that the men who had the most experience in this kind of work should be in charge of specific tasks. Thus we created a hierarchy and delegated authority. Each jefe chose the group of workers he wanted in his team, but the priest and I weren't chosen. We were to be in charge because we were both outsiders, not part of this crowd. I had come from somewhere else. I didn't know what his story was.

Although we had no task assigned to us, we joined the bricklayers. Side by side we worked, but it took me a while to learn how to work with a group. Nothing I had ever done prepared me for the kind of labor I was doing here. I had always worked alone, dependent only on my own ability to decide for myself what I wanted to do. To lay a brick here, I had to depend on somebody else's measurements, and as soon as I put down my brick and scooped up the cement oozing from all sides, somebody else would come along to lay another brick beside mine. I was working with men whom I had never met, yet everything depended on how well we could work together.

It was simple, this notion of how things worked. All a person had to do was roll up the sleeves of her blouse and go to work, side by side with the rest. Men seemed to do that well everywhere. Cities and nations rose out of nothing because of this ability they have to work together and do it well. So how could they also fight and destroy with so little regret what they had built? How could they fight each other when they worked alongside each other so well?

In front of me the priest stretched to his full length. The sight of him called me out of my reverie. He was obviously not used to hard work. At this hour the sun lashed us with an intensity that made us all red. Sweating over the bricks, each of us reached out for the water bucket almost blindly, and poured its contents over our heads to cool off. Being hosed down by the kids who made a game out of soaking us was more satisfying, but the hose wasn't long enough to reach the site and no one wanted to walk more than he had to. We settled for the buckets the women lined up near the site.

"Ya vas por el cubo," *You're going for the bucket*, the men would yell at each other and catcalls would follow. Then they would laugh along with the women, who turned their backs on them feigning annoyance when in fact they were smiling, making faces at each other as they carried the empty buckets to the hose to keep the line supplied.

"El mío ni lo pienses," *Don't even think about mine*, one of the women called back. They must have assumed that I'd missed the pun, the similar sounds between cubo and culo, bucket and rear-end.

"Que el tuyo está llenito," *But yours is so much fuller*, a man with a missing front tooth called out as a short, plump woman blasted him with the water from her bucket. The other women clapped. It was plain to see that her bucket had been spoken for, and all she had to do was keep it coming back.

"Traeme el tuyo, vieja," *Bring me yours, woman*, some of the men yelled as they acted out fainting spells. "¡Que me mata el calor!" *The heat is killing me.*

The women went back and forth carrying their buckets, and the ones who were just standing around watching and joking would join in the laughter about whose bucket would save which man from instant death and which man would go to his grave thirsty and hot.

The priest stretched and looked over at the people involved in the bucket game. He neither laughed nor even smiled at the good-natured fun going on around him. When he caught me staring at him, he gave me a worried smile. I stretched too, turning my head to stretch my neck muscles. He followed my example and stretched his own neck. Then he looked back at me with a conspiratorial smile and resumed his work.

I looked around me. The bucket game had fizzled out as the men returned to work, and in spite of all the joking and the kids running through the site as we tried to work, the foundation of the wall was now discernible. Brick by brick the church was rising out of the ground. It was such an ambitious project for a town this size, whose people were so poor. I admired their spirit, their willingness to give up their time for a building—a church, but nothing more than a building to me. For them, religion apparently satisfied more than the soul. They were sacrificing everything to build a church that would meet not only their religious, but also their aesthetic needs.

The priest had told me he thought that he wouldn't be able to replace the old church with one equally as impressive, that he would have to put up a much smaller brick church, a poor imitation of the one that was destroyed. He found out differently; the people had demanded nothing less than what they had lost, which was why he said they came from miles around to work on this project. It had to represent their collective conception of God's grandeur, no matter what it cost them in money or labor, which explains why the humblest border town has a church like a palace, fancier than anything its residents could afford.

Still, not a single one of them is ever heard begrudging Him the gift because it means as much to each of them as it must to Him. The truth of the matter is that most of us have a need to gaze at something grand, bigger than the self.

Zemi appeared among the group of kids riding around the site after three o'clock. She seemed happy and excited to be with her friends, and she rode her bike with careless abandon.

"They look like ants," she told me. I knew she was talking about the workers.

"No, they can't. Ants are black. These guys are all dressed in white."

"They do too look like ants," she argued. "Mom said so."

"You mom's here?"

"Over there," she said, pointing to the sidewalk across the plaza. No one was there. "I guess she left."

"Did she pick you up at school?"

"No! Nobody picks me up at school."

"You're too big for that."

"Sure, I'm six."

"That's pretty big."

"Hope nobody burns it down again."

"Who burned it down the last time?"

"Luz! Everybody knows that."

"I don't know that," I said. She shrugged away my ignorance, unconcerned. The trail of cement buckets on the floor of the church made an enticing course for her. Already someone had dunked his foot in a bucket by mistake, which had caused a big commotion among the women. "Who was Luz?"

"Just a kid."

"Whose kid?"

"Maria's."

"Your mother's?"

"No!" She was exasperated. Perched on the bike's seat, her slim, wiry body was ready for action. I must have sounded pretty stupid asking all those questions. "She's older than Mom."

"Ah, excuse me, but everybody's named Maria around here."

"Are not. My name's Zemi, and besides, she's not even here now. So there."

"Where is she?"

"I don't know," she shrugged. "She left."

"Why?" She shrugged again, and the right side of her lip curled down. "Was she a friend of your mom's?"

"Sure, and Miriam too."

"So your mom probably knows where she went."

"Ask her," she suggested, implying that the discussion was closed.

"I will."

She couldn't contain herself any longer. The rest of the bike group had circled the site a few times while we talked, and now it was her chance to join the action.

Miriam walked across the plaza as fast as she could. She didn't want the priest to think she was checking up on him. She had heard a thing or two about the construction work, mostly from Maria, but she had made a point of staying away from the plaza. Even without trying Miriam could see him, the black spot in the distance among all the white-clad bodies bending down, straightening, carrying things; she couldn't tell what.

He still wears a frock, she thought. Even in this heat. And she knew he did it to prove who he was, God's representative on earth, this particular part of the earth. That's what the frock told her.

"It's the uniform," she whispered. But that's his problem, she thought. She had never made any claims to being anybody's representative on earth. Only the church made such claims. As far as she knew, God had no need of representatives.

"Miriam!" Cora's voice called out to her. Miriam shaded her eyes with her hand and followed the sound of the voice. She found Cora standing at the street corner across from the plaza, keeping an eye on the work.

All those men, thought Miriam as she walked towards Cora, the sight of her becoming clearer as she approached.

"Vieja, where are your glasses?"

Miriam dismissed the question with a wave of her hand. "How's your life, Coralia?"

"Oh," said the woman whose eyes were still red from crying. "It could be worse, you know?"

"¡Ay, mujer! What makes you say that?"

Miriam kissed her.

"You heard from Clarita?"

"Sí," said Cora, affectionately. Miriam always remembered. "She sent me some drawings she did of me."

"She's getting to be a big girl," observed Miriam. "And you?"

"I'm a big girl too," Cora said and laughed. She had straightened out Miriam's poncho and pushed back her hair. Miriam waved her hand at her, trying to get her to stop.

"How are you, malcriada?"

"You talked to Maria?" demanded Cora. Miriam nodded, eyeing the black spot that she still saw out of the corner of her eye. "So you have to ask?"

Miriam sighed. "No, I don't. But I wish you'd do something about it. Time vanishes." She wondered why young people had to be told the obvious.

"I know all that," Cora said before Miriam finished. She had a pain, like a knife stuck in her chest, and she couldn't get it out.

"You all right?" asked Miriam, her eye still on the church. She had wanted to tell Cora about how quickly the child would grow, become a woman, but with the priest a few steps away and all the noise from the construction crowding the silence out of her ears, she told her nothing.

"Are *you* okay?" Cora asked. Miriam seemed edgy, nervous, unable to concentrate. She saw her sneak a look at the construction across the street and understood the problem.

"The way they're going, they'll be finished in no time."

"Looks like it."

"You think she'll come?"

"Who'll come?"

"Maria, the good Padre's been saying he's gonna have a mass. You know...for her soul."

"A mass won't bring her back," Miriam said, sadly.

"Maria?"

"Luz."

"¡Ay, vieja! Nothing'll bring Luz back, but her mother could come to the mass. It's the least she could do."

"Is it?"

"I think so," said Cora. "Everybody thinks so. Ask Maria. He said Luz's mass is going to be the first after the church is finished, with painted walls and all."

"Maybe so."

"No 'maybe'. This is real. I think it's kinda nice."

"Maybe so, maybe so."

"I don't like the man any more than you do, but you have to admit it'll be nice to give the poor girl a mass."

"I'll admit it," Miriam said jovially, "but masses are for the living."

"Oh, all right." It always annoyed Cora to argue with Miriam.

"Coralia," Miriam said. She was going to tell her so many things.

"Give it up, old woman."

"¡Ay, mi hija! Tú sabrás." *You should know.*

"Yeah, I know. And if you don't tell me nothing I'll come over tonight and brush your hair."

"My hair doesn't need brushing, but you can come over anyway. Show me those drawings." Miriam hugged Cora and turned away. Disoriented, she faced the church.

"Están lindos." *They're beautiful.* Cora's face brightened as she remembered the drawings.

"¿Qué?"

"The drawings."

"Ay, sí," Miriam nodded. "That man's never gonna make things right, try as he may."

"Maria says he knows that."

"He knows it in his head," Miriam said as she tapped her temple with her fingers, "but he doesn't know it here," she added, touching her chest, "where it counts."

"He'll find out," Cora told her as she shrugged her shoulders. She was thinking of her own pain but she was also eyeing a young man who had stopped to look at her.

"Mmm," said Miriam, who had seen the young man too. "But by then it'll be too late."

"Too late?" wondered Cora with half a mind, her body responding to the man's eyes.

"For some people, yes." Miriam turned and cut through the alley between Gloria's restaurant and the row of dead cars in Gloria's garage. She was glad to be gone. The noise from the construction made it impossible to hear anything clearly and Cora needed some talking to.

Maybe she'll come tonight, Miriam thought, and decided to wait until they were alone to talk about Clarita.

At home that night, the priest was restless. His body was sore from the work, but what bothered him the most was Miriam's appearance at the site.

"Miriam came by today," he told Maria.

"Oh?" she answered, her eyebrows raised inquiringly.

"Was she here?"

"She doesn't visit this house," Maria answered, defensively.

"Not when I'm here." He knew Maria wouldn't respond, talk back to him, and yet he wanted her to. Seeing Miriam near the site had filled him with a rage that he couldn't explain. He knew what he looked like in the eyes of the people when she was around.

"Will you eat now?" Maria's voice startled him.

"Yes, of course."

He looked at the clock. They had worked until dark, and now that he was at home he had to eat alone. Maria had left his plate on the table for him. He pulled a chair back but waited until Maria had finished serving dishes before he sat down. She would not sit with him.

It's just as well, he thought. She wouldn't discuss Miriam. Her loyalty to that woman seemed to him beyond reason. It was true that Miriam had taken her in once, but it was also true that Maria had earned her keep. She had cleaned the house, washed clothes, planted vegetables, worked the garden in Miriam's sandy plot. She wasn't the type to take without giving, which was why it pained him to know that Maria cared for that woman who used her.

No better off than a servant, he thought. Even after little Zemi was born, Maria had worked. He remembered the sweat in her eyes as she worked the garden when he dropped by to see her that first time. The more she wiped her eyes, the more the sweat slipped down her brow into them. At Miriam's house she did the work for nothing other than the handouts that woman gave her, until he had hired her, given her a job, a home and a little money to spend. He was the one who helped her, not Miriam, but she still thought the sun rose in that woman's eyes. Her face became a mask of anger or defiance whenever he brought up Miriam's name. It was just as well that she wasn't talking because he wasn't in the mood to discuss anything else. He didn't like talking just to hear his voice.

"How's the work coming?" she asked. It took him by surprise that she should even ask. He swallowed.

"Very well," he answered. They both waited. Maria took a casserole and carried it to the kitchen. "She's going to work out much better than I'd thought," he added loudly so that she could hear him. "She doesn't mind the hard work. At least, she doesn't complain. And the people like her, looks like."

"I'm glad," she said. He waited. Nothing else came. She had started him talking, but she wasn't saying anything.

"If things keep up like this, we'll be finished in no time, before the rains come, even."

"So soon?" Maria said, surprised.

"There's an army of the faithful in this town," he said, taking her surprise as a challenge. "They've come to build the Lord a home. There's no time to lose."

"Well," she said, "I'm glad she's working out." Again, nothing more from Maria.

"I thought I'd tell you. The first mass—it'll be for her." He set his fork down as Maria came back into the room.

"Luz?"

He nodded.

"That's a good idea," she told him, as if she had not known that he had talked about it with some of the crew. Someone had told Cora, who had then told her, and now she felt sorry for him, sitting there waiting for her to guess what he wanted to say. She didn't have to guess. She knew he would not ask her, but she knew what he wanted. She was to find Maria Selene and ask her to attend. He had no way of knowing that she had kept in touch, and if he had known he would probably have objected. It would have created another silent argument, another excuse for talking without saying anything, so she never let him find out that she wrote to the woman regularly just to keep in touch.

"I'll write to Maria," she told him. He didn't answer. She stood with her arms folded under her shawl. Obviously, with the kitchen work already finished except for his plate, she was through for the evening. He picked up the fork and resumed eating.

As the days passed, I became more and more impressed with the zealous devotion that my ragged army of church builders demonstrated. Artisans, carpenters, and bricklayers, without being asked, came to me to offer themselves. They came from everywhere, even from towns with churches of their own, to lend a hand. The rebuilding of the church in Pozo Seco must have been the main topic of conversation for people in towns like this one all over the Southwest. A new church was being built, and everyone wanted to contribute. Since most of them had no money, their own sweat was all they could afford to give. They came to sweat, as if their very salvation depended on how hard they worked.

And they kept coming. I couldn't help but wonder why they had not come before, although it did seem as if at this point they were all making something like a ritual penance out of the journey that brought them here. Crossing themselves, the men removed their hats and bowed their heads over the rubble as soon as they jumped off the truck that dropped them at the site, and it never failed that someone would pick up a piece of burned wood or brick stained by smoke and water, and stare at it in silence. Then, the man would shake his head and show the piece around to "¡Qué lástima!" from the others in the group. Before too long, they would be talking, crouched over the rumble of their voices toward each other because it didn't seem right, because it seemed to them as if talking about Luz and the church fire was something that could only be done in whispers. Even men whose voices normally thundered through the open plaza, could only whisper.

"You'd think he would've done it before," one always reasoned. The others offered their opinions simultaneously in a great show of hands raised and brought down upon an open palm, insistently, to make a point. The general consensus was that he could do nothing alone, that the church was one thing but the people were something else. As they argued they would nod toward the priest and fall silent. Before long, slapping their hats against their thighs as if to shake off the dust, they would walk away from each other and join the ones already at work.

The priest seemed not to notice. He saw them jump off busses and pickup trucks onto the plaza, but he acted as if their arrival had been expected. He was never impressed nor surprised, as I was, by the many men who surrounded us. When a group arrived he simply looked in their direction, sometimes waved hello, and continued what he was doing. Had I been in his place, I would have run to shake their hands, gratefully, as some in the crowd did when they recognized a familiar face. Whatever the reason that brought them to Pozo Seco, he was uninterested and didn't question. It was building him a church.

7

In Pozo Seco she was the voice of prophecy. She had been for years. Those who were not of the sand were sometimes unnerved by the sound of her voice, often like a hiss, but the townspeople had learned to listen for it. She had marked them all with visions time and time again, and even those who were the least inclined to believe dared not deny. She was as undisputedly a part of them as the sand that defined them; it was about them everywhere, their essence.

"She's possessed," some would say, and sign themselves with a specious cross to exorcise themselves of whatever influence this knowledge had on them.

"It's her gift," the ones with courage whispered. Yet others, who claimed not to believe, swore over bottles of beer that she came by her voices through the dead. This frightened even the toughest of them, for the dead sleep lightly when they lie in sand, which sifts and shifts and splits open before you. Yet Miriam saw no reason to argue where her vision came from. The dead and the old could testify for her.

Yet she did not always want to see the future. Those nights she had visited the pregnant Maria Selene, she would go against her conscience and all her voices when, leaning over Maria's shoulder, she saw the unborn child draped in fire, seeking her. The child's features were so familiar that she loved her even then. But she could not speak the truth. How could she tell Maria that her only child would suffer so?

The desert sand dripped off her body as she entered out of the evening breezes into the silent room and squatted on Maria's dirt floor. The spirit flowed about her and the mother, Maria Selene, who saw no vision of flames. Instead, a vision of the girl, no longer in fire but draped in night colors, merged with the shadows and rested her hues against the open window. The moon's half-light was her silent benediction, slipping through the haze that lingered about the house.

"You listening again?" Miriam spoke from the darkness.

"You know I am," replied Maria Selene, all smiles as she thought of the coming child. "You think she'll be healthy?" she wondered aloud. Her skin stretched over the growing life within her like light over a shadow.

"She'll be fine," said Miriam. Her skirt, as she rose, stirred dust off the ground to envelop Maria in flickering sparks of light.

"Lay your hands here," said the mother. "You'll feel her." Her arm stretched forward to welcome her friend. Had she brought her visions?

"Tell me what will be!"

"Nada, vida, there is nothing to tell."

"A moon and a breeze keep whispering outside like there's something to tell."

"You hear better than me," said the woman whose visions were of fire. She would have done anything to shed this knowledge, to not have been the one who knew. She knelt beside the bulging crest of Maria's stomach and felt for the life.

Maria studied the deep vacant light in Miriam's eyes. She could only guess at the source of what troubled her for her friend had assumed more burdens than most people could bear. But Maria knew something was not right.

"Name her Luz," Miriam said.

"Luz," Maria repeated. She liked the sound. A breeze broke through the cracks in the old walls and slipped out of the room with half a voice. It rose to the sky on a beam of light to caress the moon's ears, as the woman leaned against the grace of darkness and whispered to unholy visions, "Luz."

Zemi had told me the little girl's name the day she had bicycled through the site, but that and the mother's name were all I had been able to find out about Luz. And it wasn't for lack of trying either. I asked anyone who'd listen about the fire at the church and the child, but these people weren't talking.

"Manolo," I'd say, "what about the fire?"

"Such a shame," he'd tell me.

"How do you mean?" I'd insist.

"Oh, terrible, terrible," he'd reply, but I couldn't get another word out of him. I began to think that something more than a simple accident had taken place the day Luz had died by fire.

"Did you know the kid who died?" I asked Cora over dinner once. When the spirit moved her she would tell me a few things about the town.

"The sky was orange," she said in a soft voice.

Swell, I thought. You ask about the kid and you get colors. I leaned forward to act equally mysterious. "The day she died?"

"Nah," she shook her head. "The day she was born. Wouldn't you know it?"

I wouldn't, but I nodded and made appropriate sounds. "But the sky is always orange in these parts," I added. "At sunset, anyway."

"No, no, no," she told me, shaking her head. "Not like that. That day you could tell something was up, something special was happenin', you know?"

"Like what?"

"The birth, whadaya think?"

"Did you know her?" I asked again.

"Everybody knew her," she said, waving her fork around.

I went back to eating my dinner, wondering if I should tell Cora to stop waving her fork at me when she got excited. But I didn't say anything; she was already acting funny as it was, keeping an eye on the men at the bar, fidgeting with her clothes, and shaking her hair back so that it threatened to fall in my food. I couldn't tell whether she wanted to be picked up or left alone, but I had had enough.

I finished my dinner quickly and excused myself. I thought of visiting Maria Soledad to ask more questions, but I'd heard so many useless answers already that I didn't want to risk any more. I went to my room instead. It was just as well, because the moment I sat down on the window ledge I saw Cora run to Maria's house.

I couldn't imagine what those two had in common. Could Cora be Maria's confidante? Impossible. It probably was the other way around. Maria looked like the type who could tell other people what to do. Cora probably ran to her every time she had a problem.

I had a sudden urge to run to her house and be told what to do, too. "Get over it," I told myself. What would Maria think of my predicament, a grown woman attracted to another who had no use for her.

"She'd tell you you were looking for your mother," I told myself, "and that you'd better give it up."

Fat chance, I thought, but it got me going. I set up my easel and sat down to draw her features from my memory. In a world where the answers were less than satisfying, I could always make the real seem less threatening.

"¡Oye, Maria!" called out Cora.

"Come on in. The coast is clear."

"Gracias a Dios," Cora said, faking religious fervor, "and where's the good father?"

"Picking up supplies for the church."

Cora crossed herself. "A saint," she said, and bowed her head.

Maria, sighing, pulled her in by the hand. "Get in here. I'm still in the kitchen."

"You live there," complained Cora, for whom cooking was a punishment.

"I like cooking."

Cora made faces. "And I like eating, but I don't make a life out of it."

"Oh, I don't know." Maria slapped Cora's thigh playfully. Cora squirmed away from Maria's reach.

"Hey, it's eating with that woman that got me these."

"You ate with her again?"

"We're regulars. You should see Gloria's face. Pure envy. She can't even hold it no more."

"And did you ask her?"

"Mujer! Give me some credit! She's not even painting yet."

"But Father Arroyo says it won't be long; the church looks almost finished to me."

"Don't rush me, Maria. I'm not gonna say a thing till I'm ready."

Maria shook her head and sighed. She knew Cora might never speak to Carole about being her apprentice. That was her way of dealing with life; putting it off. She didn't want to give up on Cora, but her friend's reluctance to do for herself disappointed her. She herself would never have allowed time to slip by her, almost unnoticed, the way Cora did. She lived as if she had all the time in the world, but for what? When Luz died in the fire, Cora decided to smuggle her own baby into the country any way she could. She talked about it constantly, and she even asked Maria to write a letter for her. Maria had written Cora's mother then and explained what would happen as soon as Cora said the word. However the letter had never been mailed. Cora addressed it and stamped it and told herself she would send it the minute she had the money to pay the Coyote, but she had laid it on top of the dresser where it still sat, accusingly.

"Anyway," Cora said, "I'm not sure I'll be good at painting. I never did nothing like that before."

You never did anything like anything, Maria thought, but said nothing. She didn't want to argue the same point again and risk antagonizing Cora. She was also hoping Carole would drop by, so she wanted to end this conversation. "So how was Carole?" she asked.

Maria's question surprised Cora who wasn't used to losing her attention. "Tired, I guess."

"Is she drawing yet?"

"How should I know?" shrugged Cora.

"Don't you ask her about her work? You eat with her every day. What the hell do you talk about?"

"Lots of things. She's real curious."

"About what?"

"You, for one thing."

"Me!"

"And Luz, and Miriam, and everything. She's got a question for everything and I mostly answer. What's with you, anyway?"

"I just wonder what she's doing. It must be exciting, knowing you have all that work to do, and look at the kind of work it is. Those walls could last forever."

"Unless somebody else burns them."

"That's right, Cora," snapped Maria, "look at the bright side!"

"Damn! What am I doing here?"

"Getting screamed at! What are you going to do about it?"

"Leave; you're too worked up about somethin'."

"Ah, Cora, stay."

"No way. I'm getting out of here. I told Miriam I was gonna do her hair, pull some of them gray ones out."

"You and Zemi are going to pluck that woman's head until she's bald."

"She likes it, okay?"

"Okay, but don't go telling her I chased you out of here. It's not as if I haven't ever screamed at you before."

"I tell 'em like I sees 'em," Cora called from the door.

She left wondering about Maria's interest in Carole. If I didn't know better I'd say she was jealous, thought Cora, and grinned to herself. "¡Ay, pero que zorrita!" *What a fox she is!* Cora said aloud, anticipating what Miriam would say.

 One day, Zemi and I went for a stroll around the town. It was Sunday, the sky was gray with clouds, and neither one of us had anything better to do. I also took any chance available to visit Maria, and hanging out with Zemi made it easier than finding excuses to drop by. Zemi probably would have been happier riding with her friends, but she seemed happy enough to ride beside me and tell me tall tales about Pozo Seco's history.

"I don't believe that cockroach story for a second," I told her. She had apparently seen one as big as a turtle. She shrugged her shoulders as if she didn't care.

"Ask my mom."

"I will."

"You know Paco? The one at the garage?" she asked, a wicked smile on her lips.

"Yeah."

"He chased after it with a hose."

I laughed. "I'm going to ask your mom about that," I said, and then I wondered aloud why so many men had come over to help build the church.

"To help you," she said. "Why do you think?"

"But don't they have work of their own to do?"

"Maybe they don't care."

"But nobody's going to pay them."

"Ask my mom," she said again. "She says people are funny. She says they do funny things, like when they're mad or afraid, and sometimes they even do bad things."

"Your mom's pretty smart."

Zemi and I reached her house. Maria was waiting for her at the door, her green eyes as gray as the sky.

"I thought only cats did that," I told her before I even said hello.

"Did what?" she asked, her eyebrows characteristically raised to punctuate the question.

"Change the color of their eyes," I answered, enjoying the nearness of her body as she stood in the doorway, blocking my path.

"It's the weather," she told me. Zemi leaned against Maria's legs in a long hug and buried her face in her belly. Maria simultaneously hugged her and tousled her hair, signaling for me to come in after her.

"We've been discussing cockroaches," I told her.

"She doesn't believe it!" Zemi yelled.

"It's true," Maria assured me.

"How big was that cockroach?"

"Huge," Maria assured me, a wide grin making her lips tremble.

"And there was just one of them?"

"Back then," she assured me.

"But you never know," Zemi pointed out in her most serious, conspiratorial voice. She winked at her mother. The cockroach story had entered the mythical realm. My questioning its veracity was an exercise in futility. Mother and daughter, clearly, were speaking with one mind, one voice, united on the cockroach issue.

"Okay," I said. "I give up."

"Thanks for playing with her," she told me.

"We didn't play, Mom. We just walked."

"I enjoy it," I admitted. "It's very educational. I not only learned about the cockroach, but I heard about the desert, and the pozo, and all kinds of interesting things."

"The pozo?" Maria demanded, staring at Zemi inquiringly.

"¡Ay, mama! We didn't go."

"She just told me about it," I added.

"She can talk about it, but she's not supposed to go that far into the desert."

"I wouldn't dare," I admitted. "I'm scared of the desert."

"She's scared of everything."

"You've got cockroaches as big as turtles!" I yelled at Zemi in self-defense and tried to catch her, but she squirmed, giggling, out of my reach and threw herself solidly against her mother's body. Maria bent over, laughing, to form a shell of arms and hair, and Zemi kicked at me from Maria's protecting arms. Eventually, I gave up trying to touch her, and Zemi calmed down slightly, enough for Maria and me to collapse on the sofa, out of breath, to recover. Zemi ran into the bedroom.

"I don't see how you survive getting slammed into like that," I told Maria.

"You get used to it," she told me. "You just get bruised." She laughed again. "She's pretty strong."

"I'm worn out," I confessed, "and all I did was walk around with her. I can't even imagine taking care of her all day."

"Ah," she waved my concern away with her hand. "It's getting easier and easier now that she's grown."

"You mean it was worse?"

Maria nodded, smiling. "You never heard about the 'terrible twos'?" I shook my head. "Well, Zemi was two for about three years." We laughed, but stopped as Zemi came in pushing her bicycle. "She's just growing out of them now."

"See you later," said Zemi.

"Hey, what about dinner?"

"You're gonna stay?" she asked me as she leaned her bicycle against the wall.

"I don't know."

"Please do," Maria insisted.

"You have enough work already. I don't want to impose," I said.

"You're not imposing," she said warmly. I felt a tiny little string being pulled inside me. I couldn't leave.

"Okay," I said. As Maria headed for the kitchen, Zemi dragged me by the hand into the dining room, turned on the lights as we passed a light switch or a lamp.

"Can I help?" I called out to Maria in the kitchen. I heard her say no.

"It's dark in there," Zemi told me. "We don't want you to be scared." She was grinning as she stood behind the chair where a third plate had been placed. "This is yours."

I also grabbed the chair before she had a chance to pull it away and sat down, but Zemi hadn't meant to pull the chair at all. She looked at me as if I was acting strangely and went into the kitchen, giving me awkward glances as if to make sure that I was still there acting strangely. Before too long, she brought in a large casserole that turned out to be chicken empanadas. Maria followed her with the rest of the dishes.

"Ooh, my favorite," I said.

"I know," Maria admitted. "A little bird told me."

"I'm not a bird," Zemi pointed out. "If I was, she'd get scared of me too."

"You'll never live that down," Maria told me.

"I'm not afraid to admit I'm scared," I told Zemi, even though Maria was the one who had spoken. "It's a lot better to be scared than be eaten alive by a snake." I knew she would scream "snakes don't eat people!" and she did, but I was ready for her with my own incredible story.

"I knew someone who was eaten by a snake," I said.

"Do not!"

"The Little Prince?" asked Maria. We smiled at each other knowingly.

"What prince?" Zemi demanded.

"But was he eaten?" Maria asked. "or did the serpent just help him get back?"

"His body was never found," I explained. "Remember? The last drawing is one of the desert without him. I'd like to think that he flew away."

"You must be a romantic," said Maria. "Even if he did fly back to his rose, the chances are slim that the rose was still alive."

Zemi was listening closely. "Nobody flies away just like that," she exclaimed, "or gets eaten either!" She had become more and more concerned about this prince.

"The Little Prince did, mi hija."

"How come I never heard of him?"

"You were too busy chasing cockroaches," I reminded her.

"We haven't read that book yet," Maria told her.

"Don't they have it at the library?" I asked. I was still wondering about her comment that the rose would have been dead by the time the Little Prince reached her side.

"They have other books," Maria answered, "but not that one."

"Next time I go to town, you must come with me. We'll get this skeptical little girl a library card."

"And she'll learn all about a Little Prince who flies, and his precious rose," Maria said, winking at Zemi. "And then when she disappears, I'll know where to look."

"Oh, Mom!" complained Zemi, but Maria was happy about the many stories she could see in Zemi's future.

Dinner at Maria's was a feast, but I was not allowed to help because I was a guest. It made me feel both flattered and ill at ease, because I didn't think anyone should sit while someone else worked.

"I hope you didn't spend the whole day making empanadas."

"No," Maria said. "They don't take long."

"Yes they do. My grandmother used to make them for me. I know how long they take."

"When you get the hang of it…" she began to explain. I was still shaking my head. Since she didn't finish her sentence, I wondered if she was beginning to get nervous again.

"The women in my house spent most of their time in the kitchen cooking," I told her.

"But they probably enjoyed it. Women who don't like to cook find a way to stay out of the kitchen."

"Are you talking about me?" I teased her. She started picking up dirty plates in a hurry, but she didn't leave. She just stood there holding them. They kept her hands from flailing.

"What makes you think I don't like to cook?" I asked her.

"Nothing. I was just saying something. I have no idea what you like to do."

"I do cook, you know. As long as I don't have to do it every day, like my mother and grandmother did. It's role playing."

"The woman as nurturer?" I nodded. She was staring at me again.

"We're not the only ones involved in nurturing. We shouldn't be expected to do all the caring," I said.

"I wonder."

"About what?" I asked. Zemi's eyelids were drooping, heavy with sleep, but she was trying hard to stay awake so that she could hear the rest of the conversation.

"I just wonder if it is role playing when someone does it naturally," she said, her right hand flying out from under the pile of plates that she was still holding. They rattled against each other, out of balance, and Maria carried them to the kitchen.

"Which most women do," I called out after her as I also got up to clear the table.

"Don't do that," she told me when she saw me. I ignored her. She was standing behind me, and I turned to face her.

"I'm playing a role here." She nodded, smiling. I could smell her breath mingled with the scent of her body. It sent tingles through my stomach, my legs, all the way down to my toes.

Maria continued clearing the table. "I had a friend once who was raised by her mother. She never met her father because the man left shortly after she was born, but of course when 'daddy' got old and needy he decided to go home."

"I know what happened," I said.

"She was thrilled to have her daddy back, but her mother was furious. After she had spent most of her life raising her kids, this man waltzes in and sweeps his children off their feet, not just my friend but her brothers as well."

"I saw the same thing happen with someone I know."

"They all said the mother was being selfish and unforgiving."

"The B word," I said. She nodded.

"But after a few months they realized they had picked up a stranger. They didn't know a thing about the man, and he wasn't very good at getting to know them. He had missed out on their lives."

"Like the Little Prince," I added.

"Exactly," she said. Zemi had heard enough of this flying prince.

"Where's the flan?" she asked.

"Coming," Maria told her.

"Flan!" I winked at Zemi. "I'm so glad you know all my favorites."

"Mine too," she said.

From the kitchen Maria called, "So he was just there, playing daddy, the role, but he really didn't have it in him."

"Because he probably couldn't have cared less," I explained.

"He may have cared," Maria corrected me, "but he had no way of knowing how to show it. He didn't know those people. The mother was the one who did the caring in that house."

"Did the two of them get back together? The man and your friend's mother?"

"Don't they always?" She grimaced.

"How tacky," I said. She brought out the flan. Zemi and I made appropriate excited noises.

"Half for me and the other half for you guys," Zemi said.

"¡Qué glotona!" Maria told her. "We're going to cut it in eight slices, and you're going to get one of those slices."

"But we don't have eight people!" Zemi complained.

"That way you'll have slices left over for tomorrow," I explained.

"I guess," Zemi grudgingly agreed.

"You told me once that your mother was from Spain," said Maria.

"From Toledo."

"Is that the reason for your Spanish accent?" she asked. I nodded. "Where was your father from?"

"I don't know exactly." I didn't like to talk about my father.

"Not from Spain?"

"No. I think he was from around here."

"This part of Texas!" Maria exclaimed.

"Yes, but he changed his Spanish name and dropped the language."

"Ah, a lot of people do that."

"They think it's the only way to get ahead."

"Ahead of what?" Zemi asked.

"Of the rest, I guess."

"How can you get ahead if you can't speak Spanish?" she asked.

"You've taught that kid well," I said to Maria, who was grinning at her daughter in pride.

"Do I get another slice?" Zemi asked, innocently.

"I guess you deserve it," Maria told her. Zemi's eyes flashed wide open, as she smiled.

"So that's how you get an extra one," I said.

"Zemi's going to know several languages when she's grown," Maria told me.

"Mom's teaching me," Zemi added.

"So how come I never hear any Portuguese?" I asked. "Aren't you from Brazil?"

"Yes, but Zemi's learning English at school and Spanish at home and with her friends in the playground. The Portuguese and the French will come later."

"Four languages! I'm impressed. When I first met you, I had no idea. I assumed you were one of those illegal aliens who come across the border with nothing but the clothes on their backs."

"That's all I had when I came in, illegally, but I also had an education."

"In what?" I said. "I mean, what was your major?"

"A thoroughly useless one," she admitted, laughing.

"Can't be as bad as mine," I said, joining her laughter. "Art."

"Philosophy."

"Oh, that one's pretty bad. You win."

She nodded. "My mother used to tell me they can take just about anything from you, including your life, but they can't take away what you know. It's like your past. It's there. It's who you are," she said seriously.

"She was right, of course."

"I'm a wetback philosopher," she added, smiling.

"You're a lot like my mother," I said, although the thought had only just occurred to me. She was waiting for an explanation, so I continued. "You remained who you were, and it cost you a lot."

"It would've cost me more to have done what your father did."

"He gave up his past to create a new one that makes absolutely no sense to who he is."

"How does he feel about it?"

I shrugged my shoulders. "Who knows. He never talked about the past. I wish he had."

"Not even to your mom?"

"I'm sure he did, but I couldn't tell you. The strange thing is that he went and married a Spaniard who made sure that her children learned her language."

"Sounds like poetic justice. The kind of thing that a romantic like you would appreciate."

"I do."

"But it doesn't make you happy?"

I tried to explain, but I wasn't sure that someone as self-assured as Maria would know what it meant to have no ancestry. "The problem is, I can't be sure of anything. I speak Spanish with a Spanish accent, although I've never been to Spain, and I know I'm Mexican-American, but I don't know from where."

"Just be who you are. Don't worry about it."

"But I want to know," I told her. "The place she came from was important to my mother. It should be important to me."

"I know what you mean. Sometimes I wonder if Zemi wouldn't be happier south of the border, growing up the same way I was raised."

"She looks happy enough here," I said, and the two of us noticed that Zemi had rested her head on the table and fallen asleep.

"One of the advantages of letting her run around town on her own all day long," said Maria as she strained to pick up Zemi, "is that she's too exhausted to stay up late at night."

"She does this every night?" I asked.

"Almost," she answered softly as she carried Zemi to the bedroom. I finished clearing the table. I didn't know what to do with the leftovers, but I had a wicked desire to throw them away before the priest got home and ate them. Instead, I started washing the pile of dishes on the counter. I was almost finished when Maria returned.

"Why did you do that?" she demanded.

"It was the least I could do," I said raising my finger to protest before she could register her next complaint. She started drying the dishes I had washed to keep herself busy or to let me know that she hadn't given in entirely.

When we finished in the kitchen and I had refused a cup of coffee, we walked to the living room. I picked up my poncho where Zemi had dropped it earlier and thanked Maria for dinner.

"You're leaving?" she asked. She seemed disappointed.

"Isn't it late for you?"

"No," she shook her head. "I don't get a lot of visitors."

"What about the priest?"

"What about him?" she asked, a little too quickly.

"Well, I guess he's not a visitor."

"That's what I wanted to talk to you about," she said. I waited, puzzled.

"Between the two of us. It's not what you thought."

"I didn't think anything," I lied. I was sure she knew I was lying.

"The first day you were here, you thought something. You saw him here, with Zemi and me, and you assumed there was something between us."

"I made a mistake."

"Yes," she said. "I'm the housekeeper. Nothing more. I don't want you to think anything of it."

"I won't," I said. Why should she care what I thought of her?

"He's not my lover, and Zemi's not his child."

"Ah, well," I mumbled. "Thanks for the scoop, but you didn't have to tell me that."

"I wanted you to know," she said and looked me in the eye.

I didn't know what to do. A part of me wanted to run away from her as far as I could, but the other part wanted to kiss her, to apologize, to make sure she knew I had thought about her connection to that man more often than I should have.

"It must have rained," I said, looking out at the wet street instead of at her. "I didn't even notice."

"I did."

"I probably should leave before it rains again," I said. She didn't ask me to stay. She simply nodded and walked me to the door. By the light of the street lamp, I saw that her eyes were their mysterious, brooding green again.

The construction of the church became for Carole an obsession. The people who came to help worked like the condemned, and she had to work to keep up with them, lacking their emotional commitment. She was determined not to be outdone by the volunteers because she thought she had to prove to them that there were reasons other than guilt to motivate a person. But working side by side with these men, whose heads were perennially cast down, made her feel that she too had been marked by their fate. During the months of labor, a bond was forged between her and those men. It was true that they seldom spoke to her directly, and that she had heard them refer to her as "la gringa"—in spite of the fact that her Spanish was better than theirs—but it was also true that she was beginning to think of herself as one of them.

A black shape approached her and broke into her thoughts.

"Reality's been licked, hasn't it?" it said. She turned her head slightly, and her wind-filled eyes discerned a familiar windmill beyond the black robe.

"You remind me of mirrors," she said, her eyes itching with tears the wind had created. He recognized the allusion and laughed aloud.

"Why do you laugh?" she demanded. He shook his head.

"You take things too seriously, you know," he said. "But if you need to talk..." he invited without finishing the thought.

"You want my confession?"

"Not necessarily, but you've been here for months and kept yourself apart."

"How do you mean, apart?" she demanded, a sudden rush of anger rising within her.

"I mean, other than Maria, who do you talk to?"

She shrugged. She wasn't about to satisfy his curiosity, but didn't he know she ate her meals with the town's most notorious personage?

"You know where to find me," he added, pointing to the church.

Fat chance, she thought, but said nothing. She was aware that Father Arroyo had already moved into the church and was beginning to use the finished rooms. It seemed somehow unfair that, while the others worked, he had stopped and was playing priest.

"Some people have all the luck," she mumbled loud enough for him to hear, but if he understood, he made no comment.

He nodded a goodbye. His eyes, guileless, measured hers with one quick glance as his black robe swayed in the gentle caress of the desert wind. She had a grudging admiration for him, and he knew it. The months of labor side by side had made her think of him more as a man than a priest, and as a man he didn't seem to be a bad sort. As a priest, however, he lacked something she couldn't quite describe. He was too distant, too intellectual, too unlike the people whom he sought to minister. He was just not one of them. He walked through Pozo Seco with confidence, exuding a self-assurance that no one else possessed, leaning slightly forward as if his aim were to get ahead of himself or them. There was something in that walk that made her doubt him. Whatever power he had over his flock, he had none over her.

She remained standing, observing the church in spite of the cold, and she noticed for the first time that her hands had grown dry. Flakes of skin could be peeled off them. They were dirty and rough and sadly overworked, but the work that made them that way was now completed.

It'll stand forever, she thought. The grooves between the rock blocks had fused themselves into patterns that no one had designed, just as the priest had predicted they would. How had he known?

Her dry hands pained her and the cold wind chilled her. Who would've thought the desert could be so cold, she thought. Even the sun shone cold, and only the very foolish or the most tenacious dared to stay outside, out of the warmth. In the distance she noticed a view so familiar that she had in the last few months taken it for granted. Cactus plants stood in the desert like forsaken hidalgos, isolated greenery claiming the vast sands. With the grace of an ancient race that had long ago assumed its possession, they flourished, even in this desert, for it was their inheritance, the land to which they had been born, and as lilies grace fertile fields, they graced it.

Carole contemplated the green cacti and bowed her head. It never ceased to overwhelm her that she should find so much greenery in this desert land, for it reminded her that everything and everyone around her were somehow thriving, flourishing. Unlike her. She slid her blistered dry hands under her poncho where her armpits warmed them. She tightened her arms about her body in a welcome shudder. It would suffice her now that the walls were standing and her hands were temporarily relieved.

From a sheltered sidewalk several houses to her right across the street, Carole was being watched. A woman was following her every move, but this time it was not the one who came with a child to watch her. It was someone else, and she seemed familiar. Both she and the woman with the child had spent the last few months observing the progress made on the church, but they seldom came near enough to be identified, although Carole had long ago assumed that the one without the child was Cora. From this far away, Carole found it difficult to focus her eyes on the woman's face, but she noticed the skirt undulate in and out of shape every time the wind mischievously changed.

"It is Cora," she said aloud, amused at recognizing the characteristic stance with which Cora attempted to demonstrate her lack of interest in things. Carole had already noticed that Cora was fascinated by the work that she was doing, but she had also noticed the woman's reluctance to commit herself to anything, even admitting to like someone's work. During their meals together, Cora always brought up the subject, usually because, as she claimed, Maria had asked her about something, and she couldn't answer it.

Yet in spite of her interest, Cora would neither visit the site nor volunteer to do some work herself. Carole had asked her, but she restricted her involvement to asking questions about the walls' progress and admiring them from across the street. It annoyed Carole, however, to see Cora hustling her body, day in and day out, across from the site where the church was being built. Infidel that Carole was, she still felt that Cora's business would probably be more profitable somewhere else.

Running the periphery of the town, I saw her. She was coming from Miriam's house, and Zemi was rushing ahead of her on her bicycle. I had the choice of turning back and being considered rude or running into her and striking up a conversation that would make us both uncomfortable. I kept running.

"Hi," I said as I got closer.

"Oh," she said, sounding surprised, in spite of the fact that she had seen me coming. "How are you?"

"Visiting Miriam?" I asked, but Zemi cycled back to me and put her finger to her mouth.

"It's supposed to be a secret," she whispered.

"Ah, of course!"

"My bike needs air," said Zemi.

"Yeah, that rear tire's low."

"Can you fix it?"

"Zemi!" implored her mother.

"Sure," I said, happy to help. "Let's take it into town and get it fixed."

"No," said Maria. "Don't do any such thing."

"Why not?" I asked. I wondered if she was upset over our last conversation. "I'm going into town anyway."

"But you don't have to take her," she said. "Pancho'll fix it like he always has," she told Zemi.

"I guess," Zemi agreed. "You wanna come with me?"

"Okay," I said. "But we still have to go and get the books," I reminded her.

"Some other time," Maria said, obviously pleased to know that I hadn't forgotten. "But you shouldn't let her take up so much of your time." Zemi made a face, put her body into pedaling, and rode on ahead. She didn't like to hear her mother say anything against her.

"She doesn't," I assured her. Maria walked beside me in silence, but I could almost hear her thinking. Or maybe it was the noise in my head that I could hear and assumed to be hers. I had gone out jogging to ease the strain of a bad night spent dreaming of lions, and facing Maria didn't help.

"I hear there's going to be a wedding," I commented.

"Yes."

"The first one in the church." She nodded. "What happened to the mass everyone was talking about?"

"Father Arroyo's changed his mind," she said.

"That's what Cora thought. She says it'll hurt him, in the eyes of the people."

"I don't know. Maybe. Some of us wanted that mass very much. It's part of our culture, you know, to have a mass for the dead."

"I know," I told her, annoyed that she was explaining this to me. "So if he refuses to hold the mass?"

"Some of the people here won't like it. They'd think he's doing it to spite them."

"And is he?"

"I don't know," she said. "It's hard to tell with him. He's not one of us."

"He's not Latino?"

"No."

"But what about his name?"

"I guess it doesn't mean much. His name is Spanish, all right, but that's all the Spanish in him."

"But he speaks the language."

"Not very well. He learned it in school, which probably hurt him more than it helped him." I looked puzzled. "It got him sent here," Maria explained, laughing, "of all places."

"Doesn't he like it here?"

"We're too Latin for him, too uncontrollable. He would like us a lot better if we could be more...what's the word?"

"Malleable?" I suggested.

"Good one. If we could just be more malleable."

"How did he react when the accident happened?"

Maria's eyebrow shot up. "The accident?"

"The fire."

"That was pretty bad," she said sadly. "He really cared for that child."

"He cared for her?"

"Don't be so surprised. He loved that child."

"But I thought priests weren't supposed to allow that," I observed.

"How can anybody help it, allowing himself to care?"

Maria walked silently by my side. I was finding it hard to believe that Father Arroyo had had a soft spot for someone—for anyone.

"He's just a man," Maria said.

"He's a cloistered man," I argued. "He betrays the church if he lets himself get involved."

"And maybe that's what happened. I don't know, but when Luz died he was devastated. At first, he could hardly hold mass. Some people criticized him because they thought he couldn't say mass without a church; that he was too proud. But it wasn't the church."

"Is that why he didn't get the church rebuilt until I got here?"

"That's one of the reasons. He couldn't get the faithful to put their faith in him. Everyone in town was shaken by the fire and Luz's death, and there is a lot of superstition in a town like this one."

"Did they blame him?"

"Why would they?"

"I don't know," I said.

"No, I don't think they blamed him, but he was too hurt to relate to their hurt, to their sense of arbitrary loss, so he sort of lost them."

I was beginning to see Father Arroyo in a whole new light. If Maria was right, and I had no reason to doubt her, the poor man was not as empty as he seemed.

"That's really incredible," I said.

Maria didn't answer. "Would you do me a favor?" she said.

"Sure."

"It's not for me," she said. I waited. "It's for Cora."

"Cora?"

"She has a bit of a problem. When she grows up, she wants to be just like you."

"How flattering!" I joked. "But I don't think she can choose that."

"She wants to be a painter," Maria confided.

"A painter!" I was relieved.

"In fact," Maria continued, "I was kind of hoping you could use her as a helper or something."

"A helper?"

"You're going to need someone."

"I am?" I hadn't thought about it. She was staring at me as if I were arguing her point. "Well, I suppose I will, but..." I objected, not knowing why. She noticed my reluctance to agree and looked away. We walked in silence again until we reached the house.

"I just don't think Cora can do this," I tried to explain.

"I understand," she said, and she bit her lower lip. "It's a bad idea."

"It's not a bad idea," I protested. "It's a great idea! It's just not a very realistic idea."

"Well, you know what Cora is, what she does for a living." She looked away, but nodded. "I can't deal with that," I confessed. "I couldn't work with her knowing what she does. I mean, I can hear her from my room, for God's sake."

"Have you told her that?"

"No, I don't even want to talk about it, and it's not easy to sit at the same table after one of those nights."

I knew I was saying more than I should say, and I also knew that what I was saying wasn't entirely clear. I ate with the woman every day, so why shouldn't I work with her?

"But what if she changes?" she demanded. "What if she gives it up?"

"She hasn't done it yet," I observed.

"If she had a reason," she argued, almost with herself.

"You think she would?" I wondered, but I was also wondering what she thought of me for being as intransigent as I was.

"I'm sure she wants to change her life, but she needs a little help."

"I guess I could do that," I said. "I do like her, you know."

"I like her too," she laughed.

"But it's kind of uncomfortable."

"I know."

"So maybe she'll come by the church some day, if she really wants it."

"Let's hope so," she said, smiling.

From my window, I watched as hailstones covered the desert floor. Dark clouds blocked the light of the sun, the storm had come up suddenly, unexpectedly, and now the rain was falling, almost selectively, here and there over the desert. People had told me that a storm like this one could dissipate as quickly as it had come, but I was hoping that it would stay because as long as it stayed I wouldn't have to work. Rain was as good an excuse as any to stay away from the church. I didn't want to get up and walk across the plaza to face a blank wall because facing blank walls always led me to ponder the nature of blankness. It was simpler to hide in my room and look at the desert and the rain.

I told myself that I wasn't hiding. My body simply wasn't used to the new order of things. I went to bed at night expecting to get up and carry on with the labor, but the church had been finished for ten days. Father Arroyo was already planning the first mass, and the moment I most dreaded had arrived. I was supposed to start painting church walls, but I wasn't at all pleased with any of the drawings I had made. It was more fun to sit and draw Maria's features, which was what I had been doing with my time. There was something about the way Maria's lips curved in a smile that fascinated me. I didn't think the priest would appreciate my drawing Maria's features on his walls, much less her smile. He wanted religious themes, not the likenesses of women I loved.

Staring at the blank walls didn't help any. It just made me run my sweaty hands through my hair as I marveled at the monumental dimensions of my task. "What in the world possessed me?" I would ask myself. What made me think I could paint a mural on this man's walls?

In spite of my confusion, or maybe because of it, the pattern of the rain soothed me. Out of the clouds, drops broke loose and followed their trajectory with a simple purpose, to fall. People weren't so simple. I wasn't. I had been in Pozo Seco for nine months, probably longer, and I hadn't yet determined what my purpose was. Painting the walls was just a job, a chore, but the purpose of my visit eluded me. It didn't seem right that drops of rain should have a purpose when I didn't.

"So what am I supposed to do?" I asked myself. "Paint the damn walls," was always the answer. I resolved to do the work quickly, if not well, and get the hell out of Pozo Seco without further investment of my time or emotions. If the priest wanted saints on his walls, I would have to give him saints even if what they stood for was as foreign to me as the purpose of the rain.

Since I could hear through the thin walls of my room that Cora was otherwise occupied, I walked down to the restaurant to plot my quick exit out of Pozo Seco. Saying goodbye to Maria was going to be the hardest thing to do, but Maria, I was convinced, wouldn't miss me. I would miss Zemi, though. I liked playing with her.

"¿Un especial?" Gloria Peñaranda asked me from the bar. I said yes. She was used to my ordering the special without asking what it was, and I did it because even when I asked her what it was she wouldn't tell me.

I was thinking about how to break the news to Zemi when Ramón, Gloria's husband, approached my table and sat down without being asked. He was a slim, dark man who walked around with his shirt buttons undone and the tails hanging out. The sporadic, kinky hairs on his chest and belly were the first thing I always saw of him. The next thing was his long, yellowing teeth, which made me wonder why anyone would ever want to kiss him.

"Hey!" he said. I didn't greet him, because I didn't want him to stay, but he made himself comfortable anyway. I sat up straight, leaned forward. "Where's your girl?"

Thinking he was referring to Maria, I froze.

"What do you mean?"

"The kid!"

Zemi! He was talking about Zemi. "Home," I said, relieved. "It's raining."

"Yeah," he said with a sigh reeking of spirits. "And a good thing too. The birds be mating after this," he philosophized. I nodded. "The whole damned desert'll be fucking."

"How nice," I remarked, serious enough to make a sober man walk away. The barflies had heard his loud statement, accompanied by the appropriate gesture, a finger pumping through the ring of the index finger and thumb, and everyone was laughing.

"Yeah," he assured me. He had associated my seriousness with a lack of understanding. "They needs the rain for that."

"For mating?" I asked, skeptically.

"They don't do nothing if it don't rain," he explained. From the bar, men agreed and raised their bottles.

"He's right," said Cora. She had made her way to my table without my noticing it. I pushed a chair out for her with my foot. Gloria sent my lunch out with the cook.

"What if it doesn't rain for years?" I asked, raising my eyebrows.

"They wait." As she sat down, Ramón got up to leave. There must have been some agreement between Cora and Gloria that kept Ramón off limits to Cora. I found such a concept interesting because Cora was an attractive, voluptuous woman whose company men sought. Ramón, obviously, was not one of those men.

"Why would they want to do that?"

"So they can feed their young," she said. That made sense. I smiled. "There's not much food out there."

"Ramón said they would all be fucking after the rains," I noted.

"He would!" Cora exclaimed as she looked towards the bar where Ramón had perched on a stool. "Men don't know nothing," she assured me with a wave of her hand. I nodded. "What they'll be doing is courting."

"Birds?"

"Sure. They need the rain. They don't get a whole lot of action the rest of the year. You know, when it's dry."

"I see," I said.

"So as soon as the rains come, they start the courtship."

"I think that's kind of nice," I said.

"Nice!" she exclaimed, and heads turned. She lowered her voice. "Hell! It's beautiful! Those little creatures really know what romance is all about."

"Looking for romance, Cora?" Gloria called from the bar. The barflies roared.

"I'm just explaining," Cora yelled. The cook came back with another special for Cora who was still settling herself in the chair after sending a few nasty looks in Gloria's direction.

"We should all be as smart as the birds about our young," I said, and Cora suddenly grew very quiet. Not even the laughter from the bar could make her say more than a few words again.

After lunch I went outside to watch the rain from Gloria Peñaranda's veranda. The inn had a lovely, wide porch with marble floors that seemed out of place in Pozo Seco. I often sat on the wide veranda with Zemi or Cora to talk about things. Today I was hoping to see the actual mating, but I could only hear the thunder and, through its rumble, the sound of the birds' singing. I couldn't name the singers. After having lived in this town for nine months, scaled quails and cactus wrens were the only birds I knew by name. There must have been hundreds of little creatures out there then whose very existence depended on the rain, but I knew nothing about them. I hadn't even seen them. The rain, with its small fingers, could draw them out.

Talk about a purpose, I told myself and strained to remember the poem in which the rain had little fingers. I wanted to be one of those characters who knew all about the flora and fauna of the region they live in. I had seen them in movies, sitting on a tree stump, telling a group of children fascinating things like the one Ramón had told me.

"¡Cabrón!" I said at the thought of Ramón. In spite of his vulgarity, Ramón was one of those men. He could reduce a beautiful thing to a crass act, but at least he knew about it. What did I know?

"When the rain stops," said Cora, who had come up behind me and was now leaning against the building beside me, "the desert'll bloom."

I didn't answer. I just sat there next to Cora, looking at the rain and smiling.

"It makes you sad?" Cora asked. I wanted to explain, since she also knew about sadness, but I was suddenly tired, scared, oppressed by the weight of my emotions, so I shrugged and shook my head. Cora must have thought I was ignoring her, so I slipped off the railing and laid my hand on her shoulder.

"Thanks," I told her, and I left her to wonder what I was talking about.

The rains didn't stop. Not for days, anyway. The water came down with a vengeance, and the storm winds managed to pick up everything that was not tied down or nailed to the ground. The desert also seemed at times as if it were going to be picked up in patches and taken away. I had grown accustomed to seeing it there, stretching before my eyes as if it were nothing more than a long, safe welcome mat. That was not what it looked like today. The rain fell in thick walls over specific areas, and I couldn't see what I was looking for. Then I saw her.

She was standing in her usual position, leaning against her front door, in spite of the rain. The soft light coming from the house enveloped her and made the features of her face fade into shadows, but the light made a screen of her white dress, and I could see through it. Because of the light, her legs seemed darker than they were. I wanted to touch them, to run the tips of my fingers over her thigh, behind her knee, then back again to the thigh, inside, where it was most sensitive. I closed my eyes to pursue the feeling, but it didn't work. My fingers felt nothing but their own pressure over the palm of my hand, where they had become a fist.

I've done it again! I told myself. And I had. I'd fallen in love with a woman who had no use for me. I liked the way she looked, the way she acted, and the way she treated her daughter but was beginning to dislike the way she held her distance when she was with me. Since our last dinner together, something I couldn't name had come between us. Sometimes I thought it had to do with what she thought I thought about the priest and her, which I had. I didn't anymore. She had cleared that up fast, but now I was pretty sure that she'd figured out, through pure intuition, that I wanted more than just a friendship to develop between us.

I looked at her again where she still stood, one leg crossed over the other, leaning the weight of her body against the upper part of her arm. I wanted her to rest on me, to lean on me when she was tired or, like today, when she was only waiting.

I was waiting too, but she was probably waiting for a man. It may not have been the priest she waited for, but I was sure it was someone like him. That was more or less the story of my life up to this point. Every time I fell in love, I fell for a woman of the heterosexual persuasion.

"Definitely, the wrong kind," I said, but a wise old queen once told me that I was falling for women who wouldn't want me because I wasn't ready to be wanted. He had learned psychology from Chinese fortune cookies and popular paperbacks, but it made sense to me, so I vowed to be ready when the right woman came along.

Maria Soledad seemed perfect. Although I thought she was straight, I had never seen her with a man other than the priest, and more than once during a conversation I thought she had been flirting with me.

You wish, I thought. And I did. But I knew straight women who thought nothing of flirting with a dyke. What could be safer?

"There's worse things," I told myself. She could be scared because she really didn't know a whole lot about me. Whatever she felt, at least I knew that she had some feelings for me. Why else would she explain about the priest? She had said plainly that she wanted me to know.

You're making too much of that, I warned myself. She had probably just wanted to make things clear, make sure that I hadn't gotten the wrong idea, which I clearly had.

I felt bad. Whatever I'd thought then had been so obvious that she had noticed. I wished Maria would care for me as I had come to care for her, but I had no idea how to go about impressing her. My impression so far hadn't been positive.

That night, I lay in bed wondering how to approach Maria. If this town had a movie house, I could have asked her on a date, but the nearest movie house was an hour away. Still, that remained a possibility. I just did not want to risk the friendship for a date. What would I do if my wanting to be more than friends offended her? Could I simply say, "Sorry! My mistake," and leave it at that? If I dared to ask for more, the nature of our relationship would change, and I could only hope it would be for the better.

After a while, I got up and headed for the bar. Gloria Peñaranda made a big fuss about my being there because she had never seen me drink before.

"What's it gonna be?" she demanded. "Milk?" The woman had a mean streak in her.

"A piña colada," I said.

"And what the fuck is that?" she asked tartly, on the defensive.

"Well," I mumbled. "Do you have wine?"

"Lots of it," she said.

"Then give me some of that."

"You sure you can handle it?" she teased.

No, I thought as I nodded affirmatively. Wine made me sick, and I knew it, but that was probably the reason why I chose it. It would give me a reason to really hurt.

Gloria brought a bottle of red wine that was presumably made in Spain and set it in front of me. While waiting for the glass, I picked up the bottle to examine it.

"A hardcore wino," she said to someone across the bar from me as she cocked her head in my direction. The men around me laughed as they always did when she said something to them. I wanted to ask her to leave me alone, but my asking would only have encouraged her.

"So what's eating you?" she asked as she moseyed by me in a cloud of smoke on her way to another customer. She stopped, turned, and slid a glass towards me. It flipped over next to the bottle.

"Nothing," I said.

"Can't get yourself a man?" she asked in a sardonic voice.

"I'm not looking for one," I said, a flash of heat burning my face as if I had been slapped.

"You can take your pick," she said with a wave of her arm encompassing the size of the room.

"I'm not interested," I responded, becoming increasingly angered at the men's laughter.

"What's the matter, girl?" she continued, speaking even louder now. "Don't you like men?"

The noise level around the bar dropped perceptibly as people waited to hear my answer. When it did not come, they resumed their own conversations, but Gloria, who had fixed me with her eyes as if I had been a worm, still waited.

"Tsk!" she said, disgusted. "I thought as much." She left my side to go to other customers.

Needless to say, I was not feeling any better, but I was nevertheless hesitant to get up and go after what had just happened. Gloria would, undoubtedly, interpret my departure as a sign of weakness on my part, and I would never again be able to escape her caustic comments.

While Gloria was bending down to pick up a few beer bottles from a box on the floor, I escaped. I left my money on the table and slipped out of the room, out of her range, for she was obviously in the mood to fire at anything she saw. I resolved then and there not to face Gloria alone again. To deal with that woman's perverse disposition, I needed Cora's protection. Cora knew how to handle Gloria. She knew how to keep her from going too far when she took to hurting.

When I opened the door to my room, there was a lion on my bed. It didn't surprise me. In the state I was in, anything was possible, but I didn't have the energy to deal with my demons then. I removed my clothes stealthily and slipped under the covers without making a sound. Then I thought I heard it pace about the room, but I kept my eyes closed and my head under the covers. After Gloria, I was not about to let a little thing like a lion scare me. There was no point in letting my fantasies get the better of me.

11 The wedding took place on Sunday in the newly built church. For almost everyone who was present, it marked the first time they had entered the church since it had been finished. It was obvious by the sounds of admiration that emanated from the women as they entered that they were impressed, and part of what impressed them was that a woman had been partly responsible for the actual construction. I had brought women's liberation single-handedly to Pozo Seco.

Lupita and Jesús, the newlyweds, left the church in someone's borrowed truck. Lupita had worn a simple white dress she had made with Maria's sewing machine and a white veil Miriam gave her. Jesús had also been dressed in white, like most of the men in attendance, which threw me into a quandary about colors and their meanings. If white represented purity, why were the men dressed in white? Lupita was obviously pregnant, so who were they fooling? I shook my head. I lost my concentration and started thinking how it was fortunate to have undisputed evidence that the roof I had helped build didn't leak. No one in the packed church got wet while under the roof, and that served as testimony to the soundness of its construction.

The wedding over, I slipped out of the church before the crowd emerged. I was well on my way to a warm bath when Jesús and Lupita came out to jump into the truck. Their honeymoon was to be spent at home, for they couldn't afford much, but their parents and their friends were throwing them a party and everyone was invited. I wasn't sure I wanted to go but I didn't want to miss seeing Maria outside the house, in a different setting, and find out once and for all whether she had a boyfriend or not. Where else would I see her dance with him, if she danced, or even simply talk with him? I couldn't pass up this chance.

On my way home, I ran into her. She must have left the church even before I did.

"Going to the party?" she asked me, water dripping from her hair.

"Don't you have an umbrella?" I offered her mine.

"No, I don't," she said, smiling, yet refusing to stand under mine. "Don't worry about it. I'm already wet."

"Yeah," I grinned. I was enjoying every minute of it. Her clothes were sticking to her skin and trickles of rain ran slowly down her face, her neck, into the not so little space between her breasts.

"So, are you going?" she asked again.

"I think so. Yes. Are you?"

"I have to. I'm bringing some of the food."

"Need any help carrying it?" I asked, hoping that she did. "We could use my car so it won't get soaked."

She considered my offer. I could tell she wanted to accept my help, but at the same time she didn't want to impose.

"That would be a big help," she finally admitted, "if you wouldn't mind?"

"I don't mind," I said, happier than I had been in quite a while. Then I asked a question that I knew would throw me into alternating periods of shame and euphoria.

"Will Zemi's father be there?" Maria grinned. She probably thought I was too curious for my own good. She shook the water off her hair suddenly, as if she had meant to shake water arrows at me, and said, "No." I couldn't tell whether she was grinning at my colossal stupidity or at the thought of Zemi's father's being at the dance.

"I was just curious," I explained. My face was beginning to turn red. I could feel the heat.

"About me?" she demanded.

"I've never seen you with a man," I confessed. "All you do is work and play with Zemi."

"Really? I hadn't even noticed."

"I have," I said, but I didn't quite believe she hadn't noticed. How could she not notice that her life was reduced to doing for others?

"Zemi's father doesn't live here," she told me. "And if he did," she said, but she didn't finish the thought. I saw her look away at the desert, the rain still striking her face, making her close her eyes and turn away.

"Do you still love him?" I asked her because I simply had to know.

"Not anymore," she answered. Then she dismissed the whole affair by claiming, with a wave of her hand, "it was just one of those things."

I nodded, as if I knew what she was talking about. I wanted her to tell me what one of those things was like, what it had meant to her, but the only thing I heard was that although she may have been in love with a man once, she was not in love with him now.

"So you're going to the dance alone," I said, cheerfully, and nearly died hearing myself saying it.

"With the food," she answered.

"Ah, yes! And I'm going to help you carry it."

"And that means you're not going alone."

"I guess so," I said.

"Well," she said. Nodding and grinning, the two of us stood soaking wet on the street corner, and neither one of us made a move to leave.

"So why don't I pick you up in about half an hour?" I asked.

"Okay," she said, smiling. I was smiling too, especially since I'd realized this would be our first date.

Maria walked away from me full of expectation. The look on her face betrayed her feelings, and I flattered myself into thinking that her last glance towards me before she turned the corner had some kind of message behind it. It told me she was making sure I would be there, if only because she wanted to know I would be.

"Oh, God! She's here!" Maria exclaimed disconcerted. "How can anybody be so punctual?"

Maria opened the door to let Carole in.

"You're not ready," Carole said, looking at Maria's robe.

"No. I've had some trouble in the kitchen, and I haven't had time to get dressed." Carole nodded, sympathetically. "Do you have a box?"

"Uh?"

"A box," Maria repeated. Obviously anxious about the time, she seemed rushed. "I need something to carry the food. I don't have enough pots to put it all in." She nearly flew toward the kitchen. Carole followed.

"What about aluminum foil?" suggested Carole. "Can you use that?"

"Sure," Maria answered, "but I don't have any."

"I'll go get some," Carole said after noticing the shape of Maria's kitchen.

"Looks awful, doesn't it?" Maria asked, disheartened. "My kitchen is never this messy, but I've been cooking for two days, and I don't have enough pots to put it all away."

"We'll figure it out," Carole said.

"I get carried away, I know."

"Don't worry about it, I'll get some foil. It'll be fine," Carole assured her.

"And a box."

"And a box. I will get a box, okay?"

"A big box," Maria suggested, sheepishly.

"As big as I can fit in the VW," said Carole. "Okay?" Maria nodded. "Leave the packing to me and get dressed."

"Don't forget the box," Maria called after her, but Carole had already left. The rain had let up a bit, and she could see Carole's VW splashing through the muddy street to the bodega.

Carole returned so soon that she caught Maria unprepared. She hadn't even had time to think about what she was going to wear, much less get dressed, so she was still in her bathrobe when she opened the door for Carole.

"Disappointed?" she asked.

"Why?"

"I'm not dressed," she admitted, which started Carole's laughing again. "Well, at least you think it's funny."

"You shouldn't worry about it," she said, carrying the box towards the kitchen. She had bought a few plastic containers along with the foil, and she was expecting to hear Maria complain about spending money on her.

"Get dressed," Carole said softly, so close to Maria that she could smell her breath. "I'll take care of this."

"Okay," Maria said, watching Carole pack the food. She knew she should leave, but she couldn't. She had to watch. Carole was wrapping dishes and putting them away one on top of the other in the box, structuring them so that bundles rested on corners and not on the dish itself. Maria felt good knowing that someone could take over, send her away to dress, make her feel as if she really wasn't alone. She hadn't felt secure in someone else's presence since Miriam took her in and made everything right.

Carole looked over at her. "You're still here?"

"But I'm going," Maria said.

"Get dressed."

Lupita's parents' house was packed with people, and everybody was dancing and having a good time. A few guitar players were walking around the room playing Spanish love songs, the way mariachi bands play at restaurants back home. The only difference was that these guys were the real thing, and they were playing the songs my mother and grandmother used to sing. I recognized so many of them that the memories came rushing back to me, and I was back again in my grandmother's arms as she sang me to sleep.

"Que las rondas no son buenas, que hacen daño, que dan pena, y se acaba por llorar," the man whom I recognized as Ramón sang. *That a night on the town isn't good, that it hurts, and that you end up crying.* That one had been one of grandmother's favorites, but I never knew if she was singing the song for herself or for me because, as it says in the song, she always ended up crying.

"What's the matter?" Maria asked me after she had laid the food out.

"Nothing," I lied.

"You look depressed. You're not upset because I was so late, are you?"

"No! It's just the music."

"The old songs?"

"They bring back a lot of memories," I admitted.

"You grew up with them too?"

I nodded. Someone handed me a beer. It was Ramón.

"Drink up, gringuita," he said.

"Thanks, but I don't like beer," I said.

"And what do you like?" he demanded in a mocking tone.

"She likes your songs, Ramón," Maria interceded. "Why don't you sing something else?"

"For the two of you?" he asked, grinning. I remembered my little run-in with Gloria at the bar.

"For everyone," Maria answered. Ramón pulled his guitar from his back and began to strum the strings.

"And you're gonna dance?" he demanded, suggestively.

"If we feel like it," I finally said. He walked away from me with the ugliest look of disdain I had ever seen on anyone's face.

"What was that all about?" Maria asked after he had gone. I didn't know what to tell her. I was certain that she would, eventually, find out about what had happened, but I didn't want to be the one to tell her.

"I had words with Gloria," I told her, "and I guess he feels like he has to vindicate her honor or something."

"Gloria's honor?" Maria asked incredulously, and began to laugh. I laughed too. It didn't seem like the kind of thing that would make Ramón want to argue. "If anything," Maria added, "it's Ramon's honor that's often defended around here."

"What do you mean?"

"Gloria gets into a fight with a different woman at every party," she informed me. "If she sees anyone hanging around Ramón, she attacks."

"You're kidding!" I exclaimed, amused. "But he's one of the ugliest creatures on earth!"

"But beauty is in the eyes of the beholder," Maria said in her most serious voice.

"You'd have to be pretty desperate to behold him as beautiful," I told her, which made her laugh. I didn't laugh, though.

"Look, there's Cora!" exclaimed Maria, waving to her friend.

"Who's that little girl?" I asked.

"Must be Clarita," she said, in a whisper. "I can't believe it."

"What? Who's Clarita?"

"She's her daughter," she told me. Then she rushed to hug Cora and kiss the little girl who stood beside her, a little surprised at all the attention.

I hadn't noticed, trying to transport the dishes in the rain, how pretty she looked. Under the yellow raincoat, she wore a light summer dress with thin straps, and she filled it. Her breasts, bulging upwards, seemed barely contained. I remembered what Zemi had said about her clothes not fitting, and I stared at her, pleased, warmed by the loving way she hugged Cora and took the little girl into her arms. She spoke softly to her as she walked towards me, followed closely by Cora.

"I didn't know you had a daughter," I said to Cora. She simply waved her hand in the air with a gesture that implied that every woman has a daughter.

"This is Clarita," Maria told me.

"Nice to meet you," I said to the girl. She must have been Zemi's age, but she didn't seem as old. I wondered where Zemi was.

"She was back home with my mother," Cora told me, "but now she's gonna live with me."

"Isn't that nice?" Maria asked the girl, but the girl didn't answer.

"Everyone around here's got a girl or two. You and I were the only ones without one," I said to Cora.

"So where's yours?" said Cora.

"In the making," I assured her, but it made her laugh so hard that she started coughing.

"So how come you're not dancing?" Cora demanded. Maria had taken Clarita to get something to eat, and I spotted Zemi playing with some kids around the table where the food was laid out.

"I don't have a partner," I told her.

"You don't need a male partner to dance here," she replied.

"How do you know that's the partner I don't have?" I said.

"Word gets around," she answered. I said nothing. "So listen," she added, "let's give these guys somethin' to talk about."

"Like what?"

"Like dance with me, stupid," she said, taking my hand.

"I don't think it's a good idea, okay?"

"Are you guys going to dance?" Maria had come back with Clarita.

"If she'd move," Cora answered.

"I'll be next," Maria added, excited. "So don't wear her down, Cora."

The thought of dancing with Maria was motivation enough to get me onto the dance floor with Cora. We squeezed between the other couples, where I soon learned that we indeed, were not the only women who were dancing together.

Cora had a wicked grin on her face. "Don't you know Spanish girls dance with girls?" she asked.

"No, I didn't." I had heard that European women danced with each other in public, but nobody had told me about the Spanish.

"Well, now you know," she said and laughed. "Nobody thinks anything of it," she added suggestively, "so you can dance with anyone you want."

I practically dragged Cora to the side when the song ended, and as soon as we got there I stationed myself near Maria. I didn't want her to forget about her asking for my next dance.

"Is Cora a good dancer?" she asked me.

"Yes, she is," I answered. Actually I'd had fun dancing with Cora.

"Well, don't expect the same from me," she told me.

"Maria has two left feet," Cora joked. "Or is it right?"

"Maria's feet are just fine," I said.

"That's what you think!" Cora practically yelled as she slapped her thigh emphatically. "You better watch out!"

"¡Ay, Cora!"

"Yeah, Cora. ¡Ay!" I said. Cora laughed even harder.

"She'll tell you she can't lead, and then you end up following," Cora told me, her hand on my arm.

"All right, already!" Maria complained.

"And most of the time you don't know what you're doing," Cora continued.

"That's okay. I'm not that good," I told Maria.

"She just has this thing about leading," Maria said, opening her eyes wide, trying to stare Cora into silence.

"It's your turn to play mother," Maria told her.

"So where are the kids?" she asked.

"They're trying to eat as much as they can. So keep an eye on the table."

"Yes ma'am!"

"The music's starting," I said to Maria, and she took my hand. That little spot of feeling I had in my stomach leaped uncontrollably and made my nose itch. I felt the rush of feeling rise all the way to my head.

I could die from this, I thought to myself, but I danced around until we reached a spot in the middle, away from Cora's laughter.

"Cora's right, you know. I'm not very good at this," she whispered.

"I'm not either," I said, but it must have been obvious to her because I'd stopped dancing and was just standing there looking at her.

"Is something the matter?" she asked. I shook my head. I wanted to kiss her. Just this once. I didn't care if she never spoke to me again. I wanted her then, looking the way she did, with her crazy long curls frizzy from the rain and the sweat on her chest slipping down her cleavage into places I couldn't follow. That's what the matter was. I wanted to follow the little drops of sweat down the curves of her body to wherever the curves took them, sliding down her belly to her crotch, her thigh, but I knew I couldn't. Not now. Probably never. So I sighed deeply and started dancing again, moving so slowly that she asked me again what the matter was. Luckily, the band was playing a slow song, which made dancing easier, even in such a crowded room when the person dancing wasn't paying attention. The hard part was just being there, dancing in the arms of this woman whose very presence enthralled me, mystified me.

I must have been missing steps, because she leaned away and smiled at me. Then she leaned closer against me and led me around the room.

"What are you thinking?" I asked her.

"You're a good dancer," she told me. "You dance like this where you come from?"

"Not like this," I admitted, but I didn't want to explain the past. I wanted to lose myself in the smell of her, her hair, the skin of her shoulders. I wanted now to last forever, so I closed my eyes and locked the rest of the crowd out of my mind. She shook her head and smiled. Then she started singing softly in my ear. It tickled me and made me smile. Eventually she looked at me again and switched positions. She wrapped her arms around my waist and stared at my face.

"Not fair," I said. I missed every step. She laughed and went back to leading me.

"Are you all right?" she asked. I nodded. The pressure of her body against mine was causing havoc deep inside me. My knees were weak, and since her dress had straps for shoulders I didn't know where to put my hands.

"Would you rather stop?" she said.

"No," I answered, and I moved closer to her in spite of all the signals my body was sending me.

When the song ended, Maria thanked me.

"I haven't done that in years," I told her.

"Me neither," she smiled, radiant. A few strands caught in one of her shoulder straps as she shook the mane of her hair. People pushed by us to reach the food table. Their presence brought me back to that room in someone's house where I shouldn't even dare look at her the way I had. After a while, I mumbled something about it having been my pleasure, but for the most part I just looked at her.

I sneaked out of the room and ran home through the muddy streets. I left the keys to the car with Cora and asked her to help Maria. She said she understood. I didn't. I just had to be alone.

Once in my room, I sat in the tub to think of her. I had the smell of her body on me, and if I closed my eyes I could feel the pressure of her arms around my waist.

So why didn't you stay? I asked myself. I could have danced with her again and again. I knew that, but I was either too nervous or too scared to do what I wanted to.

I should have told her I liked her, I thought, but then a little voice in my head said I was a fool. The only reason she danced with you, it said, is because you helped her out of a jam today. She'll be back to being her usual self tomorrow.

I hope not, I thought, but she would, and I knew it. I would be on my own again. Lately I had been wondering why I was the only one who was always left out. Everyone around me lived as part of a family, but not me, and now even Cora had a child whom she could call her own. I had no one, and tonight I was in the mood to feel sorry for myself.

I rose from the tub and dried my body in front of the mirror. I had the strong legs of a runner, and firm muscles everywhere. My mother used to say I was too nervous a person to get fat. She said I sweated everything out in fear, and she was probably right, but my running helped, although she would never have admitted that. She thought it foolish of me to run when I was already slim.

"Mom," I said to the mirror, "what would you think of me now?" I could not tell. "I danced with a woman tonight, Mom," I said to her. "And I liked it. I danced to one of the songs you used to sing, and she put her arms around me and I melted."

The mirror didn't answer, and I was beginning to feel like crying. I remembered then how someone, a poet, had asked the Lord to send his roots rain. "Birds build—but not I build," the poet said. "No, but strain, time's eunuch, and not breed one work that wakes. Mine, O Thou lord of life, send my roots rain."

I looked out my window towards the desert. The birds must have been mating now, for the rain was falling on them. Was I also what the poet called himself, time's eunuch? Was I destined to not breed one work that wakes? Did He not send the rain for everyone? The awful little voice inside my head said, "You pays your money; you takes your choice."

"Cynic," I said aloud. "Why shouldn't I want rain?" I whispered softly as I slipped under the covers. I crossed myself in bed to keep away the dreams I knew would come. I would dream of lions tonight, and of falling, and I would wake with the emptiness that dreaming of such things always left in me.

"Mine, O Thou lord of life, send my roots rain," I prayed, and closed my eyes to wait.

The rain had hit the town on Wednesday morning and cut Pozo Seco off from all communication. The town, like an island between highways, seemed far away. Maria Selene was coming home that day.

Home again! she thought as her eyes searched the station for a familiar face. There was the dying sound of footsteps as people found each other in the silence and rushed into the rain. No one was expecting her, but then she had told no one that she would be here today.

She felt the grip of the suitcase stick to her cold hand. The skin, tight and rough, shed layers of translucent silk to the touch. Maria Selene walked about the station to keep herself warm before venturing out into the rain. She wished she had someone there to meet her.

I should've told them I was coming, she thought and looked toward the spot where the sun should have been. Robbed of its light by the sudden cold, the sky had paled, or maybe it was too early yet for light. Maria remembered this type of morning from her youth, when she lived here and she used to sneak out of her parents' home with Miriam to make a ceremony for the light of day.

The thought of Miriam made her smile. She of all people should know I am here, she thought sadly. But maybe she's changed. Time can do that to people.

From the muddy road, she watched the train pull out, like time itself, slow but ever moving. She fixed a hat on her disheveled hair and started the long walk to town. But the train returns, she thought, thinking about time and her own journey home. Sí, she argued, but trains don't have no memories, she argued with herself. Not like hers, and she knew that once she entered Pozo Seco she would have no control. The past would rush to meet her everywhere she went. It's why I left, she reminded herself. 'Cause it was just too hard.

In the distance, she could see the plaza, and in her own memory she could see her daughter running through the puddles as she chased her, playing a game of tag. She stopped, closed her eyes, and then saw Luz running out the front door as Maria called after her, "Niña, ¿a dónde vas?" *Child, where are you going?*

"¡Ay, mamá!" Luz complained.

"She never answers," Maria said to Miriam, who was standing beside her.

"Es la edad, María," Miriam explained. *It's her youth.* And she called after Luz, "Don't go near the church."

She knew, Maria told herself now. Years later, she was still convinced that Miriam had seen something, some sign of Luz's death. But she didn't say a word.

"I have to make light," Luz yelled back from the street, and Maria laughed now as she and Miriam had then.

"Se está burlando de mi inglés," *She's making fun of my English,* Miriam said.

"What a thing to die for," Maria whispered now. She shook her head and adjusted her coat. The rain had soaked through the layers of clothes. When Miriam sees this, she's gonna yell at me, she told herself. She smiled at the sky as the water poured down her face, remembering Miriam coming to her house that last rainy night.

"Cariño," Miriam had said then when she finally found Maria, wrapped in a wet poncho on the kitchen floor.

"Not now, Miriam."

"Pero estás mojada y cubierta de churre, María. Te vas a enfermar." *But you're wet and covered with dirt, Maria. You'll get sick.*

"I don't care anymore."

"Pero a mí sí me importa, María. No haces nada con eso. ¿Quieres un buchito de té? Te lo hago calientito." *But it matters to me, Maria. You'll solve nothing this way. How about a sip of tea? I'll make it warm.*

"¡Ay, Diós mio! Que mujer más insistente." *My God! What a persistent woman!* Maria had said. And I just sat there like a fool, ignoring her.

She shook her head again. Through the years, the memory of her life with Miriam, the laughter and the anger, had sustained her. Away from Pozo Seco, she had had time to think about herself and Miriam, about their many years raising Luz together, about their friendship.

I didn't see a thing, she told herself and started walking—only to stop again as soon as she remembered her own words to Miriam.

"You knew, didn't you?" she had demanded then.

"How did you get so wet?" Miriam asked, and she spread a blanket about Maria.

"Did you know?"

"¡Ay, María! No sé lo que sabía." *I don't know what I knew.*

"But you warned her. You told her to stay away from the church!"

"And I had warned her before," Miriam argued. "Didn't I? I just didn't like her going to that place."

"Liar," Maria had said then. It made her cringe, as it had every time she reheard herself saying that word to Miriam. She could still see Miriam's eyes fill with tears as she ran her fingers through her hair and sat next to Maria in silence, looking away.

I shouldn't have said that. Not to her, she thought now. But after Luz's death she had been crazy with grief. She could still remember herself crying and yelling, trying to break through the crowd of people in the plaza. They had held her back. They had kept her from rushing into the blaze because they didn't believe her when she said Luz was inside.

"¡Ay, Jesús!" she cried aloud as her body shivered, shocked by the memory of Luz's pain. "That she should die like that."

It was then that she had cursed them. She had forgotten all about the curse, which had been nothing more than words spoken in anger. But Maria Soledad had mentioned something about it in a letter.

Maria's a good friend, she told herself. Over the years, Maria had written letters and kept her informed. In one, she wrote how the people were worried. They'd had some problems with the crops, and the young men were leaving town before they came of age. Even the weather had turned against them, from what she said. During the summer, the winds had uprooted old trees, and now the rains threatened to drown most of the livestock. It made them think of the curse.

She smiled slightly to think of their fears. Most people in Pozo Seco had been less than kind to Luz. They had all realized who had fathered her, and they had made her feel different. They blamed the mother and child, not the father, for the illicit birth. And after her death they must have blamed themselves because they felt the curse as if it had been real.

So they went and built themselves a church, she thought wryly. They probably need it. But she wasn't so sure about the mass. Maria had said that the first mass would be for Luz, to lay her soul to rest.

She thought again about the night she left, about the awful pain she had carried with her, and the hurt she had seen on Miriam's face. She didn't think Miriam would ever speak to her again, not after she had called her a liar and Miriam turned away, tears dropping to her knees from her face. And yet here she was. Maria Soledad said that Miriam had told her to write, and she should come and stay with Miriam because Maria Selene's old house had a hole in the roof.

She probably never even got angry, Maria guessed and she smiled sadly remembering Miriam's confusion that night, her trembling hands, as she drank the tea she had made for Maria. She thought about how many years had passed before she could see her friend's weakness through anything other than anger, before she could accept that Miriam had been as powerless as she was to prevent Luz's death. She's just a woman, Maria could admit now, even if she sees a little better than most.

Maria noticed people were walking toward the plaza. She wondered if she had been speaking aloud and if her voice had carried. She hoped they hadn't heard her talking to herself—the crazy woman who cursed them.

I was just walking out the door when Cora stopped me. We had eaten breakfast together, and she had talked nonstop about Clarita, so I didn't expect her to have anything left to say. I was, of course, wrong. Cora's supply of anecdotes on the subject of Clarita seemed to increase as my patience wore thin.

"See that woman?" she whispered to me. Gloria Peñaranda was keeping an eye on the woman.

"The one with the suitcase?" I asked. She nodded.

"You know who she is?"

"How the hell am I supposed to know who she is?" I demanded. Cora's many mysteries sometimes made me angry.

"Hey, if you don't wanna know," she told me.

"I want to know, Cora," I argued. "I'm dying to know."

"Forget it."

"Okay, I'm sorry," I added, softly. "Tell me. Who is she?"

"Luz's mother," she said after an appropriate silence.

"The kid who died?" She nodded. "What's she doing here? I thought she was never coming back."

"Who told you that?"

"Zemi," I answered.

"You should ask me about these things," she said. "Zemi's just a kid."

"So what's this woman doing here?"

"Maria sent for her," Cora told me, her right eye almost closing as she nodded her head. I knew that the eye signal meant something important.

"Why?"

"There's the mass, you know."

"But Father Arroyo's already changed his mind about that," I reminded her.

"Yeah, but if you ask me, Maria's got something up her sleeve."

"What do you mean? She's got something up her sleeve?"

"There's something going on that she's not telling."

"If you don't talk!" I threatened, pointing my finger at her.

"I don't know what it is!" she exclaimed. "It's just what I suspect."

"About what?" I almost screamed. Gloria Peñaranda was puffing away on her cigar and laughing at me. Cora's association with me had never pleased her.

"About Maria," Cora whispered, her eyes fully open. "I think she's trying to pair Miriam and Maria up."

"How do you mean?" I wondered, confused.

"Maria Selene," she told me, pointing at the woman with the suitcase, "used to be Miriam's best friend."

"So?"

"They lived together," she explained, "even though Maria had a house."

"And?"

"And they had an awful fight before Maria left, after Luz died. Maria kind of blamed Miriam, because you know how Miriam can tell you the future when she feels like it and you ask her nicely."

"Actually, I didn't know that."

"Well, she can," Cora said, "which is why Maria got angry at her, I guess."

"Because she told her the future?" I asked, thoroughly confused.

"No, because she didn't tell her."

"Now I'm really lost."

"Maria thought Miriam knew," Cora explained.

"About the fire?"

Cora nodded. "So she blamed Miriam when it happened. Well," Cora reasoned with herself, "she really blamed everybody."

"For Luz's death," I added. Cora nodded, a strange frown on her face.

"Luz was pretty wild," she said. "Not like Clarita."

"I'll be damned!"

"You are," she assured me, "if you live in this town."

I laughed. "It's not so bad."

"Yes, it is. Maria Selene put a curse on us before she left."

"Go on!" I said. "You don't believe that stuff. Do you?"

"Hey!" she said. "I believe a lot of things."

"A curse?" I asked, frowning. "So now you think Maria Soledad's trying to get this Maria and Miriam back together to get rid of the curse?"

"Could be about the curse," Cora admitted, "but it could be much more than that."

"You're making this up," I said. Cora had a way of sounding as if she knew more than she knew.

"She was the one who wrote the letter asking her to come."

"Maria?" I asked. "Our Maria?" Cora nodded. "That's wild," I said. "And kind of nice. Don't you think?"

"Maybe," Cora answered. God forbid she should agree with me.

"And it's kind of wicked too," I added, "because it could create all kinds of problems. What if these people don't want to get together?"

"They probably do," Cora argued.

"Yeah, but..." I didn't know what else to say.

"It's the timing," Cora added.

"I didn't think Maria had it in her." Cora shot me an "I told you so" expression. I waved goodbye to Cora as I walked away. I had to think about what this new information meant in terms of what I knew about the people in this town and what I had learned about Maria Soledad.

Disturbed by the silence, Miriam looked out the window at the rain. "¡Que día está haciendo para ella!" *What a day for her!* she said out loud, thinking of Maria Selene. She knew in her bones that her friend was at this moment making her way home, alone, and she wished that she had not listened to the other Maria, the young one, who had begged her to stay home so that Maria Selene could make her decisions alone.

"No entiendo esa necesidad que tienen de estar siempre solas." *I don't understand this need they have to be alone,* she said to her cat who had jumped on the window sill. "¿Y tú?" *Do you?* The cat looked back at her. "Claro que no, tú y yo somos de un otro tiempo." *Of course you don't. You and I are from the old school,* she told him as she ran her hand over his fur, "y eso quiere decir que yo debí de haberla estado esperando en la estación. De estamanera, va a pensar que estoy brava, aunque le dije en mis cartas que no lo estaba. Nunca lo estuve. Si alguien podía comprender su dolor." *Which means that I should've been waiting for her at the station. As it is, she's going to think I'm angry, even though I've told her before in my letters I'm not. I never was. If anybody could understand her pain* ...she said, but she didn't finish the thought. The memory of Maria crying over her dead child intruded.

"Quisiera poder olvidar el pasado, sacármelo de la mente." *Sometimes I wish I could just forget the past, put it out of my mind.* It wasn't possible. Her past and Maria's were linked through the birth of her child, the love, the years. A fit of anger at the wrong time couldn't change her feelings for Maria.

"¡Ay!" Miriam exclaimed as she saw through her window a woman who looked like Maria approaching her house. "It can't be!" But the woman had the same full hips that she still remembered and that way of walking as if she were tired and about to stop at any minute. Tears flooded her eyes, and her hands instinctively covered her mouth. Then she stepped outside to make sure that her eyes were not deceiving her.

"María!" she called out to the woman who stopped and smiled at her. "¡No te mojes!" *Don't come out in the rain!* Maria yelled, but it was too late. Miriam was already walking, arms stretched out, towards her.

"Vieja testaruda." *You're a stubborn old woman,* Maria said. "¡Ahora estamos las dos mojadas!" *Now we're both wet!*

"Let me look at you," Miriam whispered as she stared at her friend through the rain and the tears. "Just the same," she said. "You're just the same."

"You're right. I was wet when I left."

"¡Ay, María!"

"Espera aque se me seque el pelo para que veas las canas." *Wait till my hair dries and you can see the gray,* Maria said, smiling, because meeting Miriam now with the soft raindrops caressing both of them made her feel as if time had stood still and nothing had changed.

"Tú eres la que no has cambiado." *You're the one who hasn't changed,* Maria added.

"Just because you told me not to come out in the rain doesn't mean that I'm as stubborn as ever," Miriam argued.

"Yes, it does, old woman," Maria teased her. "And I'm sure you have some warm tea you won't give me."

"What are you talking about, mujer?"

"The day I left!" Maria exclaimed. "You drank my tea."

"I did no such thing," Miriam argued.

"You did! I've been laughing about it all day. You offered it to me, and then you sat there and drank it."

"What was I thinking of?" Miriam asked.

"We both had a lot on our minds that day," Maria admitted.

"I'm so sorry for you," Miriam said.

"I feel better now."

"And you're home," Miriam said, and they hugged for the first time in five years.

"Tengo tanto que decirte." *I have so much to tell you,* Maria whispered through her own tears, and words she never thought she could say spilled out of her mouth into Miriam's ear.

"Don't be sorry!" Miriam said as she ran her fingers over Maria's face to wipe her tears. "You're here. That's all that matters."

"But I said so many things," Maria argued as Miriam led her out of the rain into the house.

"And I didn't say enough," Miriam answered, for she had always regretted her silence about Luz's destiny and about her own feelings for Maria. To protect the friendship, she had sacrificed her love, but when Maria left she thought she had lost both.

"We'll just pick up where we left off," Maria said. Miriam agreed.

                         I practically ran to the church that morning. My little talk with Cora had finally shed some light on the mystery surrounding the accident, and on top of that it had told me something new about Maria Soledad. I had spent the night thinking about her, trying to interpret what had happened between us at the dance, but I had come to no conclusions. The best of my interpretations told me that it was brought on by friendship, not love, so my mood when I met Cora for breakfast that morning was anything but jovial. Her story, however, changed that. It was encouraging to think that Maria had enough respect for the love of two women to attempt a reunion between Maria and Miriam.

It's probably not sexual, I told myself. In spite of Cora's insinuations, I still found it hard to believe that the two women had been romantically involved.

Everybody's not gay, I reasoned, but Miriam's being gay would explain Father Arroyo's contempt for the woman.

But if Miriam and Maria Selene had in fact been lovers, then where did Luz come from? Whatever I may have wanted to think, the fact remained that Maria was Luz's mother, which meant that a man had been involved at some time.

It could've been a mistake, for that's what I kept hoping had been the case for Maria, my Maria. She had probably just met a man who swept her off her feet and got her pregnant. It had happened before.

Makes sense, I told myself. I simply didn't want to think that Maria could love a man. The thought made me cringe.

"Ouch!" I said, as Zemi did when I said something wrong. This is just ridiculous. First I think she is; then I think she isn't. I don't know what to think. And I can't ask her about it because I'm too big a coward.

I stood in the middle of the church and stared at the walls. I had come to measure the walls where I wanted to start drawing, but my mood had changed. I was too angry even to care if someone had heard me, and I wasn't too happy about the drawings, either. Father Arroyo had seen the sketches I had made and, since he neither approved nor disapproved of them, I had decided to use them. Looking at them now, however, they seemed somehow inadequate. Chills ran through me.

"Damn!" I said. If it isn't one thing, it's another. How the hell can I concentrate on this when everything else is distracting me? Too much was happening. Not only had I fallen in love, but I had also gotten myself involved with Cora, Clarita, Zemi, and now Miriam and Maria, whom I didn't even know, not to mention all those women who came to look at the church.

My room was full of drawings of Maria and other women whom I had seen around, but I had not taken my role as church painter very seriously. My rendition of the Stations of the Cross put even me to shame.

I never believed this job was real, I reasoned. What else would have led me to spend months drawing everything but what had to be drawn?

I left the church wondering about my work. If I was to do the work, I had to come up with something more than copies of other painters' works. That's what my drawings were, which is why Father Arroyo, when he saw them, had simply said, "interesting." He must have realized then what a mistake he had made. I had never painted anything out of the ordinary, much less particularly original. Any well-trained eye could have seen the influences latent in my work.

I've just never dared, I thought, and I rushed up the stairs to gather the courage to dare.

The next two weeks I spent in my room with the Bible. I felt like a sinner who suddenly got religion, because from the moment I opened my eyes in the morning to the moment I closed them at night I thought about Jesus. I wanted to get the feeling of what He must have been like in order to do Him justice, but the stories in the Bible made him seem unreal, and I was left with cartoon versions of His life. I couldn't find the third dimension that would let me paint him the way I felt he should be. I was depressed and suspected that I was really a lousy artist.

Father Arroyo was no help. He sent messages with Zemi, who usually came with Clarita, to find out what was wrong with me. I entertained the girls every time they came, but I also sent them back to him with no news at all about my problem. I couldn't tell him that I couldn't draw him a Christ, try as I may. I knew I was close, but I was so far, too.

Eventually, he came in person. I went down for breakfast at a time when I knew Cora would be busy with Clarita, and I found him at my table, waiting for me.

"Good morning," he said. I couldn't believe he was sitting there.

"Hi," I answered.

"Are you in hiding?" he asked.

"No," I told him, but said nothing else.

"I thought you were eager to start on the walls," he commented. I signaled the cook, who had sneaked a peek through the kitchen door, for the day's special. "Why haven't you started?"

"I don't like the drawings," I told him. He frowned. "And you didn't like them either."

"They were good enough," he tried to reassure me, but he wasn't very convincing.

"Not for me," I argued.

"So now what?"

"Now I study the subject until I can come up with something I like," I told him.

"Is that what you're doing in your room?" he asked.

"What do you think I'm doing there!"

"I don't know! Nobody's seen you in two weeks. We were wondering what happened."

"I've been reading," I said, asking myself if Maria was one of those people who were wondering.

"The Bible?" he asked. I nodded. "Don't you think it'd be easier to talk about it?"

"With you? Are you an authority?"

"Some people would say so, yes." He answered without losing his temper.

"Sorry, but I think I want to get the unauthorized version."

"This is a church you're talking about," he reminded me. "Those walls are supposed to remind the faithful of God's suffering, show them what He did for their sins." I nodded, amused. "You do believe, don't you, that Jesus died for our sins?"

"I'm Jewish," I informed him, which was not a total lie. My mother had been Jewish before she married my father, and after that she had been nothing at all. Their children, however, had been sent to Catholic school by my father, who never went to church himself. In the end, we all went through life with a rather muddy concept of what it meant to have a religion.

"Jewish!" he exclaimed in disbelief.

"Yeah." I was really in the mood to irritate him.

"So, you think you can do this?" he asked, concerned. "I mean, if you don't even believe!"

"I'm not converting, you know? I'm just painting."

"But this kind of work requires devotion, the kind a true believer has."

"You don't paint with devotion." I argued for no reason, because I knew that he was, if not right, almost right.

"But you've got to feel it," he insisted. "You've got to be able to move these people with God's passion."

"I don't need your religion to paint your God's passion."

"So why haven't you started?"

"Because I'm not pleased with what I have now," I told him honestly. "I'm beginning to see what I want to do, but it's still rough, not fully formulated."

"I want to see it," he said.

"You'll see it when I'm finished," I snapped back at him. He didn't argue. He simply raised his hands in front of him and cracked his knuckles, a gesture I had seen a million times already. Today, it meant resignation. At other times, it had meant impatience. I saw the calluses on his hands, and I felt my own. My face must have turned red with shame.

"Oh, come on," I said, and rose to leave. He didn't quite understand. He probably thought I was angry and calling the conversation to a close, but I nodded towards the stairs and he followed me. In spite of the foul mood I was in, I couldn't keep him from his precious sketches. If he wanted to see what I had done, I had to let him. The months of hard labor spent side-by-side had bought him the right. I was also convinced that the sketches I had now were far better than the ones he had seen before. They still showed no evidence of any passion, but for the first time I believed that the passion would come.

I went to work a week after Father Arroyo's visit. Having him look at the work, even though he seemed puzzled, had allowed me to look at the drawings from a different perspective. I still wasn't totally satisfied but I figured it was now or never. I wrapped the sketches into a bundle and went down to breakfast at what had once been my usual time. Cora must have been listening by the door for a sound, for as soon as I stepped outside my room she stepped out of hers.

"How's Clarita?" I asked. She put her finger to her mouth asking for silence.

"Sleeping."

"Coming down?"

"Claro," she answered. "I've missed eating with you," she added.

"I ate at odd times," I said. "Whenever I felt like it. You must've been busy with Clarita every time I went down."

"That's probably true," she agreed. "Having a child keeps you busy. If it isn't one thing, it's another."

"I bet," I said, and rushed ahead of her into the restaurant.

"Well, look who's here," exclaimed Gloria Peñaranda when she saw me. I had actually stayed away from the restaurant during the last two weeks because I was too scared of facing her on my own. The few times I filled myself with courage and went down to eat, I'd had the good fortune of being served by the cook, not her.

"Can it, Gloria," snapped Cora.

"Yes ma'am!" Gloria exclaimed. "Whatever you say, a fine lady like you. I should be honored you should eat at my table," she answered and laughed. Her regulars laughed too. Cora, her eyes icy slits, cocked her head to look at Gloria.

"You've got something to say?" she demanded, hands on her hips. Gloria Peñaranda considered the situation.

"No," she said, almost meekly.

"'Cause, if you do," Cora added, "you better say it now."

"The usual?" Gloria nodded towards me.

"Scrambled today," I said.

"You?" she said to Cora.

"I want mine raw," snapped Cora, who was still upset.

"¡Ay, chihuahua!" Gloria complained, apologetically. "You know we don't serve no raw eggs."

"Give me the usual, then," said Cora and waited until Gloria had left to sit.

"You didn't eat, did you?" she asked. I shook my head.

"Not here," I said. "I had some stuff upstairs."

"You're really a coward," she said.

"I like to keep out of trouble, okay?"

"So you stay away," she pricked.

"I have my way of dealing with things and you have yours," I said. She didn't answer. She sat instead and sulked. "Is Clarita in school?" I asked, although I knew she was. She herself had told me during one of the visits she had paid me with Zemi.

"Yeah, but she can't read," Cora told me. I looked puzzled. "Maria's teaching her to read at home."

"But isn't she Zemi's age?"

"So what?" she asked. "There's no schools where she comes from."

"It's a good thing you brought her here, then," I said.

"Yeah," she answered. "Before she ended up like her mother, right?"

"You mean you can't read either?" I asked, surprised.

"Didn't I tell you we had no schooling back home?" she snapped.

"But I didn't realize," I mumbled, at a loss for words.

"Knock it off, okay?" she asked. "I know what I am, but I want better for my girl. As soon as she learns to read, she'll start going to school, and then she can learn English."

"That poor kid's got her work cut out for her," I said.

"She can handle it," she said. I couldn't help but smile at her new attitude. Clarita's arrival had made a difference in Cora. It was beginning to show.

"I'm sure she can," I said, and watched her eat her breakfast with her mind a mile away.

I had pretty much decided what to do about the drawings. I spread them out around the church in the proper order of the Stations and stood back to admire. For the first time in my short career as a painter, my work pleased me. The faces in the drawings didn't look like faces I had seen in other artist's works, but they were familiar. They belonged to the people whom I had seen almost daily since my arrival in Pozo Seco almost a year ago. I didn't recognize anyone in particular, but they were all there in different shades of brown and with slanted, heavy-lidded eyes.

"They look good." I heard Maria's voice and almost missed what she said.

"You startled me," I said, happy, trying not to smile, but nervous to see her.

"I know," she smiled, pleased to have gotten some reaction out of me. "I didn't mean to. I just wondered how you were. I mean, I haven't seen you since the dance."

"Didn't Zemi tell you what I was doing?" I asked.

"She said your room was messy and could she keep her room like that."

"She was right," I laughed, "but it was mostly because I had drawings all over the room. It's taken me a while to come up with something I can use."

"Are these the new drawings?" she asked, gesturing towards the walls with her hand. I nodded, grinning with pleasure. "I like them," she said, looking at me intently. I wondered if I should mention our dancing together. I wanted to, and I was about to say something when she looked away at the walls again. "Father Arroyo liked them too," she added.

"Really?" I asked. "He didn't say very much of anything when he saw them."

She bit her lip and nodded. "That's his style. He can't admit to anything."

"Like Cora," I suggested.

"Right," she agreed.

"I haven't forgotten what you asked me," I told her. She looked puzzled, as if she had asked me too many things for anyone to remember. "About using Cora as my assistant. It's really a good idea, especially now that Clarita is here."

"But wait until she asks you," she warned me. "Don't ask her."

"Why? I'm going to need an assistant, and we both know she's willing."

"But give her the chance to ask you," she told me. "Cora's the kind of person who has to do things herself. It takes her forever to get the courage to do it."

"Cora?" I interrupted her. "You've got to be kidding!"

"She acts tough, but that's because she's had to be tough all her life. But she's not that tough. She's really very scared about a lot of things, and she has to think about things for a long time before she actually acts."

"Like her bringing Clarita?"

"Precisely. She agonized for years about having left her little girl behind."

"Why did she?"

"Because she ran away from home, and she didn't have any money, and it seemed the right thing to do at the time. But when the years started passing and she still had no money..."

"She realized that things weren't getting any better and she was wasting her time," I interrupted her again.

"More or less, but I think the real deciding factor was her own upbringing. She left her daughter with her mother, in the same environment that she was running from. That's what really did it."

"She mentioned something about that this morning. She said she wanted something different for her daughter."

"Don't we all?" Maria said, and I wondered what her story was. What was she running from? She must have read my mind because she changed the subject right away. "Where are the windows?"

"Father Arroyo is having them made," I explained. "The ones we had up for the wedding weren't ours."

"Are you going to paint them too?"

"No," I answered, pleased to think that she thought about me and my work. "That's a specialized kind of work. There are only a few people in this country who still do it. I'm just going to do the Stations of the Cross."

"Well," she said, as if she were thinking of leaving. "That's still a lot of work. I guess I should leave you so you can get started."

"I have time," I said. "And besides, I don't have to be alone to work, so you can stay if you want to. They do." I signaled towards the women who had taken their posts across the street from the church.

"What are they doing there?" she asked.

"They've been there from day one. And it looks like they'll stay while I paint the walls."

"They just stand around and watch you?"

"Uh hum," I smiled. "And when I say hello to them they get all embarrassed and shy and hardly ever say anything."

"You think that's funny?" she asked, a little upset.

"No," I defended myself. "I think it's sad, because they're obviously impressed by what I do, but they're too insecure or just plain ignorant to do something like it themselves. And that's a shame."

She didn't respond, but she shook her head as if she had thought of something negative.

"Maybe your being here will make a difference for them," she said.

"I don't see how; they don't even talk to me, and it isn't because I haven't tried." She let out a sigh.

"Maybe that will change," she said and walked towards the door.

I followed her, wondering if I had upset her by calling the women ignorant. I was thinking of a way to reopen the conversation when she turned and asked me to come to dinner. I accepted immediately, of course, but I feared that my insensitive comments had spoiled the evening already.

After she left, I refused to put off my work for another second to sit and think about the conversation. That was my usual practice after talking to her, but today I had more pressing matters. I still had to transfer the drawings to the walls so that I could begin painting. I rolled up my sleeves, put Maria and the women who watched me from across the street out of my mind, and went to work.

14 I made it to dinner at Maria's that night, and she asked me back for the following week. During the meal, she asked me all sorts of questions about the work I was doing in the church, and I was only too happy to tell her about it. It helped me clarify things, define lines, give the faces meaning. As an artist, I knew my limitations. Maria made me surpass them by providing me with something I'd never really had, a past.

From Maria I learned what some of the people in Poco Seco, especially the women, thought about. The people themselves never talked to me, and I still didn't know why. I also learned from her some of the narratives behind their lives. Every single one of them had a story, and much of what I imagined they felt ended up on my drawings behind the very same faces I saw every day as I walked to work. The stories Maria told me were the difference between the drawings on these walls and the stuff I'd done before I came to Pozo Seco. If nothing else, she gave my work depth.

I had been drawing for three weeks when Miriam came to see me at the church. I had heard a lot about her from Zemi and Maria and even Cora, but I didn't really know her. I knew only that Maria and Cora trusted her, but the priest did not. That she lived all alone in the desert made me think of her as a sort of wild creature, but the day I met her she wasn't even as tall as she seemed when I had seen her from my window. Age had obviously bent her, slightly, as only time can, but she still carried herself with the agile ease of youth. It gave her a mysterious aura. Her eyes, with eyebrows like fur, seemed heavy with the knowledge acquired over the years.

"You the painter?" she asked me.

"Yes," I said. "What can I do for you?"

"What do you here?" she asked, irritably.

"Painting," I told her. "Oh, you mean 'what' as in, why am I here?" I asked. She nodded. I gestured to the walls. "It's my work." She walked around the room and stood in front of every one of the drawings, but she showed neither approval nor disapproval. Then she made a few gestures as if she were struggling with something, and I realized that she was looking for the right English words to say what she came to say.

"Si quiere, puede decirlo en español," I told her. *You can speak Spanish if you want.*

"You speak Spanish?" she asked me in English, skeptically, although she had just heard me speak the language. I nodded. "Good," she said.

"Me enseñó mi madre," I told her. *My mother taught me.* She smiled and kept an eye on the drawings.

"Esas caras no parecen muy santas," she said. *These faces don't look too saintly.* "¿Y al padrecito le parecen bien?" *Has the priest approved of them?* "No son suyas. Son del pueblo." *They're not his. They're the people's.*

"Pero estás pintando al pueblo, mi hija," she said almost in a whisper. *But you're painting the people, child.* "Y esa, ese diablillo, se me parece al cura." *And that one, that devil, looks like the priest.*

"Las cosas no son lo que parecen," I told her. *Things are not always what they appear to be.*

"De eso mismo vengo a hablarle," she told me, examining me again. *That's what I came to talk to you about.* Her mysterious demeanor was making me curious, but I couldn't imagine why she wanted to see me.

"People tell me things," she said. "Soy una vieja, ¿sabes? Y los viejos como yo lo oimos todo porque la gente ni cuenta se da que estamos escuchando." *I'm old, you know? And old people like me hear everything because nobody notices we're listening.*

"De acuerdo a lo que me han dicho, a usted nadie la ignora." *According to what I've heard, nobody ignores you.*

"Ah, sí. Ni cuenta se dan que estoy entre ellos." *They don't even notice me among them.* "Soy como la arena. Ahí estoy a sus pies, pero nadie me ve." *I'm like the sand. I'm there at their feet, but they don't see me.*

"¿Y qué quiere decirme con eso?" *What are you telling me with that?*

"Que oigo más de la cuenta," she admitted, coming close to me. *That I hear more than I should.* Arms crossed, I was standing beside her. She laid her hand on my arm. "Y he oido que haces preguntas, una detrás de la otra. ¿Por qué?" *And I hear you've been asking questions, one after the other. Why?*

"¿De Luz?" *About Luz?*

"¡Ay, mi hija! Déjala en paz," she told me and crossed herself. *Leave her in peace.*

"I'm curious about her, about her death."

"Fue una muerte muy dolorosa," she told me, her eyes closing as she shook her head. I wanted to believe her. *It was a painful death.*

"Pero esta gente, los que hicieron la iglesia, se sentían responsables, como si fueran culpables de algo." *But these people, the ones who came to build the church, felt responsible, as if they were guilty of something.*

"Eso está en tu mente," she assured me, shaking her head. *It's all in your head.* "La gente me han dicho lo mismo, que les culpas de algo, pero nadie es culpable, ni siquiera tu diablo." *People have told me the same, that you blame them for something, but nobody's guilty, not even your devil.*

"What happened, then?"

"There was a death," she said, "and the people had to stand by and watch. The fire was too big for anyone to go in. They had to hold the mother back."

"And it was nobody's fault, right?" She nodded. "¿Y por qué se sienten culpables?" *So why do they feel guilty?*

"¿Quién puede responder por sus demonios, o los tuyos? Solo les digo de qué guardarse, como le digo ahora. El desierto no es ni tan grande ni tan malo como lo ves, y tampoco lo son sus hijos." *Who can answer for their demons, or yours? I can only tell them what to beware of, as I'm telling you. The desert is neither as wide nor as wicked as you see it, and neither are its children.*

"Pero no soy del desierto," I said, which only made her argument seem more sound. *I'm not of the desert.*

"Pero los que somos," she said calmly, "preferimos no tener que estar siempre explicando lo que somos." *But those of us who are would rather not explain ourselves to you.*

"I gather I'm supposed to stop asking questions."

"No si tienes que hacerlo, pero date cuenta a quién preguntas." *Not if you feel that you have to. But keep in mind who you ask.*

"But what about the death?"

"What about it?" said Father Arroyo. He had been standing in the penumbra of an adjoining room all along.

"What is it to you?" I asked. His presence made Miriam restless, like a wild animal about to become someone's game. I wanted him gone.

"You're in my church," he said to Miriam.

"She was admiring my work," I informed him, and I wondered if he had understood our Spanish conversation.

"I'm fond of her devils," Miriam told him in her best English, almost defiantly.

"Then worship them elsewhere," the priest snapped. "This is the house of God."

"It's very pretty," Miriam said, "and empty, but it's curious, you know? You think I can find the devil here. Why not something else? Why not Luz?"

"There are no spirits here."

"But you worship one," she said.

"A holy spirit," he said. Miriam nodded, smiling and staring him down. She knew.

"I leave now," she informed us. I made a motion as if to speak, but she stopped me. "Don't worry," she told me, her kind eyes telling me that I was not to blame for his presence. "We meet again."

"I hope so," I said, and I walked her to the door. Once outside, she was surrounded by dogs that capered about her legs in excitement. I stood at the door and watched her walk away into the desert, just as I had watched her so many times from my window.

"That wasn't very Christian of you," I said to Father Arroyo.

"And it takes a heretic to show me the way?" he snapped back.

"I was wondering when that would come up," I said, casually. He let out a scornful sound and strode out of the room into the shadows from which he had emerged.

I sat on the floor to think. If, as Miriam had suggested, Luz's ghost were here, why could I not feel her? If Father Arroyo had loved, truly loved, that girl, why did he not seek her spirit out?

Given what I had just witnessed, the morbid pangs of guilt that I had occasionally felt about having used Father Arroyo's face on some of my devils seemed like a waste of good human emotions. His actions towards Miriam confirmed what my instincts had already told me, that there was something not quite right about this priest.

He doesn't even believe in spirits, I lamented. A light breeze teased the papers scattered on the floor. It lifted them and dropped them like giant butterflies playing in the air. I wondered if Luz had heard me.

"That woman is a demon," he practically screamed when he saw Maria.

What woman? she thought, but said nothing. It was one of her fears that he should learn about Carole what she, herself, suspected, and she wondered how he would react.

"She was at church!"

"Who?" she asked, innocently.

"Miriam," he hissed back at her. "It isn't enough that she defies me everywhere else, but she has to come to me, to the house of the Lord."

"She has every right," Maria cut him short.

"Right?" he yelled, his face tight and red.

"He's her god too," she said.

"Her only god is a fallen angel."

"You can't know that," she said mildly, "because you've never talked to her. She worships the same God you worship. None other."

"And how would you know that?"

"Because I've known her for seven years." She knew full well that she was admitting to her disobedience. The priest nodded repeatedly, his face distorted in anger.

"You never stopped seeing her," he told her.

"You know I haven't. She brought my daughter into this world, and she let me stay with her when no one else would help me."

"Anyone could've done that."

"Maybe, but no one did. It takes somebody like her, somebody who's really kind, to do something like that for a stranger."

"She has her motives for being kind," he said, his jaw trembling.

"Ulterior motives? If she had them, she never asked me for anything that I wouldn't have gladly given her. She's not a witch, like you think she is. She's just a woman with a gift, a God-given talent."

"Don't you tell me what God gives! You're not His instrument! Nor is she!"

But you are, she thought. And a troubled one at that.

"You're not to see her again," he told her.

"I can't do that," she said.

"You can too. And if you want to stay here," he threatened, "you'd better not."

"I won't stay then." She was angry now. He felt her words like a slap in the face.

"What do you mean, you won't stay?"

"You don't own me. I owe you the work you pay me to do, but nothing else."

"Do you know who you're talking to?"

"To a man," she answered. "Are you anything else?" He had no answer. He simply sat by the window and rubbed his chin.

"You don't know what it's like for me," he finally said. "Everywhere I go, she's been there before me. Everyone I see has been touched by her."

"She was born here," Maria tried to comfort him. "The people know her."

"And they would know me too if I didn't have to contend with her," he reasoned.

"She is not against you," Maria assured him. "Never has been."

"She's not with me!" he exclaimed contemptuously.

"You haven't let her be with you. You're afraid of her, but she's not afraid of you."

"So she holds mass at home," he said despondently.

"She needs it. She's a very spiritual woman, and you've locked her out of your church, God's church, so she worships at home."

"She's not a priest!" he exclaimed.

"What's a priest?" she asked. "To the people who come to hear her, she offers the word of God as they know it."

"The word of God isn't flexible. It doesn't change with every congregation."

"Well, maybe it should. The world isn't made out of white men who hate women." He looked at her as if for the first time. Although there was no anger in her statement, it told him more about Maria than he had ever known.

"That's what you think priests are?" he asked, his face drained now. She nodded. "Regardless of what you say, she still can't preach. She hasn't been annointed."

"And she never will be, not in your church. Not as long as it is run by men like you."

"You blame me!" he said, amazed.

"You said it yourself. If you're not with me, you're against me, and you can't deny that in your church women aren't much more than servants."

"I'm not going to argue theology with you," he said, defeated.

"Why should you?" she asked. "My opinion counts for nothing where you come from."

"And you blame me for that?"

"Who else can I blame? Aren't you God's instrument on His earth?"

"I'm a priest," he said.

"And you enforce the church's laws, the same ones that keep women like me down. Have you read the work of the church's fathers?"

"What are you talking about?" he snapped. The woman was questioning him.

"How can you read theory and not think it applies?"

"Nobody believes that anymore," he argued.

"It's still the law!" she yelled. "Where do you think your attitude comes from? You think a woman's silence in church refers to the ones who sit in the pews?"

"It's not for us to question."

"Ah, right. Don't question. Accept. And as far as I can tell, accepting makes you as much to blame for those laws as the men who made them."

"Is that why you don't keep the Sabbath?"

"Not in your church, I don't."

"At Miriam's?" he asked.

She nodded. "I will not be silenced," she told him. He nodded also, but his nod was one of dawning awareness.

"This little talk of ours has certainly been enlightening," he said with a tinge of worry.

"I'll be gone by morning."

"No," he said. "Please don't leave."

"It's best."

"No it's not. Not for me. I was wrong to say what I said," he admitted, his head turned away from her. "Please, don't leave me. I...." but he couldn't finish.

Maria stood by the door, defeated. She didn't know what to say after having revealed so much of herself to him. Nothing will ever be the same, she thought, for she had to wonder how she would face him the next day and in the days to come.

"Good night," she whispered before she left the room. The priest, left alone, wrestled with the thought of Miriam, Maria, the law. He had never questioned, but the women in this town seemed to do nothing *but* question...and defy. From little Luz, who had never stopped asking him why, to Miriam, who thought her answers made the most sense, and now to Maria, who had the force of her intellect behind her.

"Amazing," he said. Maria had read the work of the church's fathers and questioned them, defied them. He had simply interpreted them, but never questioned them. He remembered reading St. Thomas Aquinas' "The Production of Woman" and noting that Aquinas seemed to be questioning God's intention, but he had been told in no uncertain terms that Aquinas hadn't questioned God, as it seemed to him. He accepted what he was told, and stopped asking questions that could make him seem too different, too daring.

Maria would have asked, he thought. It made him wonder about her upbringing, her education. He didn't know anything about either one although he had known her, lived in the same house with her, for over six years.

"What am I to do?" he asked aloud. Having raised the building, the church, was good, but not good enough for him. The people still trusted Miriam. On Friday afternoons and Sunday mornings, they followed her to the edge of the desert where she held a simple mass. He had seen her from the distance. Had wondered why they followed her. What did she give them that he didn't? What did they find in her devotion that they couldn't find in his?

This is blasphemy, he thought, but he couldn't help but wonder what in the world he must do to gather the town around him.

Father Arroyo left the house that night without having decided where he was going. Something inside him insisted that he visit Miriam, but at the same time something else told him that he couldn't. The years of antipathy and hostility had taken their toll, marked the path that they were both to follow. Still, he knew that if he wanted to change religious practice in Pozo Seco, he had to deal with Miriam, speak to her about the masses, question her about her preaching.

"Blasted woman!" he grimaced, knowing that he had to talk with her. Doing it, however, could prove costly, even dangerous. He didn't trust himself with this chore. He simply didn't know that he could control his temper, his bad feelings towards Miriam. Almost automatically, he set his eyes on her house, the little speck sitting out beyond the edge of the town, but he simply couldn't walk in the direction of the place.

What did he know about her? Maria had accused him of judging Miriam from his ignorance. He knew that she could be Indian, although she lived apart, away from the rest of the Indians in the area. She did have constant contact with the people at the reservation, so she must be acquainted with their ways, their religion.

He had left the house angrily, slamming the door. He hoped Maria hadn't interpreted the slammed door as anything relating to their previous conversation. Why should I care? he thought. It troubled him that he did, because he had never cared what she thought before.

"That's all I need," he said. "To go around wondering what she thinks."

As he wandered about town, Maria's words came back to him. He had never known her to care so passionately for anything; she had after all, offered to leave his house, her job, even though she knew full well that there were no other jobs available in Pozo Seco. Such behavior, Father Arroyo believed, was reckless, and it was also doubtlessly a direct result of whatever it was she felt for Miriam. There was no other reason, as far as he was concerned, why a person should risk everything over a disagreement.

Father Arroyo frowned and turned away; his hands made fists. His own words to Maria had been offensive. He knew that now. He wished he could take them back, but he couldn't. What would it look like? But the thought of losing Maria, and Zemi, of having them move back to Miriam's house or even away from Pozo Seco made him cringe. He had never told her, of course, because the opportunity had never presented itself, but he respected the woman. He couldn't even imagine doing what she had done, crossing the border alone, coming from wherever it was that she came, and making a life for herself and her daughter on what little she earned. He hadn't known then about her education, about her having studied the same works he had studied.

"In any other profession..." he said, but he refused to finish the idea. If I'd told her I respected her, he thought, things would have been different. But he knew that telling her would have been impossible. Maria and Zemi had come into his life out of convenience, his convenience, and the pattern of their relationship had been established then, when he offered her the job and she took it. She was to be his housekeeper, which made him her employer regardless of how little he paid her. He had convinced himself that the church would not afford him the luxury of a housekeeper, but the fact that he was helping the woman out of a bad situation somehow made it easier for him to give in.

That was years ago. To this day, nothing had come of his plans to do something for her, to help her find a real job, one that paid enough to live on. He had simply settled into an easier life with her in his house, and he had learned to look forward to Zemi's company at night. Since the day Maria entered his house, coming home was a pleasure. It had bothered him at first that the rooms were altered and rearranged, but playing with Zemi and talking to Maria during dinner had made him feel part of something special, a family.

"Something I shouldn't have," he said, but he wanted it. He had given up the chance of having his own when he entered the church and took the vows, but he hadn't known then what he was giving up. And then when Luz died....

"Let her stay," he whispered. Maria's words and the tone of her voice came back to him to remind him of her passion. He had never felt anything as strongly as she did. He had read about women who had left the church in search of justice, but the rights of women within the church had never interested him. He simply had not thought of them as a separate class, as anything at all. Maria held that this was his mistake.

Questioning the church had never occurred to him, but he was impressed by the radical priests in Latin America who did question and, in fact, defied the Pope's decrees. They interested him. Fascinated him. He read about them in newspapers as if he were reading about national heroes. In his eyes, what these men did counted, and it hurt him to think that he had been sent to Pozo Seco, the wrong place, where he faced as opposition not a military junta but an old, belligerent woman who refused to acknowledge the church as her guide. He would have been more useful somewhere else, in a place where the lives of the people were centered around the church, where the priests risked their lives to organize the poor, minister to the hungry, and comfort the displaced. He knew that he could have spoken for them with a forceful, defiant voice, but as it was he had been sent here to replace a priest who had, himself, sinned.

"Father Leal," he spit out with contempt. The very thought of a bad priest made him angry, and he had to shake his head at what he knew Father Leal had done.

Father Leal had been disloyal to the church, broken his vows, fathered Luz, and chosen to ignore his role in her creation. Father Arroyo never spoke to Maria Selene about the priest and his relationship with her, but he grew to like the child and brought her into the church, even though her mother was Miriam's best friend. That Maria Selene had been a devout Christian. She had raised Luz in the church, had insisted that she learn her catechism, had made it possible for him to get to know her. He still missed her, the mischievous child whom Father Leal's concupiscence had produced, and this confused him. He had never questioned his choice, his celibacy, but to have fathered such a child he would have changed his life.

Luz had adopted him as her friend when he first came to town, and he, aware of the circumstances of her creation, had let himself be befriended. He thought then that he was doing her a favor, that he was taking under his wing a very rebellious and unruly child in order to help her grow. She had been marked by the accident of her birth in a town where everyone knew who had fathered her; such things had conspired to make her a bit wild, a bit more daring than other children her age, but Father Arroyo knew that she was a good child. He had trusted her with little chores in the church in order to keep her around, and for all he knew it was one of those little chores that had cost her her life.

"Oye, Padre," a voice called him from the street corner. It startled him back to the present. "What are you doing out so late? Looking for action?"

"Cora, is that you?" He had been so lost in thought he couldn't focus on her face clearly.

"Were you expecting the Pope?"

"No."

"So what are you staring at?" she asked. Father Arroyo had stopped beside her and was running his fingers through his hair.

"I think you did the right thing," he said. Cora stared at him in disbelief. "Your decision to bring Clarita…it was the right thing to do."

"What do you care?" Cora snapped. "You're probably just wondering if she's baptized."

"Is she? Because if she isn't, she should be."

"She doesn't have time for that kind of thing," Cora told him. "She's got a lot to learn."

"Bring her by the church," Father Arroyo added, softly. "There's nothing to learn before baptism."

"I'll think about it," Cora answered, confused.

Unaware of Cora's confusion, Father Arroyo crossed the plaza and entered the church. Carole's drawings were covered by white sheets, but he uncovered them. He was sure she would be offended, but he wanted to inspect alone what Miriam had seen earlier. The cross, he agreed, was too big, and the devil's face looked an awful lot like his.

So that's what she thinks of me, he thought. He smiled, in spite of himself. Carole's drawings were good, and the faces on the walls were as familiar to him as they must have been to Miriam.

Everybody's here, he thought. Then he remembered Miriam's objection to Carole's questions. She had said something about how her questions were designed to draw from the people what she now had exposed upon these walls.

She must have been asking the right questions, he told himself, because the people on Carole's walls were the same ones who had built the church, the ones whom he should call his flock. The looks on their faces, however, made him stop to think about how well he knew them. He had seen them at prayer and he had seen them about town as they lived their ordinary lives, but he had never seen them feel so deeply or so passionately.

"Passionately," he said aloud, and for the second time that night he was faced with a word whose meaning he had never before felt. He understood what it meant to feel passionately, but he had never felt the fire that passion could ignite. There was fire in those faces, but there was also something, a look of commitment that he couldn't explain. On their way to Calvary they witnessed a brown Christ like themselves carrying His cross, but there was no denying that in the process of witnessing, His cross had become their own, His resurrection likewise theirs.

I have never felt this passion, he thought, and his hand came to rest on the heavy candle stand that had survived the fire. He examined it carefully by running his fingers over the edge, the very same edge that had fallen on Luz and crushed her that fateful day. How he had prayed that she had been dead before the fire consumed her body.

Why had he not been able to comfort Luz's mother then? He had locked himself in his work, away from the wailing that had so emphatically offended him, and given only cursory attention to the woman's pain. Had he not lost and grieved as well after Luz's death? When he found the ashes and tried to make sense of what had happened, did he not think his heart was about to break? Maria Selene demanded then that he resurrect the child. He didn't even try to explain, to reason with her, to help her in any way. Her mind was too far gone with pain, he had told himself, and he had barely listened as she cursed priests and the church and finally even the townspeople. She vowed her daughter's spirit would return. But he did nothing to help her, to make her see that life is as it is for reasons that not even a priest can alter.

Was I to be undone by her? he wondered, but the image of Maria Selene's pain was as clear in his mind now as it had been then. Even the look on Miriam's face came back to him as members of the congregation confessed to him that she had seen the death long before Luz's birth. He dismissed her visions then as drug-induced illusions, but he never forgot the wisdom of her passion. "What would you have gained by knowing?" she asked Luz's mother as she took her in her arms to offer solace.

Tears rolled down his cheeks as he tried to fight the memories. To silence their insistent voices, he examined the drawings. He noticed an unfinished piece and drew closer. The wounds on Christ's body were being cared for by a hand whose arm had yet to be drawn. It was a slim hand, and Father Arroyo had no doubt that the hand wiping Christ's blood, attempting to ease his pain, was a woman's hand. He could tell by the shape of the fingers, the size of the hand, the expression of compassion that he saw emanating from the hand. He looked at his own hands as they locked in prayer, and it hurt him to think that his hands had never healed a person's wound or eased another's pain.

"Father," he implored, "grant me passion!" but he knew he would settle for the gift of such a hand.

As soon as she saw Carole walk towards the desert, Cora decided to visit Maria. She couldn't wait to tell her the latest news about the painter, but Maria always acted as if she didn't care, which sometimes made Cora wonder how much she should tell. That was why she hadn't said anything about Carole's run-in with Gloria, although she herself thought it was funny, and Gloria thought it was hilarious.

Gloria had told everybody by now, which only made people flock to the restaurant. They sat around and waited for the painter to come in while they discussed the pros and cons of her condition, and everybody was very disappointed to realize that the little altercation with Gloria had scared the painter out of going to the restaurant. No matter how long they waited, the painter didn't show up. They wondered if she was eating, and the women, particularly, began a big argument about how much weight she was losing. "You'd think I pulled a knife on her or something," Gloria complained. The crowd at the bar laughed, but some of them thought Gloria may have gone too far.

"I didn't even touch her," Gloria argued, but it didn't change the fact that the painter wasn't eating and she was staying away from the place where most of Pozo Seco expected to see her.

"So go to the church," Gloria yelled at the ones who complained about her bad manners, and that got them started all over again on how some people think they have the right to push other people around. The discussion on what happened at Gloria's bar raged for weeks. Cora reasoned that Maria must have known about it, but Maria never mentioned it, even after the dance.

"It's like she don't know a thing," Cora said, but hearing herself speak reminded her that Maria had danced with Carole. "¡Ay, chihuahua!" she exclaimed and slapped her thigh. The dance must have made it clear to everybody, even the ones who thought Gloria was wrong about Carole's sexual preferences, that Maria was the same way. Everybody knew and was talking about it. Even Miriam, who never said a word about anybody unless it was good, asked her about what had happened at Gloria's bar and about Maria dancing with Carole, so how could Maria not know?

"Smart people can be so stupid," Cora told herself and shook her head in disgust. They never noticed anything unless it was right in front of their noses, and in Maria's case it was worse. "She's book smart, but she don't have the good sense God gave a mosquito, and it's really something because she says I'm thick. Thick, thick, thick. What's that supposed to mean?"

Thinking about Maria, Cora got angry. Her natural inclination was to tell her what the town was saying, but she refrained because she didn't know what Maria would make of her having told her. It didn't take a lot of smarts to know that something was going on between those two, but Cora didn't think either one of them knew what the other one felt.

"Or even herself!" she told her own hand, which, as usual, extended forward and upwards as she spoke. "¡Ay! Good thing I'm not smart."

"You said it," Cora heard someone say, and she saw someone running to catch up with her and pulling down her skirt at the same time.

"¿Y a tí quién te dió vela en este entierro?" *And who gave you a candle in this funeral?* Cora asked.

"Pues tú, chica. ¿Qué andabas hablando sola?" *You did. Were you talking to yourself?*

"Ay, Martica, I didn't recognize you."

"Pues no, con la conversación que traías." *Of course, not, what with all the talking you were doing.*

"I was thinking about something and got all worked up about it. You know how it is."

"Take care, comadre. You got better things to get worked up about."

"I know it," Cora admitted.

"What's this about being smart?"

"Not me. Maria, you know? Y la güera."

"Ay, sí. They're real smart, those two."

"Not really," Cora said.

"¿Cómo que no, Cora? Hazme el favor, no hables boberías." *How can that not be so, Cora? Do me a favor, don't say silly things.*

"¡Pero me vas a decir a mí que las conozco! *You're going to tell me about it, when I know them.* They're smart in the head, I tell you, but the rest of them is silly."

"Caramba, Cora. That's not what I hear," Martica said and started giggling. Two other women who had joined them elbowed each other and laughed.

"Pues valga quién pueda," snapped Cora. *More power to them.*

"Ay, Cora, don't get upset," one of the women said. "We were just talking."

"Sí, I know. Everybody's talking. Talk, talk, talk is all I hear."

"Hell, the painter should've punched Gloria out," Zenaida said. She had come up beside them and heard the last comment.

"She's not like that, Zenaida," Cora told her.

"Ay, verdad, and you know her. Well, I don't care. With all the work she's done, you'd think Gloria'd leave her alone."

"She's just jealous; it's what I say," Martica said.

"You're right, you know. It's because she's smart," Zenaida added.

"But Cora says she's stupid."

"Ay, Martica, no inventes." *Don't invent things.* "Na'mas dije que era silly." *I just said she was silly.* "I think all that reading she did in college burned out the really smart bones in her head." The women agreed with a chorus of "si."

"What bones?" Martica wondered after everyone, still nodding, stopped saying yes.

"The smart ones," Cora explained the obvious.

"She must still got some of it because look at that church," Zenaida argued. Another chorus of "Ay, sí" emerged from the group. Cora had to nod her head, say "sí" too, agree with the general consensus of the group, but secretly she still wondered about Maria and Carole.

"You got the smarts in the bones?" Martica asked.

"¡Ay, mujer, qué tonterias!" *What silliness,* Zenaida said. The others laughed and Martica joined in. "Knock it off with the bones already."

"I'm getting out of here before she gets worse," Cora told them. Martica was trying to locate her own smart bone by running her fingers over her head.

"El piojito, cotica," Zenaida said, laughing at Martica who looked like a parrot scratching her head. *Scratch, Polly.*

"Maybe she's got fleas," one of the women said.

"On top of the smart bones!" Zenaida added.

Cora left them laughing and headed for Maria's.

"Guess what I saw!" Cora exclaimed as she walked into Maria's house without knocking.

"What?" Maria asked, startled. She had been singing Zemi to sleep on her lap when Cora entered, as usual, unannounced.

"Isn't that kid too big to carry?" Cora asked.

"She's not heavy," Maria told her. She had almost fallen asleep herself as she sang to Zemi.

"Hmm, well, guess!" Cora repeated, cheerfully.

"If you wake Zemi up," Maria warned her, "you die."

"That kid's out like a light."

"And it took me an hour of reading books and singing to get her there."

"What's the matter with her?" Cora asked. Zemi was known for falling asleep at the table.

"She's nervous."

"Yeah? Clarita too."

"Zemi has a fever, but the two of them are up to something, and it's making Zemi nervous," Maria said.

"Pobrecita," Cora said. *Poor baby.*

"They've been skipping school."

"Ay, no," Cora said. Maria nodded.

"It's probably because Clarita's having trouble with the language."

"But she's learning!" Cora interrupted, upset to hear Maria complain about Clarita.

"It's not about learning. Clarita's getting frustrated about being left behind, so she and Zemi sneak out every once in a while."

"I'll kill her!"

"Let's wait and see what happens," Maria suggested.

"But she's going to fail!"

"I told you she would, Cora. She has to learn the language before she can pass anything."

"And what about Zemi?"

"Zemi's the one you need to kill."

"I bet it's all her idea. You know? Skipping school. Clarita wouldn't do that." Maria nodded and bit her tongue. As much as Zemi was to blame for initiating the trouble the two girls got into, Clarita was no innocent. But Cora would never see that.

"We'll just have to wait and see what happens with this skipping business," Maria said.

Cora nodded and then remembered her news. "Carole," she said, mysteriously.

"¿Qué?" Maria asked as if she had just been awakened from a dream. Cora didn't know what the problem was, but Maria seemed to be getting more and more distracted these days.

"I saw Carole going somewhere."

"Cora, that's not news. She has a car, you know."

"She wasn't riding. She was walking. Towards the desert."

"No way! She's scared to death of the desert."

"But maybe she has a date," Cora suggested.

Maria's heart skipped a beat. "What do you mean, a date?"

"You know, with somebody." Maria looked puzzled. "You've had dates. Haven't you?"

"But why should she have a date? Maybe she's studying something."

"In the desert? There ain't nothing out there but sand."

"I don't know. There's Miriam's house."

"But she doesn't know Miriam."

"She does now. Miriam was at the church the other night."

"How do you know that? You never said a thing about it!" Cora said, sounding hurt.

"There's nothing to say, Cora. All I know is Miriam went to the church and talked to Carole, but I don't know about what."

"Well, find out!" urged Cora. "When are you gonna see Miriam?"

"Tomorrow," Maria answered, wondering where Carole had gone.

"Ask her."

"Why don't you ask Carole? You eat with her, don't you?"

"I used to." Maria gave her an inquiring look as if she were expecting an explanation. "She hasn't been coming around."

"Where's she eating?"

"How should I know? Maybe she's found a better place. Maybe she has a lover stashed away somewhere."

"And maybe you'd better ask her if you're so damned curious about it!"

"Hey, don't yell at me! You'll wake Zemi up and blame me for it. I'm just telling you what I saw, which is more than you ever do."

"Right." Maria was too angry to argue. Lately, Cora had been making a point of telling her all kinds of upsetting things about Carole, and her favorite line was that Carole had a lover, as if she should care. Maria sighed deeply, gathered all her strength, and got up to put Zemi to bed.

"Besides," Cora continued, walking behind her. "I wouldn't know how to ask her. She makes me nervous, you know?"

"Yeah," Maria answered. She knew only too well how Carole could make a person nervous. If ever a woman had made her feel confused, nervous, as if she were about to do or say the wrong thing, it was Carole.

"I mean, I eat with her and all, but I don't know what to do when I'm with her. I have to speak good English, which I don't even know, and I have to say something. It's strange."

"Whatever you've been doing up to now has worked," Maria told her.

"Umm. But I can't get the nerve to ask her what I want, to let me be her helper. And it's looking so pretty. Have you seen the walls?"

"No. You have?"

"From the outside, like everybody else. It's disgusting. You should see the crowd cruising the plaza."

"You cruise the plaza," Maria reminded her. Cora grimaced.

"I went to mass Sunday," Cora admitted.

"You!"

"The good padre damned near croaked. You should've seen the look on his face."

"Oh, dear. First you. Then Miriam."

"I just went to see the walls," Cora explained. She didn't want Maria to think she had become religious. "But she'd covered them up. With sheets. Couldn't even look under or nothing."

"All the painters do that."

"You mean she didn't do it on purpose because she knew I was coming?"

"Of course not. If she'd known you were coming, she would've burned them."

"Go ahead. Laugh. I just wanted to see what she's done."

"So tell her, Cora, and ask her about teaching you."

"God! That's so easy for you to say."

"You're going to miss your chance, Cora," Maria warned her, "because if you don't ask her, I will."

"Don't you dare!" Cora exclaimed.

"I'm going to go up to her, and I'm going to put on my nicest voice and my southern belle accent, and I'm going to say, 'Carole, honey, I don't know a thing about colors or brushes or anything like that, but I would so love to learn and be of assistance to you in all your endeavors.'"

"They don't talk like that."

"This southern belle does, and I will."

"You're a real bitch, you know," Cora said. She didn't think Maria was teasing her this time, like she had before. "I'm the one who's wanted that from the first."

"So ask for it already!" Maria was too serious to be joking. "If you haven't asked by tomorrow, I'll do it myself the moment I see her."

"But why?"

"You think I want to be somebody's servant the rest of my life?"

Cora said nothing, but she was having trouble holding back the tears. Being somebody's servant never bothered her before, but now that she wanted something as bad as she wanted this, Maria wanted it too. It wasn't fair. She never would have expected something like this from her. Anybody else, she would have understood, but not Maria.

"Well," she said, as Maria left the room to pick up her sewing and check on Zemi. When she returned, Cora was gone, and the front door was open. She thought about chasing after her and trying to explain, but she didn't.

"What's with Cora?" asked Carole. She had reached the front door as Maria went out to her usual spot.

"Hi," Maria said, happy to see Carole disprove Cora's theory. "Did she talk to you?"

"Talk? She almost knocked me down. She was going so fast, she left me spinning."

"Okay, I get the general idea."

"Is she upset about something?"

"She'll get over it," Maria assured her and asked her to come in.

"Aren't you busy?" Carole asked. Maria was always doing something. "The only time you're not busy..." Carole added, but she didn't finish the thought. It would have meant admitting that she sat by her window to enjoy the sight of Maria leaning against the door.

"What time is that?" Maria asked. She was curious to find out when Carole thought she wasn't busy, but Carole had decided against talking and grinned at her instead.

"You don't say very much," she told Carole.

"Me? What do you want to know?"

"What time were you talking about?"

"When you lean against your doorframe," Carole admitted.

"Ah!" Maria smiled back at the woman who, she knew from Zemi, had painted her picture as she leaned against that doorframe. "You've been watching."

"Oh, yes. It's a beautiful sight."

"My doorframe?"

"You. I've been watching you. I like the way you look. I like the way your hair curls up about your shoulders."

"You're pretty bold today."

"Hey! For a moment, I thought you were going to say I was pretty. I'm heartbroken."

"You are," Maria admitted, feeling silly, like a giggling teenager on her first date. She had hoped that this moment would come, that they would have this conversation and end up in each other's arms, kissing, but then she stopped smiling.

"Don't go away," Carole said. "You have a way of leaving."

"I'm just thinking," Maria said.

"Think later. We're here now, and I've just told you I'm attracted to you."

"I heard you," she admitted, but she didn't think that she could say the same. She knew she had feelings for Carole. She had even wondered what it would be like to kiss her. On more than one occasion, she had come close to doing it, but that was before, when she wasn't thinking.

"I'd like to kiss you," Carole said.

"Ah," Maria said and got up to rearrange the bundle of her sewing things.

"Ah, what? Does it bother you? I know you at least like me." She had followed Maria and was standing behind her. She slipped her arms around Maria's waist, under her breasts, and held her to her, softly, as if she were afraid of scaring her, burying her face in Maria's hair. Maria relaxed in the embrace and caressed Carole's arms around her.

"You smell wonderful," Carole said. "I've been wondering all this time what your hair smells like."

"Now you know."

"It smells curly."

"That's not a smell."

"It is here. Put your nose back here," Carole said. Maria moved away, out of Carole's embrace. "So, does it bother you?"

"It doesn't bother me, but it scares me."

"I scare you?"

"Not you," Maria said, turning to face Carole. "The way I feel."

"Why?" Carole asked, and then she kissed her. Without thinking, she bent towards Maria and their lips met. Nothing could have been easier, simpler, more natural than to slip her tongue into this woman's mouth, and it didn't surprise her to feel Maria's tongue wrap itself around her own in a lingering caress. Carole would have kissed that mouth forever, but Maria pulled back within the circle of her arms and stared at her.

"I'm..." Maria said, "I'm a little confused."

"Because I kissed you?"

"Because I kissed you back. The last thing I'm looking for," she said, nervously, "is any kind of involvement, and this is all very new to me."

"But we are involved," Carole told her. "It's what we feel."

"No," Maria said, slipping away from Carole, who had leaned forward to kiss her again.

"No, what?"

"We're not involved. Not yet, and I don't know that I can. I have plans, you know."

"They don't include me?"

"They include home, taking Zemi home."

"To Brazil?"

"You sound as if I've suddenly gone crazy."

"It's just..." Carole said, her head shaking, her hand spread open, gesturing her puzzlement, but she didn't finish the thought because she didn't know what to say.

"I need time to think about all this," Maria told her.

"Does Zemi know?"

"Not yet."

"Have you been thinking about this or did it just come up?"

"Go home," Maria told her, smiling. She didn't seem upset. In fact, a chilling calm had settled on her.

"I guess a kiss is out of the question," Carole said.

"Go," Maria whispered, smiling, and pushed her out of the house. Carole caught her hand, held it.

"You don't want to talk?"

"Not tonight," Maria told her. "I have a lot of thinking to do."

Carole sighed, resigned. Maria said good night. Outside, Carole broke into a run. She circled the town at full speed before she stopped. She could hear giggles every time she passed a group of people sitting on their doorsteps or standing around and talking, but she didn't stop until she got tired. Regardless of how her conversation with Maria had ended, she had finally kissed her, and Maria had kissed back. Obviously, there was something there.

Yeah, but she's leaving, Carole reminded herself. She refused to believe it. Immigration was the other way around. People came in; they didn't go back.

It's probably just an excuse, she told herself. A red herring thrown in to give herself time. It made sense, but it also made sense that, after thinking about her feelings, Maria could choose to deny them. At the edge of town, Carole found a tree stump and sat down to think.

While I was going over what had just happened between Maria and me, I heard a noise behind me. At first I thought it was a lion, chasing after me even out in the open. But it wasn't.

"I wanna talk to you," a husky voice said.

"What are you doing here?" I asked.

"I told you already, damn it. I wanna talk to you."

"Listen, Cora, how did you know I was here? Are you following me or something?"

"What? Shut up and listen. The whole damned town saw you running like a fool."

I wanted to tell her that I didn't run like a fool, but I thought it wisest to listen because Cora's eyes were red with anger or spilled tears.

"Okay, what's up?"

"I want a job."

"Great," I said. She stared at me as if I were a cockroach sticking to her shoe.

"From you," she told me. I laughed, but I stopped very quickly.

"A job?" I repeated. Maria must have planned this too. Maybe that was the reason why Cora and I both had run out of her house this evening.

"You heard me," she practically yelled. "I wanna learn to do what you do." I was silent, still thinking about Maria's plot to get me to take Cora on as my assistant. "What's the matter? You don't think I can do it? You think I'm too stupid to learn?"

"I didn't say a thing," I said, surprised.

"So what is it? You give the job to her?"

"Who?" I asked. I had never seen Cora so intent on getting something or act with such determination. "Could you slow down?" I pleaded. "What are you talking about?"

"About being your assister," she told me, trying to control herself. "I wanna learn to do something."

"Sounds good to me," I said.

"Yeah?" she asked, surprised. She fixed me with her eyes as if she didn't believe what she had heard. I nodded. "Hey!" she snapped, "you're not just saying that to get rid of me, are you?"

"Nobody can get rid of you," I told her. "You're like a plague." She laughed and said yeah a few times.

"Like when I followed you to the restaurant. And you finally gave up."

"I gave in," I told her. "I figured if you were so damned curious, you deserved to be up close."

"So what about this job?"

"It's a great idea," I told her. "I need an assistant anyway, especially somebody who's willing to work hard."

"I can work hard," she assured me.

"For little money."

"I don't want your money," she told me. "I just want to learn."

"I'm going to pay you, whether you want it or not," I told her. She shrugged her shoulders. "Getting paid for what you do is important."

"I don't have to read no books or nothing?" she asked. I wondered what had happened to her English.

"Not unless you want to."

"So what do I do?"

"You come to church with me tomorrow morning, and I'll put you to work. If you can paint, we'll find out."

"Just like that?" She snapped her fingers.

"Just like that." I snapped mine. "You can't really learn to paint in school. What you learn there is how to polish what you already know."

"You're kidding."

"No. Nobody has to teach you how to paint. Hell, nobody can. It's something you get at birth, like a talent. And you either use it or you don't."

"Well, I wanna know if I got it so I can use it."

"Okay," I said, happy to see her so determined.

"Okay," she agreed. "I'll see you tomorrow then." She turned away as if to leave but she couldn't quite bring herself to do it. "Okay?"

"Sure," I said. "We'll have breakfast."

"Yeah."

"Is that all?" I asked. Cora was staring at me as if I had done something awful.

"Are you okay?" she asked me.

"No," I told her, honestly. I wasn't entirely okay.

"Wanna talk?"

"Not really," I said. She wasn't convinced. She sat on the ground beside me and lit a cigarette.

"I used to think it was a sad night when the moon hung so low," she confessed. I looked at the moon. It was low. "But now, I don't know."

"Has it been a good night?"

"Yeah," she said, philosophically, staring at the smoke, "and no."

"More good than bad?"

"No," she told me. "The part about working with you is good, but there's another part that's not so good."

"I don't follow you."

"Ah, hell. It's just as well," she said, keeping her eye on the moon. "You think wishes come true."

"Mine never have," I said. "Yours?"

"Not unless I've shed something for them. You know, like a lizard."

"But you're not a lizard," I told her, although I could tell that she was becoming more and more serious.

"So it wasn't my skin," she snapped back and laughed, "but it hurts just the same."

"What are you talking about?"

"People," she said. "Friends. You never know what they're gonna do. It's like, they wait until you really care for them, and then they screw you."

"Yeah," I said. "I know what you mean. Does this have anything to do with your running out of Maria's house tonight?"

"You saw me?"

"You ran into me."

"That was you?" she asked and laughed even harder. "Shit! I thought it was the priest."

"Thanks a lot," I said. "You wanna talk about it?"

"No," she said. "You're the one who's talking."

"I think I'm shedding my skin right about now, but I sure as hell am not talking."

She sighed, knowingly. I sighed too. We both stared at the moon.

"Noche de ronda," she started singing in a soft, melodic voice, "que triste pasas, que triste cruzas por mi balcón." *A night on the town, how sad you cross by my balcony.*

"I love that song," I told her. "My mother used to sing it around the house." She smiled condescendingly, as if she didn't believe me.

"Oh, that's right. You're supposed to be Spanish."

"Luna que se quiebra sobre las tinieblas de mi soledad, ¿a dónde vas?" I sang. *Moon breaking over the darkness of my solitude, where are you going?*

"Dime si esta noche tú te vas de ronda como ella se fue," Cora continued. *Tell me if tonight you're going out on the town as she went.*

"¿Con quién está?" I added. "Dile que la quiero, dile que me muero de tanto esperar." *Who is she with? Tell her that I love her, tell her that I'm dying from waiting so long.*

"Que vuélva ya," she harmonized. "Que las rondas, no son buenas. Que hacen daño. Que dan pena, y se acaba por llorar," we finished together. *That nights on the town aren't good. That they hurt. That they embarrass, and you end up crying.*

"That was great!" I exclaimed. "You're really good."

"I admit it," she said. "You know Spanish."

"Did you know that song was written by a woman?"

"You're kidding!"

"Well, maybe. Maria Teresa Lara was supposed to have written it."

"You're not sure?"

"There was another Lara, a man, so there's a lot of confusion, at least in my mind."

"I'd like to think a woman wrote it," she said.

"Yeah."

"But I wonder who she was writing about."

"Somebody who left her, I think."

"A woman?"

"I don't know," I said, evasively. "I don't know anything about her."

"You know you missed a piece when you broke in," she reminded me.

"I know," I said. "Noche de rondas, como lastimas, como me hieres el corazón," I sang. *Night on the town, how you wound, how you hurt my heart.*

"So how come you left it out if you knew it?" she asked. "Is your heart broken too?"

"Not broken. Just bruised." She leaned back against my legs and started humming the song again, her eyes on the moon.

"Those old songs are all about hurting. You noticed?" I nodded.

"Yeah."

"You think she's alive?" she asked. "You know, the woman who wrote the song."

"I don't know. I told you, I'm not really sure she wrote it."

"Imagine doing something like that. Writing a song that lives on, and it doesn't matter if you're dead or alive, because the song just goes on and on."

"It would be satisfying."

"Satisfying, my ass. It's a fucking dream!"

"Well," I said, a little amused by her fervor. "I don't have fucking dreams."

"So tell me something I don't know," she said, laughing. I had the feeling she was expecting me to really tell her something. When I remained silent, she fixed her eyes on the moon again and asked me, softly, "What do you dream about?"

"Things," I told her. This wasn't the right time to be specific.

"Any people in your dreams?"

"Some."

"Like who?" I heaved a deep sigh and shook my head. She looked up at me without entirely turning her head, and asked, "Did someone walk out on you? Like in the song?"

"All the time," I said, and I got up from the tree stump to straighten out my pants.

"Is she the one in your dreams?"

"What makes you think it's a she?" I asked.

"Isn't it?" She got up too.

"Look, Cora..." I started to say. I wasn't ready to talk to Cora about my preferences.

"Hey," she stopped me. "Qué más dá?" she said with a wave of the hand. "Sometimes I wonder, that's all, about what makes you tick."

"I don't tick."

"Okay. I'll stop wondering."

"And I'll see you tomorrow," I said, walking away, although I would have preferred to have stayed a while longer, alone.

"Sí," she said, instead of saying goodbye, and I left her in possession of the tree stump.

16

The next day, Cora went to work with me. I offered to pay her a third of my salary while I was training her, but she refused the money.

"A third of your salary won't buy me shit," she snapped, which made me wonder how she planned to support herself and her daughter.

"I can't afford more than that," I told her.

"So keep it," she remarked. "I didn't ask for your money. All I wanna do is learn."

"No, I have some money of my own. My mother left me some, and I don't need all that much, really."

"Some people."

"What does that mean?"

"Nothing. I didn't say nothing. Shit!"

"Listen, I'll give you a third of what the priest pays me now, which isn't much, but later if this works out, we'll see what we can do. You may get a raise, and get all of what the priest gives me," I joked. Cora wasn't laughing. She shrugged her shoulders as if she didn't care, as if this whole conversation about money was beneath her. I wished she would say something, but she just puckered her lips as if she were thinking a hard, difficult thought and looked away. I gave up, but I didn't like the idea of her working for so little money.

"It's all right," she said.

"Let's go, then." And she followed me out of the inn into the street. We hadn't yet crossed the plaza when I saw Maria Soledad walking towards Miriam's house.

"Maria!" I called after her. After last night, I didn't know if she would talk to me, but she stopped, waited for me, even smiled as I approached, which made me wonder what she was thinking about. I knew I was smiling because she hadn't left yet.

"Good morning," she said.

"Hi!" I said, excitedly. "She finally asked me," I blurted out in a loud whisper even though I hadn't meant to speak about Cora at that moment. I wanted to ask her if she was really leaving.

"Asked you?" Her eyes followed Cora, who didn't stop to talk.

"You know? What we talked about? She wants to learn to paint."

"Ah!" Maria exclaimed, not very excited.

"So I'm taking her on as my assistant, like you said I should. Even though I can't pay her a whole lot."

"Don't worry about it," Maria told me. "Cora can take care of herself. She's a big girl now."

"Yeah, but it's not fair. If I could squeeze a few dollars out of Father Arroyo..." I said, but we both laughed.

"You're going to teach her something. That's more important than money."

Maria seemed nervous. Although we were talking, she wouldn't quite look me in the face.

"Are you okay?" She shrugged, shook her head. "About last night."

"Well," she said. "We should talk again."

"Yeah?" I grinned. Maybe she had changed her mind, unpacked her bags, if they were packed.

"But not now."

I hated not now. It usually meant never.

"Okay," I agreed, reluctantly. "Well, I'm glad about your telling me to use Cora. I can use the help. Father Arroyo's changed his mind again about the mass. It's on."

"Luz's mass?" Maria asked, surprised. I nodded. "But he was dead set against it."

"I know, but I think Miriam's visit the other night made him think. Did you know they had words?"

"I know something happened. He was very upset that night."

"She taught him a thing or two about worshipping spirits," I told her. She didn't seem to understand, so I explained. "He can only recognize one spirit."

"Miriam told him differently? And he listened? Well, maybe there's hope for him." She turned to leave.

"Are you going to Miriam's?" I asked. She looked back without stopping to nod. "And you're taking a straight path? No subterfuge?"

"Not anymore," she answered, smiling. She must have known that her smile created chaos inside me.

"Does he know?" I yelled after her. She turned around again to say yes. I would have kept asking questions just to see her turn, but I eventually gave up and just stood there, overwhelmed by the desire to hold her, and watched her walk away. When I rejoined Cora at the church, I had to make a conscious effort to clear my mind of Maria's vision because the last thing I needed was to have Cora find out about my feelings.

"She say something about me?" Cora asked.

"No," I answered, absentmindedly. I could still see Maria's generous thighs as she walked away from me.

"So what did she say?" Cora insisted.

"Nothing," I told her. "Is everything all right between the two of you?"

"Sure," Cora said. I wondered. It wasn't like Maria to say hello to me and ignore Cora, and it certainly wasn't like Cora to pass up a chance to argue with Maria.

"Well," I said, resolved. "Let's get to work. We have to finish the walls quickly so Father Arroyo can have his mass before he changes his mind again."

"What mass?"

"The one he's giving in Luz's memory."

"I'll be damned! That man changes his mind every time he pees. A week ago he was griping about it."

"I know, but now he's going to do it, and the walls have to be finished by then."

"So I came along just in time," she said, a little flattered to recognize her importance.

"You bet," I said. She was so impressed that she couldn't contain her pleasure, and broke into a self-satisfied smile that helped me start my day laughing.

At the church, Cora was like a child, fascinated by the intricate construction of the scaffold and what she called the "science" of mixing paint. When I climbed the scaffold to start working, she observed my every move from the floor. Eventually, without encouragement from me, she climbed the scaffold herself and sat beside me to watch me work. She was amazed by every stroke and moved by the simplest changes in hue. That first day of work, when she thought I wasn't looking, Cora did a lot of smiling.

Once, when I stopped working to stretch my sore shoulders, I caught her looking out the window.

"Is she there today?" I asked.

"Who?"

"Oh, yeah," I exclaimed, noticing the young woman who was standing across the street from the church holding her child.

"I guess I'm not the only one," she said, sadly. I smiled at her for no reason at all and went back to work.

"She's been coming around for a while now," I told her.

"I never saw her before."

"You used to stand on the other side, so the building stood between you."

"Hey!" she complained. "I wasn't watching. That's just where I stood."

"I didn't say you were watching."

"Sounded like it," she argued.

"Well, I didn't. I just said, she was on one side and you were on the other, but I'm surprised you never heard that kid bellowing."

"Was he the one? Shit! Why doesn't she go home, then? I mean, what's the point of hanging around?"

"Maybe she wants to be a painter," I joked.

"Everybody wants something," she snapped.

"Or maybe she has nothing better to do."

I maneuvered my way down the scaffold to the floor for more paint. Cora observed me in awe, but she hadn't yet decided that she could do the work.

"How do you know how much color to put?"

"I don't," I answered. "I add as much as I think will do the job and, if that doesn't do the trick, I add some more."

"Isn't that like leaving it up to chance?"

"Maybe, but I have a good eye for this sort of thing."

"I see," she answered, impressed by my ability. "Was Maria going to Miriam's?"

"Looked like it." She pondered my response with the kind of intensity that told me to beware of her next question. After our conversation last night, I couldn't tell what to think of Cora and how much she knew about my feelings for Maria. "She really loves Miriam," I said to keep her from asking.

"She does."

"Are they related?"

"No," she answered, shaking her head distractedly long after the answer had been given. She was keeping her eye on what I was doing.

"Listen, I hope you don't mind my asking, but I'm very curious about some of these people, and Maria especially."

"How come?"

"I don't know," I mumbled. "I just am."

"Well," she said guardedly. "I can't tell you all that much about Maria. She's not from around here, like Miriam is."

"How long has she been here?"

She thought a moment and then said, "Bout seven...maybe eight years. She was pregnant back then with Zemi. That's how they met. Miriam found her out in the desert somewhere and took her home."

"In the desert? What was a pregnant woman doing in the desert?"

"She wasn't showing or nothing, I don't think. She was just skinny. Skinny and scared, that's what she was. So Miriam took her in, you know, to help her out. She does that kind of thing, Miriam does."

"Did you meet her back then?" I asked, puzzled over the odd color that one of my concoctions had produced.

"Yeah," she answered, trying to figure out what I was doing.

"I gotta get the right shade," I explained. She nodded. "So when did she get pregnant?"

"If you ask me," she finally said, as if suddenly resolved to divulge the information, "I'd say she was raped or something."

"What?" I yelled as I jumped up from the floor. I banged my head on a protruding plank and almost passed out from the shock.

"I think the coyote left her out there to die," she said.

"What coyote?"

"The man who brings people across the border. They're scum. You can't really trust them, but Maria came across alone with one of them. I think he raped her and left her there to die."

"You mean that kind of thing really happens? I just can't believe this!" I began to cry, unable to articulate my anger. "I mean, she could've died."

"It happens all the time," Cora said, matter of fact.

"How come you're not furious!" I yelled.

"Hey! I didn't do nothing!"

"But it's so unfair. And you talk about it as if it were just another little incident in some stranger's life."

"Well," she added, shrugging her shoulders, "maybe it ain't true. I told you it was just my opinion."

"God damn you!" I exclaimed.

"In a church?" she yelled back. "You'll cuss me out in a church!"

"You mean to tell me you made up the whole thing?"

She shrugged her shoulders again, a smile dying to break out on her lips. "I said, 'if you ask me,' which you did, so I told you what I thought," she explained. "Maybe it's the truth, maybe not."

"You almost gave me heart failure."

"So don't take things so hard. You'd die if it was true, and I still think it is."

"You really think she was raped by whoever brought her across the border?"

"Why not? I was. It's the price you pay for taking the chance."

"Jesus!" I exclaimed.

"Yeah, well," she said as if to make it seem funny. "Is He in that racket too?"

"I don't know. I really don't know what racket He's in. Sometimes I wonder, though."

I had by then lost all interest in mixing paint or doing anything else related to the church. I wanted to rush out to find Maria, but I knew that it would be foolish after so many years had passed to offer any sympathy.

"Are you hungry yet?" I asked Cora, on whom my turbulent emotions had not been lost.

"I could eat."

"Let's go, then," I said, leading the way to the restaurant. "Were you really raped?"

"What difference does it make? It was a long time ago."

"Were you?"

"Yeah," she said, "but I gave the son-of-a-bitch the scare of his life."

"What did you do?" I asked, animated.

"I got ahold of his knife, and I cut him up so bad he couldn't walk. I don't think he made it back across the border."

"Are you putting me on?"

"Hell no! It's the one thing I've done for myself in my life. I'm damned proud of it, too."

"I'll be damned!"

"I just couldn't go around telling people about it cause it wasn't right. You know? Stabbing somebody and leaving him out there to die."

"It's a lot righter than what he did to you, let me tell you."

"For you," she pointed out, "but most people don't care what happens to a whore, and you know that's what I am, so I just kept my mouth shut. I like to think there's just the ghost of him out there in that desert watching as women come across the river and suffering because he can't touch them."

"You think he's dead?"

"I sure as hell hope so," she exclaimed with a laugh. Then she wrapped her arm around my waist and led me to a table.

"Close your mouth!" Gloria ordered me. "You'll swallow the flies."

"And there's no free meat in this place," Cora joked. She and Gloria Peñaranda laughed. I watched them slip easily into a jovial conversation about Clarita. My eyes filled with tears. Clarita must have been the offspring of that crossing.

That night, when I sat by my window to stare at the desert, its darkness and vastness seemed more like an omen than they ever had before. I thought I could see them, the women who came across the border in search of a better life. They were making the journey at a time when the borders in this country were closed to legal passage, so they had to trust their lives to the mercy of the desert and coyotes who walked on two legs, not four.

According to Cora, these women knew the risk they took when they made the journey, but they came anyway because anything was preferable to the uncertainty of life in their own countries. Some were running from death squads; others ran from hunger. Whatever the reason, it was basic survival. I wanted to know Maria's story.

As she crossed the plaza on her way home, Maria Soledad strained her eyes to see inside the church, but the sun was shining too brightly. A red haze formed before her eyes as she tried to focus on the objects inside the room.

Damn it! she thought. She had hoped to see Cora at her new job, learning to paint, but since their little altercation the previous night and Cora's behavior this morning, she knew she couldn't possibly walk in on her.

"Hey, Mom!" Zemi's call startled her. Zemi was riding her bicycle around the plaza at her usual demented speed. Clarita trailed behind her. Her bike was bigger, a woman's bike, and she was struggling to pedal and look over the handle bars at the same time. Neither one of the girls came close enough to get stopped by Maria.

"Skipping school," Maria said as she watched her daughter speed around the plaza on two wheels, sometimes one. Zemi occasionally sneaked out with her friend to make her feel better. Maria understood how her daughter felt, but it worried her that she was missing classes. At Zemi's age, she wouldn't have missed a day of school for anything in the world. She had had a mad crush on her teacher, "a professora Maria de Lourdes Alves," Maria said aloud in Portuguese. The sound of her own language made her eyes cloud with tears.

What's the matter with me today? she chastised herself, but she knew what the matter was. She had blurted out last night to Carole that she needed time, but it wasn't time exactly she was thinking about. It was the thought of going back, of making the journey home, that had been on her mind. She had considered it seriously for over a year now, but talking to Carole about Zemi's education made her think about the past, her own friends back home.

Her two reasons for staying in the U.S. had passed. Zemi's learned English, she told herself, and the situation back home's not as bad as it used to be. She could return safely and start a new life, practice her profession, teach Zemi her language. It all made perfect sense.

And Carole had to come in now. Just as she was starting to make plans, which was the reason for keeping herself free from emotional involvement.

"Too late for that," she said, amused. She could still see the look of surprise on Carole's face when she told her she was leaving. Her own face had probably looked equally surprised because she had never voiced her thoughts, given shape to ideas that seemed no more than dreams. She had thought about leaving and wondered if she could do it, if she could walk out on Miriam, the life she had found here after running so far from home.

The ebb and flow of human misery, she mused. Leaving Miriam would prove now the hardest thing to do, but she knew that Miriam would only encourage her, even if it hurt her.

"¡Ay!" she said. "When you think it's getting easier, it gets worse, more complicated." Then Zemi whizzed by her once more.

At home she opened all the windows, but closed them again as soon as a few flies buzzed around her in the kitchen. On the living room sofa, Father

Arroyo had fallen asleep with a book on his lap. It made her wonder if her friends had saved her books, kept them for her all these years. She ran through the titles in her head and looked forward to the day when she could start again building a library in her own home.

It's time to go, she told herself. She had felt protected in Pozo Seco, safe from the political violence that had killed her mother. The years had passed, though, and she didn't need to feel protected any more.

Maria leaned against the kitchen counter, surveying the room, sipping a glass of water. "Time to go," she said aloud and nodded. It was just a question of when.

 Asking Cora to assist me had been an excellent idea. In four months, she and I accomplished a great deal without getting on each other's nerves, and I was able to learn about the local gossip in the process. At the beginning, when we started working together, she would watch me for hours without saying much. She followed every stroke of the brush with fascination, but she refused to paint herself. However, when three weeks went by and she had given no sign that she was willing to try it, I simply assigned her a corner of the wall and told her that it was hers. She couldn't believe it.

"I can't do that!" she exclaimed.

"If I didn't think you could, I wouldn't ask you to do it."

"But you don't understand."

"You're afraid. I understand that," I assured her. "But there's nothing to be afraid of. The drawings are already in, so all you have to do is paint them."

"But what if I make a mistake?"

"You paint over it, just like I do," I said, calmly.

"I've never done this before."

"So this is your first time. Go on," I urged her. "Take that corner, and do your thing." I could tell that she wasn't amused. She gave me a nasty look and dragged herself to the corner with the bucket full of brushes and a few cans of paint. Then I left her alone to start on her own. She stood and stared at the drawings for a long time.

"Where am I supposed to start?" she demanded. Her face exposed her fright.

"Try the clothes," I suggested. She gave me the nastiest frown I had ever seen.

So she began. I was pretty certain that she could produce what I expected of her, but she had to begin working before either one of us could find out. Sighing helplessly, she devoted herself to the task of mixing colors and choosing hues. I heard the sighs, as I was meant to, but I ignored them. I was determined to let her do her work alone.

The results of Cora's first solo venture into the world of painting were encouraging. Her strokes were uncertain at first, mostly because she was trying to do what she thought I would do in her place, but I knew that her confidence was beginning to grow, which meant that she would soon forget about me and begin to paint for herself. When I reviewed her work that first day, I complimented her. She frowned as if I were humoring her, as if she knew better than to believe what I was saying. I wasn't humoring her, though. If nothing else, she had managed to achieve the realistic style I had tried so hard to create. Our collaboration would not have worked out, I informed her, if our styles had been radically different.

"You mean I paint like you?"

"Well, yes," I said, disconcerted. Those words would have been offensive to any other painter.

"Hey!" Cora screamed and slapped her thigh with pleasure. "How about that!"

"Later on you can change your style," I told her.

"What style?" she complained. "I just want to paint."

"But a painter's style is the way she paints," I explained. "The way she does things."

"I just do what you tell me," she insisted, eager to please.

"I know that, Cora. But if you're going to make art your life's work, you need your own style. And that's something you develop when you do your own work."

Cora pondered the notion. Had she not considered the possibility of doing her own work?

"Look, I'm just starting out," she told me, annoyed.

"Okay," I said. "Come on with me. I'll show you what I mean."

"Where are you going?" she demanded, as suspicious as ever. I signaled for her to follow me and took her to my room. I realized as soon as I opened the door that I would be opening my secret life to her; at that point, however, teaching her to recognize what I meant when I spoke about style seemed more important than protecting my privacy.

"Did you do those?" she exclaimed as soon as she saw the sketches and paintings of Maria that hung on my walls. I nodded. "She's beautiful!" she whispered, reverently. As an answer, I pulled a few canvases from behind my headboard and stood them on the floor against the wall.

"Hey!" she yelled, excited, "that's me!"

"Yeah, but can you tell the difference between this painting of you and those?"

"Hell! You put green all over my face, and the paint's not smooth. It's like chunks of paint all over."

"It's a different style of painting."

"It's what you get when the painter's not in love with you," she complained.

I ignored the remark.

"Don't think I don't notice you don't tell me nothing," she added.

"I'll tell you when there's something to tell," I told her and pointed to the canvases. She stood, her arms wrapped about her as if she were afraid to disturb anything in the room, and examined the paintings one by one. I wondered if she was still thinking about me and Maria and what it could mean to have all these paintings of the woman around, but I didn't know how much to tell her, so I let well enough alone, picked up a few books from the boards that were my bookcase, and dropped them on the bed.

"If you look through these books," I heard myself say, but I remembered immediately that she couldn't read. "You'll see there's a guy in here who paints with dots."

"No shit! Dots?"

"That's the way he sees things," I explained.

"And you only see one thing," she added. "Maria."

"I like the way she looks," I finally explained. She adopted an all-knowing face and let out a sound under her breath. "I like the way her hair changes, from wild and curly to straight and long. I don't know how she does that."

"It's called getting it wet," she said, rolling her eyes. "She don't have a straight hair on that head of hers."

"Yeah," I smiled.

"How come there's no green on her face?"

"I don't know," I answered honestly. "When I paint her, I usually get depressed and that makes me be more realistic. I guess."

"It's a lot like the stuff we're doing," she commented. I agreed.

"You want your painting?"

"With that green shit on my face?"

"It grows on you," I teased her.

"Sure," she said. "I'll take it."

"But the one you really want is that one." She had been holding a pastel of Maria.

"Why would I want a picture of Maria for?" she protested.

"Because she's your friend."

"I guess," she said, sadly. "But I know you're not going to give me that one!" I laughed and handed her the books.

"Listen. Hang that painting where you can see it. Don't hide it in the closet."

"I won't," she said. I knew she was looking for the right words to thank me. She was standing around looking at the floor, ogling the paintings.

"Go away!" I said.

"¡Ay! Pero gracias."

Without Maria's knowledge, Zemi and I conspired to get her out of the house for about an hour. Zemi agreed to take her to the church at exactly twelve o'clock, which was the only time of day that Zemi could read with ease because the two hands were pointing directly up at the number twelve on the clock. She was to take Maria out of the house so that Father Arroyo could sneak in with Manuel Garriga to assemble a birthday present I had made for her.

Working during my spare time in Manuel Garriga's carpentry shop, I had made Maria a bed frame. Manuel had been able to get us good oak wood at a reasonable price for Father Arroyo's new pews, and, since I volunteered to help him with the pews, he volunteered to teach me how to do a few things with wood. It was a reasonable arrangement for both of us, and I was able to replace Maria's bed frame, since I knew from Zemi that it had collapsed to the floor for the last time a long while ago. Maria had simply removed the frame and left the mattress on the floor, and Zemi had bragged about how high she could jump now that there was no structure threatening to fall out from under her.

The problem of Maria's bed had bothered me from the beginning when I, too, made it collapse to the floor. I had often thought about buying her a new one, but I didn't think she would accept it. The arrival of her birthday, though, gave me a perfect excuse for replacing the old bed frame with the one I made. What I didn't know was how Father Arroyo would react to such a personal gift from a near stranger, so I approached him about it when I started my work on the frame. I took him to the shop and asked his opinion on how to get the frame to Maria's bedroom. Much to my surprise, he was the one who suggested that I employ Zemi in my little deception while he and Señor Garriga sneaked into the house to assemble the frame.

Thus it happened that Friday, after dinner, I asked Maria to visit the church the next day.

"I'll be free at twelve," I told her, "and if you come by I can give you a guided tour." She hesitated.

"I thought you didn't want anyone to see your work until it was finished."

"That's other people," I said, smiling at her. We had both tried since the night I kissed her to ignore what had happened. "It doesn't apply to you."

"Well..." She looked away nervously, obviously flattered.

"I can take you on my bike," Zemi broke in.

"Sure. If you're sure it's okay with you," she said to me.

"It is," I assured her, enjoying the nervous smile dancing on her lips. "In fact, we probably should have a picnic afterwards."

"That would be so nice," Maria agreed. "The weather is beautiful."

"What's a picnic?" demanded Zemi.

"It's when you take your food outside and eat sitting on the ground," I explained, but I was thinking that the weather was not the only beautiful thing around. Maria was still looking at me and smiling, and I liked knowing that we would be together, away from the town, in a different setting.

"Can I bring my bike?"

"We wouldn't dream of separating the two of you," Maria said jovially.

"And what about Clarita?" Zemi almost pleaded because she wasn't certain what the answer would be.

"If her mother lets her come," Maria said, "it's all right with me."

"Awright!" Zemi shouted.

"Well, I guess that means we're going," I said to Maria.

"I guess so. I'll bring the picnic lunch if you pick the spot," she said, coyly.

"I'll bring dessert and sodas. Which kind does Zemi like?"

"Coca Cola," she offered, still smiling.

"I'll keep that in mind," I said. "See you at twelve, then?"

"You will," she agreed.

"Don't forget," I said to Zemi.

"I won't!" she yelled as she winked at me. I left the house wondering if Maria suspected something.

"What was that wink about?" Maria asked Zemi as she picked her up from the floor.

"What wink?" Zemi asked innocently.

"You know what wink, you rascal. The one you gave Carole."

"Oh, that wink!" Zemi, who had been sworn to silence, smiled mischievously.

"Yes, the one in that eye," Maria said, pointing to it. "Are the two of you up to something?"

"How come Clarita's pants fall down?" Zemi asked, seriously.

"Her waist is very small," Maria explained.

"It's the same as me!"

"Yeah, but she hasn't learned how to hold up her pants yet," Maria told her. It made her smile that Zemi had also noticed that Clarita's clothes didn't hang quite right, and she was always pulling and tugging at whatever she wore. It was clear how little of the money Cora sent home had been spent on Clarita.

"How long will you be tomorrow?" interrupted Father Arroyo, coming to Zemi's rescue. Zemi's sudden change of subject matter was enough to give away any well-kept secret.

"About an hour or two, I would think," said Maria. "Will you need me for something at that time?"

"No, not at all," said the priest. "I would just like to look forward to a bit of peace and quiet," and he gave Zemi a knowing look as he spoke.

"Have we been making too much noise for you?" asked Maria, a little ill at ease.

"No," Father Arroyo said. "But tomorrow I can use the two hours at about that time."

"It's settled, then," said Maria, a bit serious now. "We'll be out of here by twelve." It always hurt her to be reminded that she lived in this house through his generosity, as if her hard work counted for nothing at all.

"Good night," said the priest, not knowing how to correct whatever mistake he had made. He stood there thinking that he just didn't know how to talk to that woman.

"Good night," she answered, but she had no way to hide the awkwardness of the situation. Carole had helped her to do the dishes so Maria couldn't escape into the kitchen as she always did, and the dress she had been making for Clarita was already finished. So she faced him awkwardly, trying to find an excuse to leave the room while the priest waited, as if he were expecting something.

"Well," he added. "Good night," and he finally left the room.

Maria went to bed that night worried about the priest's words and her situation in general. He was good to her, most of the time, but her position in his home embarrassed her; however, short of leaving Pozo Seco, she didn't know what else she could do. The job provided her with a place to live and raise her child, but it paid no wages. She went through the same feelings every year on her birthday, much as Cora used to when Clarita's birthday approached.

"Thirty-one," she whispered, "and what have I got to show for it?" Like an obedient instrument, her mind reviewed images of the years that had taken her this far. There were the years at home with Rebecca and her mother, and the funny, loving arguments between the two as Rebecca tried to caution Lola to be careful.

My reckless mother, thought Maria. She was no longer angry at the recklessness. She told herself now that her mother had had the right to live her life as she chose, but it still hurt. To ease the pain, she thought of the years at school when she had been proud to read in the papers about her mother's political triumphs. Her classmates had praised her, but the journalists had maligned her.

Maria remembered that the newspapers had called her mother a whore even in death. A man who was never identified or found had walked into the brothel where Lola had been trying to organize a union. He simply gunned her and Rebecca down. Thirty-eight bullets pierced her body. Maria had counted them. Only five felled the more fragile Rebecca.

"I didn't even have time to mourn you," Maria thought, the throbbing in her head growing more painful and insistent. It had seemed only wise to leave Brazil even before her mother's funeral had taken place. Her mother's friends had comforted her as well as they could, but they also reminded her that the police might never release Lola's body and that too many suspicious people were following her about. They all agreed that she should leave.

That was almost ten years ago. She could see the passing of the years in Zemi, but otherwise, for her, things had remained the same. The thought of Rebecca and her mother still hurt, but she had found a sort of peace in Pozo Seco.

The next morning, Maria woke up late, the throbbing in her head as insistent as it had been the night before. She hadn't slept well. In her dreams, Rebecca's body had flown over the priest's house on its way to London, and Maria could see Lola from the front porch of her house waving goodbye. It had always troubled Maria that Rebecca's body was buried in London, away from Lola's, even though her family had long ago rejected her, just as Lola's family had once rejected her.

"Mom! What time is it?" demanded Zemi.

"It's not time yet," Maria answered, "but it will be soon."

"I can't wait!" Zemi exclaimed, and Maria could not remember the last time Zemi had been so excited.

"Run along and get Clarita," Maria told her, but Zemi was already well on her way out of the house. Maria wondered if Cora would let Clarita go now that she was upset with her.

She went into the kitchen to prepare the picnic lunch and remembered the lunches Rebecca used to make when the three of them went to the beach in Río. They were either too poor or too strikingly different or too politically correct to eat at the restaurants that lined the seaside, so they carried a picnic basket and ate underneath a tree. The food tasted better that way, her mother used to say, and Maria believed her.

She also enjoyed the people who came to see her mother everywhere they went. Even at the beach, while she was eating lunch under a tree, her mother was approached by people in need. They knew her to be their advocate and, although they lacked the courage to meet her at the women's center or at any of the other rooms with complicated political names that Maria's mother frequented, they sought her. They knew she wouldn't desert them.

It got her killed, Maria reflected, but did it really? The meetings had not killed her. The bullets had.

"God!" she exclaimed aloud. "If I don't get this out of my head, I'm going to end up crying again." Then she looked around to see if the priest had heard her.

"We're ready! We're ready!" Zemi exclaimed as she rushed into the house dragging Clarita by the hand. "Is it time yet?"

"It's almost time," Maria admitted. She picked up her basket and said, "Let's go." Zemi and Clarita ran ahead of her to arrange themselves on Zemi's bike.

At the church, Carole was waiting. She too had been looking at her watch and wondering if time had been standing still. It had taken her forever to decide what to wear, but she had settled on brown slacks and a light beige blouse.

Special occasion, thought Maria when she saw Carole, and it made her feel good to think that Carole had worn her best clothes for her. Not that she, herself, had worn anything less than her best today, but she had the excuse of its being her birthday. At least today her birthday wouldn't go unnoticed as it had for the last ten years, when only Zemi remembered to congratulate her, but then years were of monumental importance to Zemi.

Zemi rode her bicycle into the church like a storm. Maria panicked thinking of what the priest might say, but Carole was smiling. She set the basket down and waved at Carole, who gestured for her to come in.

"Are you busy?" Maria asked. Cora was working on a wall, and though she looked her way she only nodded in Maria's direction.

"It's funny," said Carole, "but I always see you in different shades of light."

Maria looked puzzled.

"When you stood at the door just now," Carole explained, "the light was behind you, so your whole body sort of emanated from the light."

"Oh, dear! I don't think I've ever done that before."

"Show me the devil," Zemi demanded.

"Get off the bike," Maria told Zemi. The child got off and leaned it against the door.

"I rode my bike in here before," she said politely. "Carole lets me."

"I don't," Maria informed her. Zemi lowered her head, embarrassed, and Carole took her hand.

"Let's go see that devil," she said, motioning for Maria to follow her across the room. "This is it."

"It looks just like him," Zemi exclaimed, although she had seen the same picture a million times before. Maria, however, wasn't impressed. She had often wondered where Carole could put a devil in the Stations of the Cross, for as far as she knew none had been present.

"You don't like it?" Carole asked.

"I do," Maria insisted. "But what's that devil doing there?"

"What do you mean?"

"Aren't these supposed to be the Stations of the Cross?" Maria asked. Carole nodded. "There were no devils on the way to Calvary," Maria said. "Only people who acted like them. Didn't you know that? There were soldiers and onlookers, but no devils."

"No devils?" Carole asked, disappointed.

"I told you so," piped in Zemi, who had actually told her.

"Well! Hell's bells! I guess I'll have to put some kind of uniform on him!" And her expletives made Zemi laugh, which in turn made them all laugh.

"Doesn't Father Arroyo object to being used?" inquired Maria. There was a wicked glint of complicity in her eyes.

"He hasn't to me," Carole said. "Has he to you?"

"Never," Maria admitted. "He has only praise for your work."

"Maybe he doesn't mind being a devil," Carole added, and they both laughed. Zemi, however, went outside with Clarita.

"They can't wait to leave."

"So, let's go," Carole urged. "Just let me call Cora."

"I'm here," Cora responded without being called. She had been leaning out the window, talking to her fans. Since she had become Carole's assistant, Cora's status had risen among the women of Pozo Seco and neighboring parishes. When they came to church, they sought out Cora as a guide, and she gladly obliged them.

"Doña Coralia," they called her, which was their way of showing their respect, so Cora took them from wall to wall to show them what she had done and tell them why. In spite of her own reluctance to show the work before it was completed, Carole didn't have the heart to stop Cora's tours, so by now Doña Coralia was a local celebrity.

"¡Hola, Coralia!" Maria said to the woman who walked towards her and Carole with a rustle of skirts.

"¿Qué hay?" *What's up?* was Cora's greeting to Maria, who simply smiled. "Do you need me?" Cora said to Carole.

"Yes and no," Carole answered. "I need to undress that devil," Carole said seriously, "but I don't have the inclination. Would you like to do the honors?"

"What are you going to put on him?"

"A uniform or something. Why don't you see what you can do?" She could hear the voices of Cora's admirers exclaim in admiration. Cora returned to them triumphantly, aware that her efforts were about to save the painter from a grievous mistake.

"What's going on between the two of you?" Carole asked Maria on their way out of the church.

"Nothing," Maria answered, and that was in fact the truth, for Cora had not spoken to her since the night of their argument.

"She was awfully cold to you," Carole insisted.

"Oh? I didn't notice, but I did notice the girls waiting for her. She's become very popular."

"I guess," Carole agreed, but she wasn't convinced that nothing was wrong between Maria and Cora.

Outside the church, Zemi was waiting near the car. When she saw that her mother wasn't smiling, she called her to watch a few tricks. She sped off on two wheels to wheel back on the rear one; then she brought the bike down on two wheels again and took some sharp corners around imaginary obstacles. Clarita was impressed, and she clapped her approval from the sidewalk.

"That's great stuff," Maria told her, and Zemi rode gallantly ahead of her towards the car. When she got off the bike, Carole chained it to the bike rack on top of the car. Clarita and Zemi climbed in the back and Maria sat in the passenger seat, still pensive, her eyes staring ahead at the road as they drove off.

18 On Highway 180/62, the same one that had brought me here once, we headed towards the Guadalupe Mountains which, by the grace of the state, were a national park. Maria wasn't convinced that the park would offer us much variety from the desert scenery to which she had become accustomed, but she was pleasantly surprised. Although between ranges the countryside was open and treeless, the mountaintop was a different story. We were grateful for its cool altitude, conspicuous forests, and clear springs.

I took the bike down from the rack and unloaded the ice chest and the picnic basket. Zemi, who had never seen so many flowers, was debating with Clarita whether they should pick some or leave them where they were.

"Si las arrancamos, se van a morir," Zemi reasoned. *If we pick them, they're just going to die.*

Clarita agreed, so they settled the matter by leaving the flowers alone and admiring them from afar. Maria and I, impressed, urged them up the path to Guadalupe Peak as gently as we could. There, overwhelmed by the view of distant mountains, we spread a blanket on the ground and sat in silence.

"It's beautiful," Maria, who was leaning against a pine tree, whispered.

"Are we going to move here?" Zemi asked. I shook my head.

"Nobody but the animals lives here," I told her.

"How come?"

"Because it's a park, it's sort of saved so nobody can tear it down. That way, when people like us come visit, it'll still be here."

"Wow!"

"Why don't you and Clarita go look around?" Maria suggested. "But be careful not to fall."

Zemi and Clarita left holding hands because Clarita was a little afraid of getting lost in the park. Zemi, with her characteristic bravura, assured her that no one was going to get lost. Maria and I simply leaned back against our respective trees to watch them.

"Do you come here often?" Maria asked.

"As often as I can."

"It's very peaceful."

"And different."

"You don't like the desert, do you?"

"Not really," I answered. "Actually, I'm terrified of it."

"But there's nothing there." I shrugged my shoulders. "I even crossed it once alone."

"You did?" My imagination was already full of what had happened during that crossing.

"Almost seven years ago," she said, with a touch of sadness in her voice.

"Was that when you came?" She nodded. "Weren't you scared?"

"Of what?" she asked, surprised.

"Of whatever was out there, in the desert." She shook her head and smiled at me. "I know you think it's dumb, but I'm scared of it. I can't help it. I stare at it from my room, and even from there it scares me."

"Why?"

"Because it's so foreign."

"You haven't come to love it in the time you've been here?" Maria teased me.

"I think I've come to respect it," I confessed, "but I don't love it. It's too much like my father's landscape, I guess. We used to get postcards from him when he went hunting, and he used to send us stupid cards of the desert."

"How stupid?"

"The cards were okay, but the idea behind them. The man was out killing these animals, and he sent pictures. He also shipped home the heads of the animals he shot during his little trips."

"Did he hang them on the walls?" she asked.

I nodded. "Pretty disgusting," I said.

"But that's somebody else's desert. Your father's, not yours. And that one was probably in Africa somewhere. You're nowhere near there."

"I'm nearer than you think. I sort of carry it with me everywhere I go."

"Because it's your past, your history. I've done the same with mine."

"You still think of the crossing?"

"Among other things. Lately I've been thinking a lot about my family." She was staring at the mountains and losing herself in thought. Sometimes it happened that she left me like that, even as I sat beside her.

"What about your family?" I reminded her.

"It's just a shame that Zemi is never going to know them," she lamented. She seemed so sad that I didn't ask her why. "My mother was a remarkable woman. When she had me...actually, before she had me...she was thrown out of her parents' home because she apparently neglected to marry my father."

"Does that kind of thing still happen in Latin America?"

"It did then."

"Did she choose 'Soledad' as her name then?"

"That's what most girls did. It must have sounded romantic to them, but it also made a statement."

"Naturally! If you're going to throw me out of your house when I need you most, then I'm not going to keep your name."

"It must have taken some kind of courage for those girls at that time to go out into the world alone. But luckily, my mother wasn't alone for very long."

"Did she get married?" I wondered if my disappointment showed.

"No," Maria assured me. "She met a very radical woman, Rebecca, right after she started school, before I came around. Mother became pregnant during her first year at the university, so she had to quit, but Rebecca helped her out."

"What was Rebecca doing in Brazil?" I asked.

"She was a business woman. I think she ran her family business out of Río or something like that, but she was also a very radical liberal. She had been arrested in London for something or other, so her family shipped her off to a country where people could be a little different without attracting attention, especially if they were foreigners and wealthy."

"Why would someone like that help your mom?"

"Mother was involved in politics, so they must have met during a political rally. After they got together, agitating and organizing was all they did."

"Were they socialists?" I asked.

"Oh, yes! Dedicated ones! They organized the dressmakers, the office workers, the domestic servants, and they even tried to organize the street walkers."

"Tried?"

Maria nodded, sadly. "They didn't make it." I watched her eyes fill with tears. "Someone killed them in a brothel." She covered her face with her hands.

"Jesus!" I exclaimed. "I'm sorry."

"No," she said. "I'm sorry. I want them to be alive, for themselves and for Zemi, but all I can do is think about them. It's what I do around this time of the year."

"Did it happen around this time?" I asked. Maria nodded.

"On my birthday. The rest of the time I try not to think about them, because it doesn't make any sense that they should be dead, and because I can't handle it."

"I'm sorry," I said. "I don't know what I would've done if anything like that had happened to my mother."

"You would've crossed the border alone, like I did."

"I guess," I mumbled, too hurt to speak. She let out a sigh and lost herself in thought again. I stared past her at the mountains, the scars of ancient paths carved into their sides, and I marvelled at their strength, her strength.

"I'm in love with you," I whispered, looking away.

"I know," she told me. Then she took my hand in hers. "But I'm not sure about anything. My life has been standing still for the last few years, and I don't know what to do anymore."

"Do you care about me?" I asked. She nodded, smiling, her eyes almost caressing me. "Then don't you think a little happiness now could help you live with your memories?"

"It's possible," she philosophized as her fingers caressed my hand.

I shivered inwardly at her touch. "I'd like to try," I told her. She neither rejected me nor encouraged me. She just looked at me as if she knew she didn't have to answer me at that moment.

"Were Rebecca and your mother involved?" I asked.

"I don't know. I never saw them touch in that way, but there was something between them. That much I knew."

"Love?" I asked.

"Probably, but there was also the work they did together. It mattered."

"Love matters," I said.

"But it's not all there is."

"What does that mean?" I wondered aloud. Maria shrugged her shoulders to indicate, perhaps, that she didn't want to know. Unsettled by the turn the conversation had taken, my stomach growled. Maria heard it.

"Shall we eat?" she asked. I agreed with a nod. As she emptied the contents of her picnic basket on the blanket, I got up in silence to gather the children, wondering how it could be possible that love didn't matter to her.

During lunch, Clarita giggled and Zemi winked at me at every chance she got. They both knew about the cake I had baked in Gloria's kitchen and they were eager to cut it. Maria made inquiring faces at the two little girls, but wasn't able to get anything out of them. I had vowed to give them no cake at all if word got out, so they contented themselves with acting silly.

"What's that?" Zemi asked, pointing at my plate.

"Potato salad," I answered. It had been one of my contributions to the picnic, but neither Zemi nor Clarita seemed impressed.

"Zemi is not used to American food," Maria explained.

"Looks funny," Zemi added.

"Está podrido," Clarita contributed. *Like it's spoiled.*

"It's not! It's just a little yellow, that's all. From the mustard."

"I don't want any," Zemi said.

"Me neither," Clarita agreed.

"She likes it." I pointed at Maria, who had already served herself some potato salad and was eating it. Maria nodded.

"She likes everything," Zemi informed me.

"You should try it," Maria insisted. "This is real American food for a real American picnic." Zemi considered it as her face contracted in disgust. She looked at Clarita, who was beginning to serve herself some potato salad. She shook her head and took some of the empanada.

"I tried," Maria looked at me with a smile.

"Next time I make something, I'm going to ask for suggestions."

"I think you did very well with the potato salad," Maria told me.

"Yeah," I complained, "but you like everything."

Clarita and Zemi laughed. They were eating as fast as they could and still acting silly.

"Eat fast!" Zemi exclaimed.

"Why?" Maria asked, puzzled. "We're not in a hurry."

"We are," Zemi answered. "We want dessert." My eyes opened wide to warn her to be silent about our surprise, but I actually couldn't expect either one of them to keep quiet any longer. They had known about the cake all day, and they hadn't mentioned it yet.

"I didn't bring dessert," Maria informed them. Zemi and Clarita giggled. Maria looked at me. "Did you?"

"I told you I would," I answered. "But you're supposed to close your eyes before you see it."

"Close your eyes!" Zemi yelled, her arms flapping up and down in excitement like wings.

"Is this a joke?" Maria demanded.

"No!" Zemi screamed with joy.

"I don't want to close my eyes."

"But you have to!" Zemi insisted. Maria finally agreed.

I took the chocolate cake out of the box and placed it in Zemi's hands. As she held it, I lit the one candle on it. Both Zemi and Clarita took deep breaths in anticipation of blowing it out.

"Okay," I said. "You can look now."

"Happy birthday!" we yelled as soon as Maria opened her eyes. Then the children and I broke into our own version of "Las Mañanitas."

"You shouldn't have," Maria said.

"It's our first birthday together," I said and immediately regretted it. How would she take it?

"Mine's coming up!" Zemi informed me.

"Yes," Maria agreed, either to Zemi's comment or mine.

"Blow out the candle, Mom!"

"But make the wish!" Clarita added.

"Okay." Maria closed her eyes to make a wish. Before she could blow out her candle, Zemi and Clarita had done it for her and were clapping and yelling with excitement.

"Let's cut it!" Zemi said as Maria and I sat smiling at each other. She cut into the cake and handed the knife to Zemi to finish the job.

"That was nice," she told me. "I haven't had a birthday party in a long time."

"Why?" I asked as Zemi handed me a piece of cake. Maria's piece had the candle in it.

She shook her head. "I guess nobody knew about it."

"I knew!" Zemi argued.

"That's right, mi hija," Maria agreed. "You did."

"But I didn't bake a cake." Zemi said.

"Mi mamá me va a hacer un cake a mí para mi cumpleaños," *My mother is going to bake me a cake for my birthday,* Clarita informed us. "Y tu puedes venir a mi fiesta." *And you can come to my party.*

"You're having a party?" Zemi asked, excited.

"Claro," Clarita answered, "but not now."

"Can I have a party too?" Zemi asked Maria.

"We'll see," Maria answered, still smiling at me. Every little nerve inside of me was doing somersaults.

"You can make the cake," Zemi told me. She and Clarita walked away from us to discuss the party. Maria and I watched them excitedly plan the future.

"They really hit it off," I told Maria.

"I'm so glad," she told me. "I thought it was going to be hard for Clarita, but finding Zemi has made a world of difference for her."

"It's made a difference for Cora, too," I added. Maria nodded, but said nothing else. "Did you have anything to do with her bringing Clarita?"

"No," she answered. "I just told her what I thought she should do, but you can't tell Cora anything. She does what she wants to."

"I'm pretty sure that's true," I said, "but whatever you did to get her to bring Clarita, I'm glad of it. Cora is a different person."

"Yes."

I brushed the hair from the side of her face, and she turned to look at me. Her face rested on my hand.

"Happy birthday," I whispered. She nodded and smiled.

After we finished the cake, Zemi and Clarita went out to explore the park again.

"The kids are having a good time," Maria observed.

"Let's go with them," I told her, and we followed Zemi and Clarita along the path.

"Tell me more about your family," Maria said.

"Like what?" I asked. "I told you about my mother already." She nodded.

"But she's not your only family," Maria insisted. "Is she?"

"No, but I assumed you and Cora had already figured out my whole life by now."

"How do you mean?" she demanded, amused.

"Don't you and Cora talk about me?"

"Sometimes," she admitted, reluctantly.

"Well, I used to see Cora run to your place every time she got something out of me."

"So you assumed she came to tell me?"

"Of course."

"You are very vain," she kidded me, but the smile on her lips told me that I hadn't been entirely wrong. "So what about your family?" she insisted.

"They're vain too," I assured her. "Especially my father's side. They came from around these parts, but they wouldn't admit to it."

"But your name is Riff."

"It used to be Río and, according to Miriam, there are some Ríos on the other side of the desert that could be related to me."

"Have you met them?" Maria asked.

"No, but I may try before I leave."

"Oh," Maria said. "It's true. Your work is almost done." I nodded but said nothing. She seemed suddenly sad.

"I guess I'll be going one way and you'll be going another." She nodded. We had reached a spot that afforded us a particularly spectacular view of the mountains.

Standing behind her, I slipped my arm around her waist and kissed her shoulder, her neck. She turned around and met my lips.

It was a long and slow kiss which left me breathless. "So," I began. "Did you make any decisions?"

"No."

"Why?"

"I have Zemi to think about."

"What does Zemi have to do with us?" I asked.

"A lot."

"Are you sure you're not using her so you won't have to get involved?"

"I am involved," Maria admitted.

"You are?"

"You know I am."

"Then, what's wrong? Why are you holding back?"

"You're going one way and I'm going another," Maria reminded me. "I'm already missing you."

"I'm still here," I insisted. "And so far all we've had is a strange kind of courtship."

"What's so strange about it?" Maria demanded. "I thought it was nice."

"Not when you're so indecisive," I told her. "Neither one of us knows what to think about the other one at any given time."

"That's true," Maria agreed, "but that's part of the charm, I think. I mean, I liked you from the first."

"And you didn't even know you were gay," I teased her.

"I knew what I liked. I still do."

"Would you like to come over tonight? I'm the one who visits you. You've never seen my room."

"I have a pretty good idea what it looks like," she said.

"But you don't know what it's like to be alone with me," I told her. "And I want you with me."

"I *am* with you."

"Alone," I insisted. "We won't do anything you're not ready for, but I want to be with you, and I don't want to be interrupted."

"I know what you mean," she said. "Sometimes I can't even finish thinking a thought without being interrupted. Which reminds me—where are those two girls?"

We looked around and called out for Zemi and Clarita. It seemed unusual to talk for so long without hearing from the children. Before long, Zemi answered Maria's call and came running towards us with a bouquet of wild flowers in her hands. Clarita had to stop to pull up her shorts.

"Oh, dear!" I said. "I thought you weren't going to pick flowers."

"These are for Mom. For her birthday."

"They're lovely," Maria said.

"And they smell good, too," Clarita added.

"Let's put them in the Igloo water," I suggested, "so they'll be okay until we get home."

"I can do that!" Zemi ran towards our picnic spot with Clarita at her heels.

"You didn't finish telling me about your family," Maria reminded me as we followed the children.

"You want to know the usual psychological stuff about hating my daddy and that's what made me a lesbian?" I asked. I wasn't annoyed by her changing the subject, but I did wonder why she had.

"No."

"Good! Because it didn't. I hated my daddy because I was a lesbian, not the other way around."

"I didn't know you hated him," she told me.

"It probably wasn't hate," I admitted, "but I didn't have very good feelings for him. I remember his presence by all the prohibitions associated with his being there. When he was home, we were supposed to be quiet. When he wasn't, we could be ourselves again, and that usually involved a lot of screaming and yelling. Mother didn't seem to mind the noise. She knew we were a loud bunch."

"How many of you were there?" Maria asked.

"Eight," I told her.

"Amazing!"

"Five boys and three girls."

"Were you close?"

"Very close. My older brothers helped me get through college, since they're now working with father in the family business."

"Is that what you're going to do when you leave here?" Maria asked.

"Work for my father?" I asked. She nodded. "No. My father cut me out of his life a long time ago. But even if he hadn't, I wouldn't work for him. I'd work for mother's business, though. It's her money that's still supporting me."

"She left it to you?" I nodded.

"I'm what Cora now calls 'privileged'." We both laughed.

"Cora thinks everybody's privileged, including me."

"Well, I am. Mom had a real estate business, and she loved it. She'd take old, beat-up houses and refurbish them. Gave me my start as a painter."

"¿Pintor de brocha gorda?" *A painter with a thick brush?* she asked.

"That's what she used to call me, until I started getting serious about it. She made sure I could at least support myself by leaving me an income. It's not much, but it helps."

"And your father cut you out?"

"Out of his life, his will, everything. I don't exist."

"Is this because of…" Maria hesitated.

"My sexual preference," I finished the thought for her. "Yes."

"It doesn't seem right."

"It's right for him. Mother and I discussed this years ago."

"Your mother knew?"

"Sure, she figured it out, but she never asked me."

"That's so Spanish."

"Would your mother have asked?" She looked at me funny. "Oops, I forgot. Your mom was probably gay, right?"

"Right," she said, but she couldn't let go of my father and what he did.

"I don't worry about it," I said. "I just learned to live with it."

"How do you learn to live with something like that?" I knew she was thinking about her own mother's expulsion from her parents' home.

"That's who he was," I explained. "He wasn't, and still isn't, a very accepting man, but I don't have to deal with it."

"You deal with it all the time," Maria challenged. "Isn't that what your lions are about?"

"I never thought about them in relation to him," I admitted.

"He's the one who shot them and hung them on his walls."

"But what does that have to do with me?" I asked.

"Maybe you feel he shot you down, too. I don't know." She laughed, mostly at herself for playing analyst.

We were approaching the picnic spot. "Oh dear! Look where Zemi put the flowers."

"It does make sense," Maria told me. I was afraid she was still talking about my lions. "We told her to put them in water, but we didn't explain about the mineral water."

"It'll do wonders for the flowers," I said, laughing.

"We just won't have anything to drink on the way back."

"What do you mean?" Zemi demanded.

"Te lo dije," *I told you,* Clarita told her. "La botella del agua es de beber, pero tú nunca crees lo que te digo. *The water in the bottle is for drinking, but you never believe anything I say.*

"It's okay, Clarita. We have another bottle in the car, and this way the flowers will get home alive."

"You see!" Zemi exclaimed.

"But Clarita is right, Zemi," Maria went on. "That water is for drinking."

"Mi mamá toma de esas botellas," *My mother drinks from those bottles,* Clarita added. "Por eso sé." *That's how come I know.*

"Okay," I said. "Let's pick up all these things and go home."

I had expected the water argument to continue, but Zemi and Clarita surprised me and Maria by clapping at the idea of going home.

"They're acting very strangely," Maria whispered to me.

"It's the excitement," I assured her. She didn't believe me.

At the house, Father Arroyo was waiting for us at the door. A broad smile on his face and a wink let me know that he had done his part.

"Hurry up!" Zemi exclaimed as she pushed her mother into the house. I was unloading the bicycle, waiting for Maria to enter the room first.

"What is the matter with you?" Maria demanded of Zemi. The girl was still pushing her towards the bedroom. Once she got her mother there, Zemi yelled, "Surprise!" I came into the room behind them. Maria surveyed the room and turned to stare at me.

"Did you do this?" I nodded, not certain whether I should admit to it or not. "Why?"

"Because you needed a bed and I had the time to make you one," I explained.

"You shouldn't have done it because I can't accept it."

"Why? It's my birthday gift!"

"It's too much," Maria insisted. "I just can't accept it."

"But Mom!" Zemi tried to object.

"Well, there's no way I can take it back," I informed her, "so I guess you're stuck with it, unless you want to throw it out or sell it."

"That's not what I want," Maria said, but at that point I wasn't convinced that she actually knew what she wanted, other than to get rid of the bed I had made for her.

"Listen," I said, deflated, "Don't worry about it. I'll ask around to see if anybody wants it."

"You do that," she told me, and I left the house wondering why nothing I did ever turned out right.

"Well?" Father Arroyo asked when he saw me outside. He had not only put the bed in but had added a quilted bedspread that had made it look even better.

"Nice quilt," I told him.

"What did she say?" he asked expectantly.

"She said she couldn't accept it."

He looked hurt and confused. "But it's such a nice gift."

"But she thinks it's too much, too big," I explained.

"Well, it is a bit large, but it's exactly what she needs. There's no point to a gift that's not needed."

"That's what I think, but she probably thinks differently. Anyway, maybe she'll get used to the idea of having it."

"I hope so," he said. "A lot of hard work went into making it."

In my room, I lay in bed with my clothes on. I was cold, but I didn't have the energy to get up and close the windows. Closing the window would make me look towards her place, stare at the spot where she usually stood leaning against the door. I wanted to keep from looking, to lie in my bed and stare at the ceiling, as blank as my head, but my head was not blank. I was fighting them, but the events of the day were repeating themselves, as if my mind were a screen on which my life played.

Exhausted and depressed, I considered Maria's words. She linked my recurring dream of lions to my feelings for my father. The thought had never occurred to me. I knew they represented something, but they were mine, not an extension of anything related to him, and I liked to think about them that way.

"All that Freudian crap is just too easy." My lions were my demons, but I couldn't claim to know, as Maria almost had, that I knew where they came from.

I hadn't always known what brought them out, what made them come. I was only aware, sometimes more so than others, that at one point or another they would leap out of me, but it was never my choice. I was simply the instrument through which they came, for whatever reason. Something in me told me, as it always had, that the lions would soon return. They were about to crowd me out of my own room, my own mind, pace about, rub the silky down of their cream-colored fur against my thighs, and disappear as they had appeared, of their own volition, into my mind, leaving me to wonder why I had been chosen to bear lions of the mind.

To find out, I neglected to look in on my work. I got up in the morning full of good intentions and headed for the church, but I didn't make it. I had a premonition of approaching lions, and it occurred to me that for these lions, teasers as they were, the plaza, a crowded church, or (God forbid!) Gloria Peñaranda's cantina could serve as stages for their wicked antics as easily as my silent room.

Until not too long ago, we had between us, the lions and me, a sort of arrangement. It was understood that they would come to me when I was alone. Lately, however, they had become daring, indiscriminate in their choice of location, as if what they really craved was to draw attention. More than once as I drew a woman's face on the Virgin Mary in the church, I felt the lashing of a tail smart my back or my thigh. I feared Cora would notice them, so I didn't look back. They must have been there, standing behind me, watching as I worked and planning the strategy that would overcome me, but I didn't acknowledge them. I didn't want a scene in front of witnesses, which is why I turned back to hide in the safety of my room. I could feel, disturbingly, within me the urgency of lions vying to leap out. I chose to provide them with a private space.

I could feel them coming, but they hadn't yet come. They often took their time. It was part of their game, the teasing game they played with my mind. They wanted me to think they had control. They wanted me to think they could dance in my head, unrestrained, until something inside me which only these lions, being what they were, recognized as a sign snapped them into life and led them to jump out.

Thus, I waited. Outside my window, the desert spread beyond the town. Miriam, or someone who looked like her, was walking towards it. The bag in which she always carried herbs seemed heavier today. I regretted that she had no herbs for me. I had once asked her, indirectly, about their power, not thinking that they could help me to appease my lions. She didn't seem surprised, but was instead offended.

"Herbs don't cure no lions of the mind," she told me, the huskiness of her voice more pronounced than usual. I didn't ask her why, but I wondered. "¿Qué son?" she asked me. *What are they to you?*

"I don't know," I said.

People told me she could read their thoughts. It had something to do with her being half Indian, or with her being chosen, somehow. I didn't believe she could see right through me as if I were water, but she did answer questions before I even asked them.

"Go home," she told me. "You'll find out."

"How?" I demanded.

"You'll find out," she repeated, as if the repetition could make it clearer to a non-believer. That was two months ago, and I had yet to learn what I was supposed to find out.

Following the course of Miriam's path, I caught a glimpse of my reflection in the glass. I looked worried, nervous, even sad.

"It's never been this bad." It hadn't. It made me think that, perhaps, this time the struggle was heading for a climax. It had to end some day. After all, other people tamed lions, real lions, and made them work for them.

"I can do the same," I said, a little uncertain, and that was when I noticed, from the corner of my eye, the wave of a tail. I couldn't help but smile as something inside me froze. They probably thought me crazy to think I could tame them. To think I could control the surging life in them. I braced myself. At any moment they could pounce, knock me to my knees, relish the fight.

From the desert, Miriam turned and looked back at my window as if she could tell that something momentous was about to happen. She set her bag beside her and squatted on the sand. How did she know that it would happen now? Did she have her own lions to worry about? I always thought she must have, but I had no time to think about her now because, behind me, a fragile tail was rising and falling rhythmically, keeping its own time and lifting to the air colorful dust particles that flickered like sparks in the light.

You'll find out, Miriam had said. But how? I lost control of my senses when lions were about. I could not even control what my legs would do. Miriam fanned herself from the sand and held a mantilla, like a shroud, over her head. She could have been one of those statues that the faithful seek at shrines.

"Are you to be my witness?" I asked of my desert vision. She gave no answer. Was I to face the lions and hope to gain enlightenment? Was I to acknowledge them? To run into the hall and never stop running? Was I to kill these lions, as my father killed his, and be forever free of having to receive them, to open up my life to the whims of the mind? What would have been the reason? Was freedom worth the price?

I turned all at once to face them, but there was only one on the bed, his body stretched along its length, his tail rising and falling, caressing the air, unconcerned about my presence. His very nonchalance dismissed my consternation. His grace, his poise, in contrast to the chaos of my feelings, made me think that perhaps I had overreacted. Then he roared, his head erect and cocked as if to dare me. He fixed me with his eyes and rose to shake his head. The hair on his mane, much like my own, stood on end then fell about the sides, and it appealed to me, this image of his hair.

"You're a lovely animal," I told him.

The lion roared again, this time at me. He wanted to make sure that he had been seen, that I had not ignored him, that I would feel his presence as he paced the room, inspecting me indirectly without getting too close or giving up that space which he had claimed as his. So he pranced, gracefully, before me, inside my silent room, his agile body taut like my own runner's legs.

"You look so much like me," I told him.

And he pounced.

"Hey!" Cora said when she saw me in Gloria's restaurant. "What's chasing you?"

"I don't want to talk about it," I said. She must have thought I was still upset about a disagreement we had had earlier.

"What's with you?" she demanded as she sat beside me. I had forgotten to wash my face before rushing out of my room, so I must have looked a mess. She looked away from me while I blew my nose and cleared my head.

"About the way I acted," she said.

"Don't worry about it," I said.

"Are you okay?" she asked. I nodded. "You sure as hell don't look it."

I ignored her and hoped she would change the subject.

"Arroyo's going to have a memorial service pretty soon," she informed me.

"I know. But he can't have the walls until they're finished."

"They're almost finished," she remarked, sadly.

"Yeah. It was a great idea, asking you to help me. You've done a great job."

"You taught me a lot," she said. I ignored her praise.

"Maria was right," I told her. "You can do good work when you set your mind to it. You just gotta get pushed."

"What do you mean?"

"Well, look at the walls! They look great."

"I mean about Maria. When did she tell you that?"

"When she told me to give you a job."

"She told you to give me a job?" she yelled. I could tell she wasn't amused by the idea. "When did she do this?"

"Long before you talked to me. She told me I needed an assistant, and she thought I should use you."

"Sounds like her."

"What?"

"Her telling you what to do."

"She was just thinking of you," I told her.

"And that too!" Cora exclaimed. "She's always thinking of somebody else!"

"Does this have anything to do with what's going on between the two of you?" I asked.

"Did she say something to you?"

"No! That's what bothers me. You won't tell me what's happening, and she won't either. But I know something's going on."

"Uhm!" Cora remarked and scanned the opposite side of the room with her eyes, her chin, resting on the V between her thumb and forefinger, turned away from me.

"I can't begin to tell you how many times I've seen you do that," I said. She raised her eyebrows but said nothing. "That's a very characteristic position for you. It usually means you're thinking."

"It means I figured out what an ass I am," she answered.

"Oh dear," I said.

"I just didn't see it. She lied, and she made me do what I did."

"Maria?" I guessed. She nodded and changed positions. This time she crossed her legs and turned away from me. "How?" I demanded. "How did she lie?"

"She told me she wanted the job," she answered, "and I fell for it. I should've known she just wanted to make me do something."

"It's a good thing she did," I said. Cora ignored me. "Look at all you've done in just a few months, and the church was finished sooner than expected. I couldn't have done it alone."

"Listen," Cora said as she rose, "I'm going now. I gotta think about this."

"Sure. I'll be here if you need me."

"You're staying here alone?" she asked, her head cocked slightly towards the bar where Gloria Peñaranda was talking to her customers. I nodded. I didn't want to tell her that going to my room was a more intimidating proposition than running into Gloria Peñaranda could possibly be.

From afar, Miriam saw them in the plaza, their arms waving, their bodies moving away and then closer, as in a dance. *Por lo menos están hablando,* she thought. *At least they're talking to each other.* It had troubled her that neither Maria nor Cora had been willing to break the silence, but now it looked as if Cora were yelling and Maria listening, trying to explain.

"Coralia," Miriam said, as she approached the two. The younger woman had hardly noticed her arrival. "¿Qué bicho te ha picado?" *What bug has bitten you?*

"Ask her," said Cora, nodding in Maria's direction.

"She thinks I tricked her," Maria answered. Miriam laughed.

"Pues claro, mi hija. No faltaba más," she said. *You certainly did. What else could you do?*

"You knew?" Cora asked.

"Pues claro, I knew. Maria y yo lo discutimos, pero solo porque no sabíamos cuánto te llevaría el darte cuenta." *Maria and I talked about it, but mostly because we were wondering how long it would take you to figure out what she did.*

"But I didn't figure it out!" Cora exclaimed. "And you should've told me instead of letting me make a fool of myself like this."

"Coralia, you didn't make a fool of yourself," Miriam answered. "De veras, Maria and I, we're very proud of you."

"You've made a lot of changes for the better, Cora," Maria said.

"Did you tell her?" Cora asked of Miriam.

Miriam put her arm around her as she shook her head in denial.

"Tell me what?" Maria asked.

"It's not time to tell you yet," Miriam informed her. "But I'm sure Cora will tell you when she's ready. Right?" Cora nodded. "Just like I'm sure your lives will go back to normal now that she knows what a fool she made of herself."

"It wasn't all my doing," Cora argued. "I had help."

"I admit to tricking you, but it was the only way to get you started."

"And now that everybody knows what the other one did," Miriam interjected, "it's time you both hugged and went home. Don't you think so, Coralia?"

Cora thought about it. She didn't want to admit it, but she had felt forsaken during the time spent without Maria's friendship. She didn't want to examine her own turbulent feelings in front of Maria but, when she met her friend's eyes and saw her welcoming smile, she rushed into her arms. This was the same Maria who had talked her into sending for Clarita, the one who had listened to her cry, year after year, for everything she was not, the one who had tricked her into changing her life, and the one who had taught her how to read and write.

"I'm sorry about it," Maria whispered in her ear.

"I'm the one who's sorry," Cora argued. "I should've known."

"You couldn't," Maria said.

"Yes," Cora argued again.

"Let's not get into another argument," Miriam said. "Let's just walk away now and resume the friendship later, as if nothing had happened."

"She's trying to get rid of me," Cora joked. "You're so selfish, old lady. You want her all to yourself."

"I have something to discuss with Maria," Miriam told her.

Cora laughed. "Then maybe I should go back to the inn," Cora said. "Carole was in pretty bad shape when I left there."

"What do you mean?" Maria asked.

"I mean she'd been crying. Her eyes were all puffy and everything. I don't know what's the matter with that woman."

"Is she ill?" Maria asked.

"Don't know," Cora told her. "But I better go back just in case she wants to talk."

Cora walked away and left Maria worried. She had not seen Carole all day, and she wasn't sure how Carole had taken her rejection of the gift.

"Te interesa esa mujer," *The woman interests you,* Miriam observed.

"She's my friend," Maria said. "What did you want to tell me?"

"Ah," Miriam exclaimed. "You're changing the subject."

"I'm not."

"Has sido muy misteriosa con lo que sientes por ella, tu Carole," Miriam said. *You've been very mysterious about your feelings for Carole.* "No. Don't bother to deny it. I know."

"What do you know?" Maria asked, then thought better of it. "So tell me what to do."

"What do you want to do?"

"I want to hide my head in the sand and never come out again."

"And what good would that do?"

"I don't know," Maria admitted. "I want to go home."

"Home?"

"But I don't want to change things. If I take Zemi away from here, she will lose her friends, and if I don't leave this place..."

"What do you think will happen?" Miriam interrupted.

"I don't know," Maria answered. "All I know is, I want a change, and it all started with her, the way I feel for her. I don't know what to do."

"Have you talked to her?"

"Some," Maria admitted, "and I told her I was leaving."

"That's encouraging."

"I haven't got much to offer. There's no point to my caring for her when I can't make any kind of commitment."

"Why?" Miriam demanded. "And what makes you think she'll get in the way of whatever you want to do?"

"Miriam, please!" Maria exclaimed. "I can't exactly ask her to move in with me."

"No," Miriam agreed, "but you can ask her to move into Maria's house. All it needs is a few repairs."

"That's *her* house!"

"She's not using it, and if the two of you can repair it....Let me tell you something, before you forget. ¡Ay, hija! No me mires así. *Don't look at me that way.* Me enamoré una vez, pero nunca tuve el valor de decir lo que sentía. *I was in love once too, but I never had the courage to say what I was feeling.* I've always regretted it because there's no way for us to bring back the time. We can redeem many things, like bottles for pennies, but not what we let slip away."

"I know what you're saying."

"¡Pues, más me ayudas!" *So much the better!* "Pero acuérdate que no te dan ni un solo centavito por el tiempo que haz perdido." *But remember they won't give you even one cent for the time you've wasted.*

"But she's back with you now," Maria said.

"And we could've had all those years."

"I suppose you're right." Miriam smiled as she walked beside Maria. "What are you smiling about?" Maria asked.

"About the priest. He's going to be more than a little surprised when this becomes public knowledge."

"Maybe it won't," Maria argued. "Maybe there's nothing between her and me, and maybe she'll just leave when the church is finished. I can't think of a reason why she would want to stay in this town. Can you?"

"Yes," Miriam asserted. "Claro que sí, y espero que tú también puedas. Si no es así, ¿por qué te disgusta tanto el hablar de esto? *I certainly can, and I hope you can think of one too. If you couldn't, I don't see why talking about this upsets you so much.*

Maria didn't answer, but Miriam was right. Talking about the future, her future with Carole, made her nervous and upset. She didn't know what to expect, and it worried her.

"Talk to me, Maria."

"I can't," she answered. "I've thought a lot about this, but I still don't know what to think."

"Then stop thinking," Miriam suggested, "y deja que el corazón te guie." *and let your heart lead you once more.* "You did before, and look at what a lovely gift it brought you." Maria knew that Miriam was referring to Zemi, to that day in the desert when she let go of her sorrow to lose herself in love.

"That was different," Maria argued. "I was much younger then, and I was very lonely."

"But you liked that boy and followed your heart. Let it be like that again."

"I don't know," Maria said.

"Yes, you do." Miriam kissed Maria's cheek and walked away. She didn't say goodbye.

"What was that all about?" Father Arroyo asked.

"She was upset," Maria answered. Zemi had gone to bed in tears, angry about her prohibition.

"But she knows the pozo seco is too far into the desert," said the priest.

"She's only six years old, and at that age knowing something doesn't mean the same thing as it does at ours. I can understand danger. She can't."

"Well, I hope you made it clear to her that she's not to go that far," the priest warned.

"I think she understands that," Maria answered, but she remembered the dissatisfaction in her daughter's eyes when she was told not to enter the desert.

"If she gets lost there…"

"She won't get lost, because she's not going."

"I hope you're right."

Maria didn't answer. She went instead to her room, where she could vent her anger on her pillow. He always assumed the worst of the child, and it infuriated her because she couldn't defend her without sounding defiant.

Maria was the first to admit that her daughter was, by most people's standards, a little wild. She rode around the town on her little bicycle as if she were being chased by something evil, and she got into fights with some of the boys because she was inclined to defend her opinion, but for the most part, Zemi was a good, well-behaved girl. If her mother asked her not to go into the desert as far as the old well, she wouldn't go. Maria was sure of that. Father Arroyo, however, was never sure of anything when it came to Zemi or any other child.

He just doesn't like children, she thought, but then she remembered about him and Luz. Miriam claimed that he had loved Luz as if she had been his own daughter, but Maria couldn't quite believe it. If he had been so caring with a child five years ago, how could he have become as distant and as uncaring as he was now?

Maybe he doesn't know how to deal with his pain, she thought, and she recognized how he must have hurt when Luz died. If it had been her daughter who had died, who had burned in that fire at the church, she would have gone crazy, as Maria Selene had, and she would have done anything to bring her daughter back.

Poor Maria, she thought. She had left the town after the funeral because she couldn't face even Miriam, her best friend. The pain had been so devastating that she had turned against everyone, even Miriam, who loved her well enough to let her go.

The thought of Miriam's love for Maria and their own conversation just now made her feel warm. They made her forget about the priest and Zemi for a while, and she remembered that Carole was probably standing by her window at this moment, waiting to get a look at her.

How could I not answer her when she told me she loved me? How could I let her be the one to express her feelings and not even acknowledge them?

"You're an awful person," she told herself aloud, but she didn't believe it. At this point in her life she simply had no other choice but to reject love, if that was what it was, until she could stand on her own, figure out what she wanted.

She left the room and went to the front door. She leaned against the frame in her usual manner and sneaked a few looks up at Carole's window every now and then. Was she watching? Maria couldn't tell. She wondered what the room looked like inside. Zemi had told her about the canvases that filled the walls or leaned against them on the floor. Most of them were of her, but she had never seen them. She was tempted to go up to pay her a visit, to see how Carole actually lived, but she didn't know whether Carole would like a surprise visit. If she had never told her about the paintings, then it was probably because she didn't want Maria to see them.

Cora said she was ill, she thought, so she probably wants to be left alone. She wouldn't want to have a serious conversation if she wasn't feeling well.

I'll go see her tomorrow, she thought. Then she saw the shades on Carole's window suddenly drop.

"She was watching me," Maria thought with pleasure. Maybe Carole hadn't taken her news about leaving seriously.

"I'll find out tomorrow," she said aloud as she decided to retire for the night.

"Find out what?" the priest asked from the living room.

"What I'm going to do with my life," she answered honestly, but she wished immediately that she hadn't said it because he frowned.

"Aren't you happy here?"

"Not entirely."

"I didn't know," he mumbled, almost embarrassed. Why was he so unaware of other people's feelings?

"It has nothing to do with you. It's me." He stared at her as if more information were forthcoming. "But I don't know what I'm going to do yet."

"Let me know if I can help," he told her.

She nodded.

 It rained intermittently during the next few days, and the desert bloomed. Flowers grew where it seemed as if nothing could take root. It was a yearly ritual, this blooming, and I had learned to admire it. Patches here and there of four o'clock and pale yellow evening primroses gave the desert a new look, an almost inviting look. I would willingly have wandered through those flowers and been lost if only to find out how deep into its wasteland the flowers grew, for I found it hard to believe that anything could grow on arid ground. However, as Cora had told me, every time it rained, the desert covered itself in colors.

Lost in the contemplation of the living canvas that spread before me, I sat on a tree stump, and I must have been distracted because when Maria Soledad reached my side I was startled by her presence.

"What's wrong?" I asked. She was extremely agitated.

"It's Zemi. Have you seen her?"

I shook my head. "Did you look in the church? She goes there a lot when she skips school."

"That's the first place I went to."

"What about Clarita? Has she seen her?"

"She's in school," Maria answered, "where she's supposed to be."

"Where could she be then?"

"The desert. She wanted to go see the well."

"Why?"

"Because of the book."

The Little Prince?

"Yes. She thinks she knows exactly where the final scene took place."

"Oh, my God!"

"So she wanted to go check it out. She said it was near the dry well."

"But she promised you that she wouldn't go that far out."

"Promises don't mean much to a six-year-old, especially someone as spirited as Zemi."

"What are you going to do?"

"I'm going to find her," Maria answered as if the answer were obvious.

"But it's so dangerous!" I was hoping and praying that she wouldn't ask me to go with her.

"It's not that dangerous, but if I stay here I'll go crazy with worrying."

"But..." I started to say.

"Why don't you go over to the house in case she returns?" she asked me.

"Are you going to be all right?" I asked. Nothing, not even Maria could get me to enter that desert.

"I'll be fine," she answered as she walked away.

"Are you sure it's safe?" I yelled. She turned back and waved my question away. I was not even sure that she had heard me, and she was walking away so quickly that I knew she wouldn't hear me if I yelled again. After a short while, I couldn't see her anymore.

I should've gone with her, I told myself, and I thought of following her into the desert. For one wild, courageous instant, I broke into a run towards the desert that had taken her. I ran over the flowers and around them as I tried to make my way. I was determined to do this, to show her I had no fear, that I could risk my life for Zemi if I had to. Then I tripped on a patch of primroses and my opinion changed. Two inches away from my face, on the ground, was a snake. I stayed on the ground, paralyzed with fear, until I realized that the snake was nothing more than a twig.

Annoyed, I stood and shook the sand from my clothes. A little twig had instilled back into my soul the fear I had so foolishly pushed aside to follow Maria. I ran back to safety, away from the desert, and decided to wait for her at the house. If Zemi got back without her mother, I could tell her what had happened and wait for Maria. If neither one got back, I could ask Father Arroyo to send someone after them.

Maria's house was deserted. After I got inside, I felt a little cold. I wondered why. Her house had always been warm and inviting, but it may have been her presence in the house, not the house, that invited me.

I sat in the chair where she usually sat to ponder this revelation. The time I had spent in this desert town had been made bearable by her presence. What would I do if something happened to her?

"That's right, Carole," I told myself. "Don't worry about her. Think about you." Actually, I was worried sick over her fate in the desert, and I hated myself for having deserted her when she needed me.

I walked into her room and looked through her clothes. I needed her shawl. I wrapped it about me as I had seen her do; then I went to the door to lean against its frame. What did she think about when she stood in this position for hours every night? She knew I watched her for as long as she stood here and that more often than not I painted what I saw. She probably liked knowing, too. She had a strange and peculiar way of keeping secrets that sort of let you know what she knew without really telling you. So even though she had never mentioned knowing about the pictures, I knew she knew. Zemi must have told her. Seeing her mother's image on the canvases had made her happy, so, of course, she had ignored the promise not to tell Maria about the portraits.

The scent of her body on her shawl was intoxicating. I wound it around my face so that I could breathe her scent, not like perfume but like the smell of a woman. I thought I would borrow it after she came back, if she came back.

"Stop being morbid," I told myself. What could possibly happen? A million possibilities rushed through my head, not the least of which was her falling down that well, wherever it was. The first time she crossed that desert, she met the man who fathered Zemi. Cora told me she may have been raped, and there was no way of knowing if Cora's coyote was still out there, good and angry about having been stabbed.

"Hey!" Zemi exclaimed, appearing suddenly in front of me. "What are you doing here? And how come you've got Mom's thing on?"

"Where have you been?"

"Out!" Zemi answered as if I wasn't supposed to be asking.

"Out? Your mom's been worried sick!"

"Where is she?"

"Looking for you!"

"But I'm here."

"But you weren't here before!" I told her. Our conversation was slowly convincing me that I shouldn't have children. "She's in the desert looking for you."

"How come? She told me not to go there!"

"She thought you went anyway. She was really scared for you. It's dangerous out there."

"It's not so dangerous. You're just scared of everything. My mom isn't. She can go out to the well and come back just like that," Zemi said as she snapped her fingers. "And I can too."

"Well, lucky you," I said. Then I stopped to think what Maria would do if she were here. She would be calm. She would be reasonable. She would stop asking stupid questions. Wouldn't she? "Where were you, anyway?"

"At Miriam's."

"No, you weren't."

"Was too!"

"Your mom went there, and she didn't find you."

"'Cause I was hiding."

"Why?"

"Because," she answered, as if it were obvious, "I was angry."

"And now you're not?"

"Nah, Miriam found me and gave me cookies. She said Mom was right about the desert, but I already knew that."

"So why were you angry?"

"Because!" That was it. The conversation was going nowhere and my concern was growing.

"Now we have to hope your mother gets out of there all right," I said.

"She's not scared."

"But I am, and she's been gone for a long time now."

"Okay, I'll go find her," Zemi said.

"No, you won't. She told me to keep an eye on you until she got back. She wasn't sure where you were, but she didn't want to go looking for you all over again after she got back from the desert."

"I don't go in the desert," Zemi said, firmly.

"Well, maybe this time she didn't know. Why don't you go to bed? You must be tired."

"No! I wanna be up when she gets back."

"But what if she's upset?" I asked. Zemi considered the possibility.

"I'm sleepy," Zemi said right away and started yawning.

"It may be better if you talk about it with her tomorrow."

"I guess," she agreed and yawned again.

"I'm convinced already," I picked her up from the floor and carried her into her room. She put on her pajamas and got into bed, slowly.

"Where do you think he disappeared?" she asked. I knew what she was talking about.

"In the desert," I said.

"But where?"

"In the Sahara."

"No. It could've been any desert."

"Like your own, for example?" I asked.

She nodded. "Maybe."

"You think he went back to his planet?" she asked.

"I'm sure of it."

"And you think his rose was okay? They die pretty quick. Mom cuts them sometimes. They die like in a few days."

"But the Little Prince came from a special planet, and roses probably lived much longer there than they do on earth."

"You think so?"

"I'm sure of it."

"You think there's a little prince on earth right now?"

"I hope so," I said. "But I know for sure there are a lot of precious roses," I whispered as I kissed her nose and ran my fingers through her hair. "You're one of them."

"Is my mom one?" she asked. I nodded. "And Clarita?" I nodded again.

"Is everybody special?"

"To somebody else."

"Why?" she asked.

"Don't you remember what the Fox told the Little Prince?"

"Yeah," she answered, smiling.

"Then that's why."

"Did my mom tame you?" she asked, innocently.

"Yes," I answered. "She did."

"I'm glad," she said.

"Go to sleep," I told her, gently, and kissed her nose again. "I'll stay up to wait for her."

She closed her eyes but held on to my hand. She wanted to make sure I wouldn't leave her, but she didn't need to worry. I sat by her bed to watch her sleep, and I thought how blessed Maria was to have had this child given to her.

Hours passed and Maria was still gone. Zemi had fallen asleep soon after I put her to bed, so I sat in the living room to wait. I was certain then that something awful had happened to Maria, and it was of course my fault for letting her venture into the desert alone.

"Where's that damned priest?" I exclaimed. If he were home, I could leave him in charge of Zemi and go out to look for Maria.

"Carole?" Father Arroyo said, surprised, as he came out of his room. "What are you doing here?"

"*Me*? Where have *you* been?"

"In my room."

"You mean you've been here all this time?"

"I live here! Carole, what's wrong?"

"Can you stay?" I asked, jumping up from my chair.

"Yes," he said, surprised.

"Maria isn't here, I'm looking after Zemi."

"Isn't she with Miriam?" he asked.

"She was, but Maria didn't know that."

"No," he said, smiling, acting as if he wanted to discuss something.

"I have to go now," I told him. Why was he talking at me when I was in such a hurry?

"But where are you going?" he asked.

"Damn it! Can't you do someone a favor without having to confess her?"

"Yes," he answered, calmly, staring at me. "But what should I say when Maria returns?" I was speechless. I hadn't thought of that. For all I knew, there was a good chance Maria would return; she had lived near this desert much longer than I had, and she probably knew her way around. So what made me think that I could help her? All I knew how to do was look through my window, mostly at her as she leaned against her door. A journey into the desert was not something I would be good at, but the thought of Maria in danger made me decide to risk it all.

"Tell her I went to look for her."

"But," the priest added as I rushed out, "isn't she at Miriam's?" Why did he ask me that again? If Maria had been at Miriam's, Zemi would have seen her, and she hadn't.

"I can't explain," I called back. He waved goodbye as I broke into a run towards the spot where I had last seen Maria. On my way there, I passed by the church. The doors had been left open, as was the custom in Pozo Seco, and the light of the moon seemed to be illuminating the altar from inside.

How could it do that? I wondered. I slowed to a walk. No windows faced the altar, so how could the light create such an effect? I had heard the women say that Luz had come back to them, that she was, in fact, in the church. Cora had mentioned it during work, and we often joked about how the brushes and other equipment that we left strewn about at the end of a work day could never be found in the same place the next day.

"La Luz is giving us a hand," Cora would say in an attempt to make a joke of our bewilderment. And she'd laugh, but not very convincingly.

"It's the moonlight," I told myself now, because I could see, through the stained glass, a silhouette. It was clearly a woman wearing a robe, and she was walking from window to window.

"Could Cora be showing the church at this hour?" I wondered. It was possible. Cora's fascination with the pictures on the walls, with how they had developed, brought her to the church so often that most people in town were talking about her change of life. Not only had she given up her previous trade but she had also started dropping by the church on Sundays with Clarita by her side. After the services, she showed her creation to the women as Clarita explained what her mother had done.

At this moment, though, the figure in the church didn't look like Cora. The colors from the walls seemed to blend into the white cloth of the woman's robe, and as she passed from one window to the other she took the images along. Before my eyes passed Mary as she followed her son, but then she faded from the light into a brighter Jesus on his way to Calvary.

They seemed more like reflections of reflections, the playful fancy of the clear moonlight, and I became almost certain, for the first time, that it must be Luz.

"Luz," I called as I entered the church. No one answered. Why should she speak to me?

"I made this for you," I told her. I wanted her to know I wasn't one of the crowd who had feared her presence in the town after the fire. "I painted all the faces of the people you knew, so you wouldn't be alone. I don't know how it happened that the people got scared, but I want you to know I'm not."

She gave no sign that she had heard me or that she was there, but I could almost feel her presence in the light.

"Help me find her," I pleaded, and as I finished saying it I thought I heard Maria's voice outside.

I ran out of the church in search of her voice, but I found myself standing face to face with the desert. Was that Luz's message? Was she trying to tell me I had to go in?

"How do you know?" I asked. As had been my experience with all spiritual matters, I received no answer. If I could pray, I told myself, maybe I would know what I'm supposed to do. But prayer had never been a comfort to me. I just couldn't believe that anyone could hear me as I prayed, although Mother always told me that I had to have faith.

"Mother," I called. "Guide me." I had no concept of a religious world, but I knew that my mother, as one of the ancestors who looked after my soul, could be depended upon to guide me. Had I not kept her memory alive with candles and water kept in clear glasses since she passed on to the spirit world?

I sat on a tree stump at the edge of the desert to collect my thoughts. All I had to do to relieve my misery was turn around and retreat to my room, where I would be safe until the lions found me.

"I can't do that," I said aloud. "I've got to help her." I knew that my mother would understand, so I closed my eyes and took the first few steps. It was easier than I'd thought it would be, but I couldn't see a thing. When I opened my eyes, I was in the desert, and I could see by the moonlight that it was as peaceful as it had seemed from my window.

The earth, rived with life, groans from her bowels. Such is the awakening of a desert morning. The sand splits, sifts centuries of winded voices through the floor, lifts them through the stasis, and brings its daily offering of life to the morning sun. The light enters, mindful of its art, caressing with its essence the very air.

The gentility of nature puzzles me, for I live in mortal fear of its violence. It seems deceitful somehow. Since entering the desert, I have learned to mistrust even the light. What appears to be flickering fingers spreading out of the sun to caress me become steel rakes that cut up the ground into sand pits and crevices. I trip over them, fall into them, and finally find myself crawling out of them, reduced to my basic instincts by a pile of hard sand.

I had walked through the night but had found no sign of her. I had called out her name often, but my calls had been answered only by the flurry of fluttering wings. Immediately I had thought of bats. I could see myself drained of blood on the desert sand after being attacked by a particularly thirsty pack, so I started walking around with my arms stretched forward to feel the air about me as I moved.

Now, from where I stood, I could see no signs of houses. I must have ventured further into the desert than I thought, so it was safe to assume that I was lost.

How the hell was I supposed to find Maria if I was lost and on the verge of tears? I tried to be reasonable and think my way out. I examined the sky. Since I'd seen the sun come up and it hadn't passed over me, I knew I could walk towards it to get back to town.

"Good logic," I told myself, and it felt good to at least know more or less where I was. I resolved then to keep looking for Maria. I had gone too far into the desert to give up on my search. Besides, I was convinced that Maria was in danger, the kind of danger from which only I could save her. I checked on the sun again. It hadn't moved, but before too long it would be directly above me, and I wouldn't know which way to turn. I decided to walk away from the town, with the sun at my back, but as I started walking I noticed something moving on top of the mountain directly before me.

The shape didn't look like an animal...more like a man. "Jesus! A coyote!" A wave of fear ran through my body. Cora's story of her rape came back to me all too cleary. I shuddered to think that Maria might still be vulnerable to this random violence—or I might be. I sat down on the ground, my face buried in my hands. A tear fell onto the dusty surface of my boot.

"Don't waste water," I reminded myself, but as I stretched my arm to wipe the tears, the ground moved almost imperceptibly in front of me. I wiped my eyes quickly. Surely, the tears were making me see things, but when it moved again my tired body bolted from the ground and ran in the opposite direction. Convinced that something was after me, I ran until sheer exhaustion made me stop, but nothing could make me sit down again.

In the shade of a hanging rock, I fell to my knees. I would have given anything at that point for a glass of water or a way out of the desert. I realized I hadn't a chance of finding Maria.

The desert is at peace now, or so it seems to me, but it could just be the time of day having this effect on me. Over its distant edge, the last remnant of the evening's light begins to fade. The colors change from orange into blue, and then an even darker blue heralds the night. If I weren't so nervous, I would let the colors soothe me, caress me into reaching some form of inner peace, but as it is I am too scared, too frightened still to sit among the cacti.

I walked most of the day, in spite of my thirst, and yet I saw neither a road out of the desert nor a living soul other than the man I had seen, or thought I had seen, earlier on top of the mountain. Once in awhile, when I would look up I could swear I saw him again. If he was there, it stood to reason that he was waiting for me to get weaker before he made his move, whatever that might be. Still, I had bigger worries much closer to me, like the ground moving, so I only kept a corner of my eye watching out for him. The rest of me had to deal with reality. I had had neither food nor water since the previous night, and my body was beginning to complain.

Although I had followed the logical course of walking with the sun at my back so that I could find the town, I hadn't found it, so it was entirely possible that I had spent the day walking in circles. I couldn't tell. The cactus plants all looked the same, more or less, and even the mountains looked like one another. I couldn't tell where they were in relation to the town, but then my sense of direction had always been a problem.

On this night, like the previous one, the desert was cold and full of sounds. Clearly, animals lived here. If only Maria—or anyone—would find me and lead me back to town, I would put this insane escapade out of my mind and go about my business as if nothing had happened. I would get in my car and take off for distant lands down a previously charted path. I would forget Maria, who was still trying to figure out what to do with her life, and go meet someone like me. Though come to think of it, I hadn't exactly figured my life out either.

I looked up. From out of nowhere, a lion sprang. I fell backwards on the ground, paralyzed with fear. Was it sitting on my chest? The pressure I felt told me something was pressing against it.

"This isn't happening!" I cried out, but I was gasping for breath while feeling that my heart was beating much too fast.

I didn't have to open my eyes to see it, pacing about me, its body, sometimes bigger than life, reducing me to nothingness. I was the Christian chosen for this evening's performance, but for whom was he performing? There was no telling. At this point, however, I was past caring. I wanted him to get it over with, to tear me apart once and for all, to do what he had been threatening to do for years. A better opportunity I could never offer him. I was weaker now than I had ever been, and I would never let myself be this weak again.

"Do it!" I told him. He ignored me. I kept my eyes closed. I could feel his tail moving, the heat of his body merging with mine, but I didn't care. I was hoping for the end.

"Hey!" Cora, her hair wrapped in a bright kerchief, yelled from the church's doorsteps when she saw Maria. "Have you seen Carole?"

"No," Maria answered. Cora's annoying habit of walking up to people and not greeting them made her cringe. "Isn't she at the church?"

"What do you take me for? That's the first place I looked."

"The last time I saw her, she was sitting on a tree trunk staring at the desert."

"Ha!" Cora laughed. "We ain't gonna find her there."

"I wonder if she followed me," Maria mused.

"Into the desert?" Cora exclaimed. "Don't flatter yourself, kid. She's scared to death of that desert."

"You're right," Maria said, and yet the thought of Carole following her into the desert didn't seem unrealistic to her. She had so many fears, so many misconceptions about things, that she had probably managed to do the wrong thing for the right reason. She was just the kind of person who would go off into a desert to rescue a damsel in distress, or at least one she thought was in distress.

"What's the matter with you?"

"¿Qué?"

"What's that look on your face? Are you sick or something?"

"No, I was just thinking."

"Yeah? About what?" Maria didn't answer. "You don't really think she went in there, do you?"

"It's hard to tell," Maria said, "but she does believe in a flying prince and other equally romantic things."

"Yeah? I was kind of hoping she found herself a lover." Maria's right eyebrow rose in inquiry. "She didn't even come home last night, you know?"

"What do you mean she didn't come home!" Maria exclaimed.

"What's it to you?" Cora snapped. "I'm glad she finally got laid. The only reason I want to see her is because I can't work without her. She calls all the shots."

"So why don't you do some thinking of your own for a change," Maria snarled, but regretted it immediately. "I'm sorry. I'm worried about Carole. She doesn't know the desert, and I'm pretty sure she followed me into it last night."

"Why should she?"

"I was pretty upset. Zemi had been missing for a while, and I thought she'd gone out to the well."

"So?"

"So, when I found Carole, I told her where I was going. She was at the house when Zemi got back, but Zemi said she was upset."

"Well, I don't know. I still think she fould herself a lover."

"Don't be ridiculous!"

"What's so ridiculous about getting laid?" Cora asked.

"That's not the only thing on people's minds. I would rather think she's lost."

"Now isn't that something?" Cora observed. "You'd rather have her lost than in bed with another woman."

"What do you mean? And how do you know?" Yelling at Cora didn't make her feel any better, but it made her feel less exposed.

"Oh, for God's sake, grow up already!"

"What has gotten into you? You're so nasty. I don't even enjoy talking to you anymore."

"Well, it's a good thing we're not talking then! Because I wouldn't want you not enjoying it."

"Cora, what's the matter with you? You're so angry all the time, especially at me."

"I can't stand the way you stand around and do nothing," Cora said. "And don't look at me so surprised! I know I did a lot of that for a long time. Believe me, I know."

"So now you've changed, so you can tell everybody else what to do."

"Something like that, yeah. You pushed me to do all kinds of things I didn't think I could do, but when it comes to you…!"

"What am I supposed to do?" Maria asked, wondering what Cora was trying to tell her.

"It's not my face on all those pictures in her room."

"Is that supposed to mean something?"

"You just can't stand to talk about you," Cora said, the sound of her voice rising accusingly.

"Get to the point, Cora."

"Don't you know Carole's in love with you?" Cora asked. Maria didn't answer. She turned away as if to leave. Cora grabbed her arm, held her back. "It's plain as day."

"So?"

"So why don't you do something about it?"

"I don't owe anybody anything."

"What the hell does that mean?" Cora snapped. Maria pulled her arm away, but Cora followed.

"It means I decide who I love."

"Fancy that," Cora sneered. "You get to make choices."

"Leave me alone, Cora. I have a lot to do."

"You always do. You don't even talk to people, you're always so busy, but we're not talking about busy."

"I don't want to have this conversation with you," Maria said, emphasizing each word, as if speaking slowly were the only way to reach Cora.

"Look, I like Carole. I don't like seeing her alone."

"We're all alone, Cora. Haven't you noticed?"

"Pues, sí, what do you take me for?" Cora grew calmer. She had been so angry at Maria that she was having a hard time controlling the sound of her voice. Now, as she had done so many times, Maria had deflated her, taken all the anger out from under her by simply bringing up her own sadness. Maria knew she was lonely.

"I can't make things right for you," Maria continued. "I can't even make them right for myself. You're absolutely right about Carole and me. She told me she loves me. I told her I didn't know what to say. I don't."

"She's going to leave!" Cora warned.

"I can't help that."

"Don't you care about her?"

"Cora," Maria almost whispered. "I don't know what I think anymore, but can we stop fighting?"

"It's all my fault, you know?" Cora cast a quick glance at Maria then looked away.

"What is?"

"The fighting. I've been talking to Carole and reading some stuff she gives me and then we talk about it.

"Good for you!"

"Yeah, but now I'm angry—all the time."

"Welcome to the real world," Maria said.

"I think I liked it better when I didn't know nothing."

"No, you didn't like it better. Believe me, I was here."

"So how do you live with knowing?" Cora asked.

"You mean knowing that the world is run by assholes, that democracy has never existed in your country or mine and will never exist because the men are too damned violent to give it a chance, that we're very insignificant in the larger scheme of things?"

"How come you can say these things when all I can do is get angry? Did you think about this?" Cora asked, but in the same breath she added, "Gloria keeps saying I'm gonna be a communist. Hell! I don't even know what that means."

"As soon as you start to think, you become dangerous."

"Does it make me a communist to want something good for people?"

"It all depends on what you advocate, but I'm glad you're reading and thinking and hoping for a better world."

"I'm ready to fight for one," Cora confessed.

"Good for you. My mother always said that things won't get better unless we change them," Maria said.

"She was a communist, wasn't she?"

"And she loved women," Maria added.

"That too?" Cora said, surprised.

"I guess it runs in the family," Maria joked.

"So does that mean you're going to say yes?" Cora teased her.

"It means I'm thinking about it, but right now I think we ought to find her."

"She won't be in the desert."

"Well," Maria said, "we'll find out."

I woke up on the ground, very much aware that I shouldn't have been there. The sun was almost directly above me, from what I could see, for clouds covered most of the sky, but nothing could cover my thoughts about the man. Was he still there? I couldn't remember if this was a new day or the previous one. The phrase "unstuck in time" came to mind, but I couldn't remember who was the character who was unstuck in time.

Maria would know, I thought, and it reminded me of my purpose, my reason for being there. Ironically, in search of her, I had found a lion, and one more real than I wanted to even think about. Although I couldn't see the lion now, I knew he would be about. He would keep his eye on me and let his presence be known soon enough. On that I could depend.

I was tired and hungry and thirsty, besides being afraid. The fear, however, I could deal with, but my body's demands were beginning to get the best of me. The skin bordering my lips was dry, like scales, and it was peeling off like dandruff from my face every time I ran my hands, out of habit, over my mouth.

I'm becoming a pillar of sand, I thought. And what for, I wondered. I hadn't even dared look back when I wasn't supposed to, which wasn't true to form, according to the new wisdom. Women looked back, like Lot's wife, and what was usually left of us was nothing but a sand pile. We weren't just following blindly the orders handed down. Maria probably believed that. I thought I did.

She and I had talked about the way women do things the day we sat around and read poems to each other. In one of the poems, the poet explains the choice made by Lot's wife was because of her neighbors, her animals. She couldn't just leave them to their death. She had to look back. Hence, her fate. I can still see the smile on Maria's face when I read her the poem. She said she wasn't surprised by the interpretation, the notion that Lot's wife had chosen death over a lonely exile. Had chosen to become a pile of salt rather than leave everything behind. Anything was preferable, she said.

That was the day we talked about being away from home and about how disconnected a person can feel, and all because one did as one was told and neglected to look back. Indirectly, we had been talking about ourselves all along, although neither one could pinpoint with any accuracy who had issued our edicts. I remember leaving and not looking back. But then, again, maybe I had. Does it count as a violation? Violating a rule without intending to?

About ten feet away from me a large brown rabbit was chewing on something. He looked wise to me and a bit unreal, since he seemed to be smiling. I sat down and watched him. He looked me over, finished what he was doing, and moved on, unconcerned. Occasionally, though, he stood on his rear legs, looked around, found me, and then started off again until he could no longer see me. He could have been a spy for one of my lions.

I looked at the mountain's edge. I was sure I saw the man again. "Damn!" The lion, almost on cue, jumped me from behind. This time I felt the force of his paws on my back as I fell forwards on my knees and told myself not to cry.

"What's the point?" I asked the sand. A voice in my head yelled, "Walk!" I got up. His superiority established, the lion paced around me. I didn't even attempt to walk away from him. Instead, I moved towards him as he paced, his tail waving, looping itself around me.

"You had me on my knees," I said to him. He roared agreement, as if he meant to tell me that that was the point all along.

"You're probably right," I answered him, but then I saw the priest sitting on a rock, laughing at me.

"What's so goddamned funny?" I demanded. He probably thought I wouldn't make it out of this desert alive.

"That's all right, I guess, but I wish I could see her before I die," I told the priest. The image of him was oozing in and out of shape before my eyes. "I want to tell her how I feel, even if she already knows."

I stopped. The lion stopped too. He looked me square in the eye. "How do I feel?" I asked him. He moved towards me, threatening to leap, take my head off. I didn't budge. He was playing his role and I mine. Both of us knew what was expected, so we walked through the day engaged in the performance. When once, ahead of us, I discerned a bright, metallic color that I thought could be water, we went as one in its direction. He tried to trip me as we approached the edge of the water. I simply walked through him when I had to.

When we reached the water, I collapsed before it to drink with my hands. There were some peculiar creatures swimming about my hands; I ignored them. I was too tired to be concerned. I drank enough to quench my thirst, and then I walked into the pool fully clothed. The lion sat by the edge to wait.

Later, perhaps at night, I slept by the water, guarded by a lion that sat, as was his habit, close enough to make his presence felt.

"One of these days I'm going to eat you," I told him. I looked about me. The man was still standing on top of the mountain. He had a perfect view of me. I finally lay down, this time of my free will, and went to sleep.

"Are you ready?" inquired Miriam. Maria Selene stood by the window measuring the depth of the desert with her eyes.

"It's romantic," she replied. "What she did." Miriam nodded, although she really thought it was foolish. That Carole had entered the desert looking for Maria amazed her. Everybody knew her fear of it.

"You look beautiful," she said. Maria smiled, flattered.

"Hace años que no me pongo esta ropa," she said. *I haven't worn this in years.* "Limpiar casa me ha dado un vestuario nuevo." *Cleaning house has given me a new wardrobe.*

"No solo la ropa que has encontrado, sino la buena idea," Miriam said. *It's not just the clothes, but the great idea.*

"¡Ay! Miriam, ya sé." *Miriam, I know.* "Pero no protestaría por más ropa." *But I wouldn't complain to find more clothes.*

Miriam laughed at Maria's coquetry as she looked through the pile of old clothes for something else worth saving. She still had the flirtatious wild nature that had impressed Miriam the first time they met so many years ago.

"No sabes lo que me alegra que le hayas dado la casa. María necesita espabilarse." *You don't know how happy it's made me that you gave her the house. Maria needs to look alive.*

"Está enamorada, sabes," *She's in love, you know*, Maria said. Miriam knew. "Claro que sabes. A ti no se te escapa nada. Por eso es que me diste la idea de que le diera la casa." *Of course, you know. Nothing escapes you. Why else would you suggest I give her the house?* "¿En qué piensas, mi vieja?" *What are you thinking about, old lady?*

"En ti," *About you*, Miriam answered, the smile on her face widening as she leaned back on the pillow she had placed against the wall.

"A de ser algo bueno, porque tienes una cara bien pícara." *It must be something good, because you have a picaresque face on.*

Maria slipped next to Miriam and kissed her cheeks.

"Se nos va la procession, Maria," *We'll miss the procession*, Miriam complained.

"¡Ay, pero cómo protesta, Dios mio!" *My God, how she complains!* "Ahora que es amiga del padrecito... ¡Ay!" *Now that she's friends with the little priest...*

"Me lo merezco," *I deserve it*, she laughed. She and Father Arroyo had spoken about Luz's mass and about religion, more than once already. It had seemed to Miriam that every time she turned around she ran into the priest either talking to himself or, worse, to her. Maria Soledad had told her that she and the priest had had words, but neither she nor Maria had guessed that the man could change so radically, so quickly.

Maria Selene examined her friend's face and saw not the woman as she was now but the girl whom she first met almost thirty years ago.

"You don't have to come," she assured her friend.

"Voy contigo," Miriam said. *I'm going with you.*

"¿Crees que se quede?" *Do you think she'll stay?*

"No," Miriam answered.

"Ya terminó la iglesia, y bien linda que está." *She finished the church, and it's very pretty.*

"But she's in love," Miriam replied.

Maria smiled. "¿Y Maria Soledad?"

"¡Ay!" Miriam said sadly, shaking her head.

"Se le ha metido en la cabeza que quiere irse." *She's got it in her head to leave.*

Miriam nodded. "¿No te recuerda a nadie?" *Doesn't she remind you of anyone?* Both women laughed.

"Tal vez sea lo mejor para ella." *Maybe it's best for her.*

"¡No seas tan buena, mujer!" *Woman, don't be so good!*

"Pero María..."

Maria pinched Miriam's rear end and helped her up on her feet. "Pero nada. Vamos a interferir. Primero le damos la casa, y luego buscamos la manera de amarrarla a algo. Así se queda." *No buts. We're going to interfere.*

First we'll give her the house, and then we'll find a way to tie her to something. That's how she'll stay.

"¡Ay, mi amor! ¿Y si no quiere?" *But, love, what if she doesn't want to?* "Queriendo se nace," Maria argued. *We're born wanting.* Miriam shook her head and pondered the statement.

"No tengo la menor idea lo que estás diciendo, pero tú sabrás." *I have no idea what you're saying, but you probably know.*

Maria took Miriam's arm and escorted her out of the house. Miriam was once again reminded of the old excitement that Maria's lively nature always created in her.

"¿Qué tienes entre manos?" *What have you got up your sleeve?*

"Ya verás," *You'll see,* Maria told her and winked at her. Life with this woman could only get more interesting.

At eight o'clock, when it was pitch dark outside, Cora and Maria Soledad waited for the procession. A group of men carried Nuestra Señora de Guadalupe's pedestal, and in front of them at a slow, ceremonial pace, Father Arroyo, vested in his fanciest robe, led the way. Followed by altar boys waving incense and grown men dressed in white, the priest prayed as he led the congregation. He seemed different, more at ease among the people. The rest of the faithful, carrying candles and singing a song to the Virgin, trailed behind them.

"We haven't had a procession in so long," Maria said.

"He must have missed them," Cora replied.

"I did too. Back home, the processions were events."

"Funny," Cora said. "I don't remember anywhere I come from."

"That's not possible,"

"Maybe I was just doing other things and never noticed them," Cora added. Maria nodded and hugged Cora to her. Cora was one of those angry poor who had turned against the church as a symbol of everything they were not. "But you know, it's nice that the church is finally being used for the right thing. We spent a lot of time working on those walls, and it was for this. It's kind of nice."

"It would be nicer if Carole were here," Maria said.

"So who told her to go into the desert?" Cora snapped. Cora couldn't excuse Carole's behavior. It had put her in the delicate position of having to do her work, finish the church for her. She knew Carole would have been furious at her if she had left the church unfinished just because Carole hadn't been around to tell her what to do. *I never would've heard the end of it,* Cora thought, but she still found it difficult to accept that Carole was out in the desert doing nothing while she made the final decisions about the church. It was Cora, not Carole, who had finished the church, and it worried her that Carole wouldn't be pleased when she returned.

"She probably had something to prove to herself," Maria commented, although she also wondered why Carole had not returned. She wasn't convinced that it was a good idea to leave her in the desert to finish what she had set out to do. She had argued with Miriam about it, pointed out that the heat alone could kill her, but as was usually the case, Miriam's decision prevailed. And to her own amazement, the priest agreed with Miriam.

"She's a grown woman," he had said. "She knows what she's doing." And Miriam had agreed! Maria thought things had been much better when the two of them weren't talking, and she told them so.

"A man can live six, seven days without water," he told her.

"Perhaps you should try it," she suggested. Miriam and the priest both shrugged their shoulders and laughed.

"Nothing will happen; she is being watched over," Miriam reminded her. Maria knew she had to trust Miriam, but she worried about Carole's fears, especially if she felt alone, not knowing someone was looking out for her.

"Let's go in," Cora suggested. The procession had already passed them, and it would take a while before it made its way about the town. She took Maria's arm, and they walked together to the church.

"It's beautiful!" Maria exclaimed.

"Isn't it?"

"You should be proud," Maria told her. Cora obviously was. She had worked on those walls for months, and in the process she had become a painter, a woman sure of herself and what she wanted.

"I love these walls," she admitted, teary-eyed. "I have so much to thank them for."

"I'm so proud of you," Maria whispered to her. Cora leaned into Maria's arms and cried softly on her shoulder.

"¡Ay! I'm sorry I was such a pain before," she whispered.

"You weren't a pain. You were just changing, and that's not easy to do. I'm just glad I didn't lose you in the process."

"Me too." Cora was now crying in earnest.

"Oh, come on. The church'll be full of people pretty soon, and I don't want them to see you like this. You have so much to be proud of. Let them know it."

Cora smiled and wiped her eyes. Maria was right. Everybody knew that she had worked on the walls, and tonight everyone would be there to get a look at what she had done. She couldn't possibly show them anything less than her best, so she had to stop crying. It wouldn't be right to let them think she wasn't happy with her new life.

"Look who's coming," Maria told her. Miriam and Maria Selene had entered the church from a side door. Miriam saw them and nodded in their direction. Maria Selene also nodded, but led Miriam in the opposite direction to the front of the church.

"I think Father Arroyo is going to ask Miriam to speak," Maria told Cora.

"You're joking!" Cora exclaimed. "What's got into this guy?"

"I don't know, but he's changed a lot in the last few months. Haven't you noticed?"

"Me? I don't even talk to the man."

"You should start," Maria suggested. "He's different. He's even talking to Miriam."

"I'll be damned!" Cora exclaimed.

"Oh," Maria joked, "I don't think it'll be as bad as all that."

"You think Miriam will do it, speak?"

"Yes," Maria said, confidently. "It's Luz's mass."

From the street, they heard the sound of footsteps and voices approaching. The procession had made its way around the town and had come full circle to the church. Father Arroyo entered ahead of the crowd, genuflected from the front door, and walked towards the altar. He held his head high and seemed totally absorbed in the ritual he was about to perform, but he stopped at Maria Selene and Miriam's pew and kissed the women's hands. Christ, from His cross, looked upon him with kindness, and the townspeople who had followed him into the church followed him to Maria and Miriam's pew as well. They too bent down to kiss the two women's hands. That was enough to start Maria crying.

"I thought you told me not to cry," Cora said, sniffling.

"I've lived to see this, but I can't believe it."

"A lot has changed," Cora said, and she blew her nose loud enough to make her neighbors giggle.

"It's about time."

It was a lake bed I walked on. In the distance, its surface mirrored the sky. They merged without a seam between the spaces. There must have been a point where all things ended, but from where I stood that point seemed infinite. Such was reality. The shadow before me had lately been trailing behind me, yet I remained the same. So it was with light.

On the lake bed, the water marks were visible everywhere, but these days there was no water here. I wondered if that also was a trick of the light.

The lion roared. Desert warriors, their weapons drawn and anger on their faces—the grimaced faces of lion-haunted men—galloped out of distant clouds and faded into thin air. My eyes followed their shapes even as they dissolved. Only the lion remained.

The clouds above us merged into each other, stretched, and pulled apart at the horizon. My tired eyes discerned the familiar features as out of the light the priest leaped into form. He crouched and stood again, much as I had seen him crouch and stand during the many months when we had worked together, side by side at the church site, linked by our desperate need to belong. This time he was calling me. The ebb and flow of vapor on this dry lake bed made his arms unfold, as if to receive me, then withdraw back into the fold of his long black robe as the form leaked out of him. His cloak, like dark, thin air, dissolved.

Night fell, and a radiant crimson mantle stretched across the edge of my horizon. Darkness tamed the clouds. The priest and the warriors were contained within them until the light gave them life again. And still nothing was what it should be. That much I knew.

That the priest's image should tease me as it had didn't surprise me. I had always thought of him as a man, not a priest, and I had never forgotten that it was in his house that Maria lived. I had also not forgiven him, or her, for that indiscretion because I had no faith whatsoever in men, and it made little difference that the particular man in question was a priest. He was just too damned goodlooking not to notice the same good looks in another person, especially if that person was Maria.

"I can't stand that priest!" I burst out, and without warning I was jumped. He used the sound of my voice, raised in anger or in desperation, as his cue. This time, because I was so weak, I felt it more than I had before. Of course, it could have been that the lion had meant to do me in this time. I couldn't help but think so. I was flat on my face on the ground, and I could feel the lash of his tail cut my skin as if I were being dared.

"Damn you!" I raised my face to find his no farther than a hair from my own. He could have swallowed me if he'd wanted to.

"Why don't you?" I whispered. He roared. His eyes sparked with anger, or was it surprise? He must have been surprised because I wasn't afraid, and this was not the way that things generally went.

"I have something to say about this," I informed him. I rose slowly to my knees. He threatened, once again, to make a run for me, his agile body circling mine with just a few steps, prancing as if to show me the stuff he was made of, but coming, always, back to find my face, to search my eyes.

"I won't let you do this." He let out a roar, a mighty argument that before had always paralyzed me. When I got up this time, he knocked me down. Then I got up again considerably slower because my body had lost all its strength. He must have realized it then, because he charged at me as soon as I got up, my exhausted body leaning towards the ground. I saw him come at me, but I avoided him. Somehow, he missed me not just once but twice, perhaps even three times. He leaped at me again and again, from every corner of my field of vision. I was finding it dizzying to keep up with his charges and withdrawals, his attempts to surprise me or simply knock me down.

"What's the matter with you?" I cried. I was almost dancing, following his rhythm, chanting as he charged, "Not this time! I won't fall!" and laughing at his rage as I managed to avoid one attack after another. Eventually, however, I did fall, from exhaustion, to the ground. I landed on him, a shock to both of us, and I felt his body tense beneath mine, so I grabbed that sand-brown mane of his.

"Let me be!" I pleaded. He failed to roar this time, although I expected him to. His lips pulled back in a grimace, as if he were in pain. I felt sorry for him. He made no attempt to scratch me or get away from under me. He simply lay there, embarrassed in surrender, as if he had been made of air.

I rolled over on my back to release him. I wanted to conquer him, not kill him. He rose, majestically, and shook his mane. I watched him walk away into the light until I could no longer hold my head up off the ground. My eyes ached with the pain of dry tears, and I cried silently for all the other lions who had, like him, been conquered only to hang, stuffed, on walls.

I didn't know what happened after the lion left me, alive, in the sand. I did feel my body rise from the sand again, not of its own free will but through the will of a force greater than my own. I was moving, and my body was once again lingering in midair, falling off that cliff from which the lions had chased me countless times before throughout my life. Expecting to see their hairy faces again, I opened my eyes to examine the edge of the cliff from which they had always watched me as I fell to the ground, but the edge was empty, merging with the color of the sky, fading into light.

How could I be lingering in midair when no lion had chased me off the cliff? How could I be falling on my own? I couldn't tell, but I knew I was falling, floating down the precipice. Laden with the weight of years, with the certain knowledge that I would always linger, always be arrested in perpetual fall, my body hit the ground once and for all. I groaned and gasped for air. Crashing down felt like the wrath of years had conspired to grant me, at long last, peace.

**22** Startled into consciousness at daybreak by a bolt of lightning, I sat up in bed. At first I didn't recognize the room. It was dark and my eyes had trouble adjusting to the early morning shadows of a rainy day. I covered my face with my hands. The skin felt warm, as if I were running a fever. I must have been ill because my eyes itched and my body ached. I felt at ease, though, as if something monumental in my life had been concluded. Then I remembered I had to finish the church. My monument. I would have to get up. Thunder rolled outside.

I looked around me to see if the place was real. It was Maria's room, and my eyes clouded with tears when I realized what must have happened. She must have found me in the desert, much as she found me the first time she met me, unconscious on the ground. And to think I had gone into the desert to look for her, to save her from harm.

As I had seen her the first time, so long ago now, she was nestled in the old armchair before the window. Wrapped in the same old silk robe she had worn before, she moved me to tears. It must have been the fever, for I don't cry so easily. But I couldn't seem to help it now.

More than ever before I felt alone, lonely. She simply would never have me for anything more than a friend. Our courtship would be over with just a kiss and a dance because she was afraid. She had the opportunity to say yes to me, to let whatever she felt for me grow into love, but she couldn't make up her mind. She could pick me up off the ground and put me in her bed when I was unconscious, but she wouldn't risk doing the same thing when I was conscious. Choosing my love was dangerous, it made outrageous demands, asked for the kinds of decisions that Maria didn't want to make.

I wished it could be otherwise. I wished I could offer her the kind of security that Pozo Seco, tucked away from the rest of the world, offered her. But life with me wouldn't be safe, not when we would be daring an angry, insane world to give us what was ours: the chance to live in love. And Maria had rejected that life to go back to a homeland where the political climate had temporarily settled and where she would be temporarily safe. She may have been her mother's daughter, but she didn't have half her courage. And yet, I longed to go with her.

"You're up," Maria said, softly. She must have been observing me. "How do you feel?"

"Tired. How did I get here?"

"One of Miriam's friends found you," she told me. "He apparently kept an eye on you all the time you were there."

"From the top of a mountain?" I asked. She shrugged that she didn't know the answer. "So why didn't he just show me the way back before I fainted?"

"Evidently he thought you were performing some kind of private ritual and he didn't want to intrude."

"Why would I go into the desert for a ritual?"

"That's what I told Miriam, but she was adamant about our leaving you alone."

"Miriam doesn't know everything," I complained.

"Maybe not, but she said you had some kind of demon dance to perform. Did you?"

"I guess."

"Then we were probably right to leave you alone."

"But I could've died out there."

"I don't think he would've let you. He knew you'd found water."

"With bugs!"

Maria laughed at my complaining. "Did you go in looking for me?" she asked.

I nodded. "Pretty silly, isn't it?"

"I don't think so. I think it's kind of nice, romantic even."

"Oh, yeah. You're still calling me a romantic. It would've been really romantic if I'd died. All the old queer stories end like that."

"With a dead woman in the desert?"

"With the lesbian heroine, and I am the heroine in this case, dead just as her life is about to change for the better." I had no idea what I was talking about, but I was on a roll. "They couldn't possibly conceive of lesbian life beyond that first kiss."

Maria avoided my eyes. "What was your demon dance about?"

"About exorcising them."

"But what kind of demons do you have?"

"The real kind," I answered. "I told you I was afraid of the desert, but I didn't tell you I was also afraid of a host of other things."

"Like what?"

"Like my imaginary lions," I told her. She smiled. "Don't laugh. They were real enough to me."

"I know, Carole. But how were they real?"

"They came up out of nowhere when I least expected them. Actually, I did expect them, because their comings and goings had a lot to do with how secure I felt about myself."

"And they came out in the desert?" I nodded. "So Miriam was right."

I ignored the comment. I didn't care to know how right Miriam could be. I thought I heard drops tapping on the tiles. "Is it raining?"

She nodded, gazing out the window. Then she turned to me, eyes serious. "What do you do with lions?" She asked.

"You live with them, until one day you get into a struggle to see which one of you is going to decide what's what. Luckily, I won."

"The dance?" she asked.

"Yes, the dance."

We were both silent.

"I guess you know by now that Zemi was safe, that she had been at Miriam's all along."

"Yes," Maria told me. "I went to Miriam's too."

"So Father Arroyo was right!" I said.

Maria nodded. "He told me he tried to tell you where I was, but he said you wouldn't listen. I think you hurt his feelings."

"He has feelings?"

"He's beginning to develop them," Maria smiled at me. "Are you hungry?"

"Starved," I told her.

"You want me to bring breakfast here?"

"No, I'll go to the inn. Cora is probably waiting for me."

"Cora knows where you are," she said. "If she wants to see you, she knows where she can find you."

She seemed so determined that I didn't complain. I had no reason. It didn't make sense not to eat in her house after I had already eaten there so many times before. The problem was, though, that I was a bit depressed to be coming back for more of the same uncertainty, the same distant look in her otherwise gentle, warm eyes. The rain should've soothed me, but it didn't help. It just made me sad.

I watched her leave the room and then closed my eyes, listening to the rain. It felt good to know that I was once again within the scope of her eyes, within the boundaries of her world, even if that world was contained within the priest's house. Wherever Maria was, a sort of loose order reigned. She made me feel safe.

My own world was very different. I had no boundaries, which was why I'd floundered into this place so many months ago. Like the desert, my life had no set pattern. It would have been more logical if I had stayed out there, still trapped in the sand, than to be brought back to this room where I wished so much to fit in, and knew I couldn't.

"How come you're still in bed?" Zemi asked. She had sneaked in quietly while I was thinking. "Are you sick or something?"

"Something," I said. I had been wondering how long it would take her to get up this morning.

"Are you crying?" She sat close to me on the bed.

"I was, but I'm not anymore."

"Is it because you're sick?"

"I guess," I replied. She dried my eyes with her small fist.

"You want to eat breakfast here? I do sometimes, but it's hard not to spill things."

"I know," I said. "I'd rather get up."

"You find the spot?" she asked.

"You mean, the one where he disappeared?" She nodded, excited. "I saw a place that looked like it, but the book says..."

"I know. The Sara desert."

"I'm afraid so."

"Where's that?"

"Far away," I assured her. "You know where my clothes are?"

"Cora brought you new clothes." When I looked surprised, she added, "Yours were torn up and stuff."

"She just loves to get in my bedroom. She probably messed it up, and now I have to go up there and clean," I said in mock anger. She laughed. If anyone knew my bedroom was never clean, it was Zemi. "So where are these clothes?"

"In the bathroom, I guess."

"Breakfast is ready," Maria came in to announce. She offered me a robe.

"Maybe I should just go over to the inn," I said again.

"No!" Zemi exclaimed.

"You would rather face Gloria than me?" her mother kidded me, smiling. That settled it. I got up and put the robe on. Zemi took me by the hand and led me to the dining room. I felt weak, and being led by Zemi's little hand seemed like an act of infinite kindness. I realized then how much I would miss her, and my eyes teared again.

At the table, Father Arroyo hurried to help Zemi with the chair. I let him push it forward as I sat. Once his act of chivalry was accomplished, he sat at the head of the table and smiled at the rest of us. He looked like a man who was hiding something.

"I had all kinds of hallucinations about you," I told him.

"Is that good or bad?" he asked. I shrugged.

"What's that?" Zemi demanded.

"It's when you see things that aren't real," I explained.

"He's real," she informed me.

"But he wasn't in the desert," Maria said. She handed me a plate. I wasn't sure I could eat. "If you can't handle it, don't worry. It's hard to eat after you've been without food for a while."

"So," Father Arroyo commented, "did you enjoy yourself out there? I heard you were doing something. Dancing, was it?" Maria laughed softly behind the hand that covered her mouth. The original scene of my arrival was replaying itself in my head. I knew what to think, now, but I still didn't answer his question.

"Is that where you get your ideas?" he continued. "For work, I mean."

"Sometimes," I lied. Yes, I thought sarcastically, since I've been here, I've often gone to that desert looking for inspiration. That's why it was so damned easy not to get lost this time, padre. I was in a great mood.

"Milk?" Maria asked. I nodded.

"The church is practically finished," I told him, since I wasn't about to tell him about my lions.

"It's a miracle!" he said.

"Well..." I wanted to argue, but I didn't have the energy.

"It looks better than it did before," Maria added. Father Arroyo nodded as he swallowed.

"We changed a lot of things for the better," he said. "It feels like a church now, and the people are grateful."

"I'm glad," I said, and I really was glad. Erecting the church and subsequently painting its walls had given me the confidence I had always lacked. I couldn't deny that I was walking out of Pozo Seco as an artist, which was definitely not what I had been when I walked in.

"What will you do now?" Father Arroyo asked.

I shrugged my shoulders, shook my head. "I haven't thought about it."

"There's time to think about that," Maria said to me. Father Arroyo nodded as he chewed. I didn't remember his being such an energetic chewer. He was looking from Maria to me, and he seemed to have something else to say, but he didn't say it.

"You're going to carry stuff?" Zemi asked.

"Zemi!" Maria chided her. "She's too tired."

"What stuff?"

"Ours," Zemi told me. "We got this house, and we're moving everything. I already took my books on the bike." I looked at Maria for an explanation. She nodded.

"Maria Selene's house has been empty all these years, so she's letting us use it."

"But it needs repairs," the priest told me. "A new roof, for one." He pointed up to the ceiling.

"Well, yes," Maria agreed, staring at him as if she thought he shouldn't be talking. I was wondering why she was moving if she was still planning to leave.

"You're not leaving?" I mouthed so that the priest couldn't hear me. She shook her head.

"Not until Zemi finishes with school," she told me.

"What?" Zemi asked.

"Brazil," Maria told her. Zemi looked at me, probably wondering how I knew.

"We're going there," she told me.

"I know."

"It's gonna be great! There's a beach and everything."

"You want to get back to bed?" Maria asked me. I nodded. The priest got up to offer help.

"Relax, padre, I can still walk," I told him. He laughed. We had been friendly adversaries for so long that he no longer objected to the way I talked to him—without the gratuitous reverence his position usually got him. In fact, today he was acting like a solicitous waiter, which made me think the damned priest was enjoying my being an invalid, so I walked by myself to the bedroom just to spite him. Then I collapsed on the bed.

"Great bed," I told Maria. She rolled her eyes at me. "Are you taking the bed frame?"

"It's a birthday gift," she answered.

"Hey, that's great," I said. She grinned. "I'm glad you and Zemi get to have your own place."

"It's your place too, if you want it."

"I beg your pardon?" I said. I thought I'd left the hallucinating in the desert.

"Don't," she told me. "I'm the one who should beg your pardon. I should've said yes from the first, when you asked me. Instead…I don't know what happened."

"You told me you were leaving," I reminded her.

She nodded and sat on the bed beside me. "Yes, but I really do know what happened."

"You got an urge to run."

"You know about running?"

"I'm an expert runner," I told her, "which is why I've decided to stop running and follow you, if you'd let me."

"What!"

"Can you drive to Brazil?" I asked.

"Be serious."

"I'm dead serious." I was. Caressing her face, I said, "I can live anywhere, and if we can't drive there, I can always leave the car with Cora."

"You've thought about this?"

"It's all I've thought about since you told me you were leaving, but wait," I said, before she interrupted me, "there's more. I can help you live there. There's my mother's trust, you know. It's not a whole lot here, but it'll amount to much more in South America."

"Millions!" Maria joked.

"Not millions, but something."

Maria got serious again. "I don't even know if you'll like it there."

I knew she wouldn't recognize my feeble attempt at being practical, since she could only think of me as a romantic. "Why wouldn't I? I'll be with you." Her mouth was hanging open, and she let out a sudden breath that told me she was having trouble believing what I'd told her. "Surprised?"

"Yes," she admitted, looking at me strangely.

"Come here." I patted a spot much closer to me on the bed. She lay down facing me and took my hand, covering it with hers.

"You're cold," she said.

"It's all the heat I picked up out there." We laughed.

"I love you," she told me. "I don't know why it took me so long to tell you."

"Taming a person takes time," I told her. She smiled. "Every night, I stood by my window and waited."

"I guess I waited too," she admitted, "but that's because I didn't think I could love again."

"Zemi's father?"

"Not really. It's really Mother and Rebecca. They were my world and now they're gone. It's hard to love somebody when you don't know what's going to happen."

"But we never know what's going to happen."

"I know, but it doesn't make it any easier."

She was beginning to get that distant look of hers. "What are you thinking?" I asked.

"About Zemi's father. You asked me about him once, but I didn't answer."

"I know," I said. "You don't know why."

She laughed. "Actually, I thought you were being nosy."

"I was curious about the competition."

"There's no competition. I hardly even knew him. We met on the way here before we crossed the border."

"Was he Brazilian too?"

"No, Chilean, but he was coming across for pretty much the same reason, and it just happened. I was so lonely, I thought it was love. It wasn't."

"Where is he?"

"I don't know. I don't even remember his name."

"I don't know what to say."

"Say you'll stay until the end of Zemi's school year, and then we'll see."

"Okay," I said.

"You're easy."

"Fast too. Besides, it'll give me time to find out a few things about these people."

"Like what?"

"Like the guilt thing."

"What guilt?"

"The town's," I told her. She cringed her eyes and looked at me. "I had a funny feeling about those men who showed up for work even though nobody paid them."

"They came to build the church."

"That's what Zemi said, but I know better. It's gotta have something to do with the curse."

"Maria's curse?" she laughed. "What's Cora been telling you?"

"It makes sense," I told her. She was still laughing. I liked the way she leaned towards me and smiled at me. I caressed her face, kissed her hair. When she finally stopped laughing, I asked, "You think there was no curse?"

"I think you should stick around and find out how much things have changed while you were gone." She kissed me hard.

"Ooh, you make me tingle." She laughed again. "And you certainly are in a good mood."

"What do you expect? I've got my girl, and my other girl, and a house with a leaky roof, and plenty of promises to keep. But you'd better get some rest because, as soon as it stops raining, Zemi and I will come in here and take this bed out from under you."

"Oh, no!" I exclaimed in mock horror. "No sooner have you put me in bed than you're pushing me out."

"We can always carry you on it."

I laughed at the thought. "What would Gloria Peñaranda say?"

"It'll give her something to talk about, won't it?"

"You realize I won't be unconscious the next time you get me in bed, don't you? Something other than sleeping may take place on this mattress."

"I certainly hope so."

"I love you," I whispered.

"Hey! What's going on in here?" Cora entered the room yelling. Maria sat up. I hid my face behind her body.

"My God!" I complained.

"Your God!" Cora practically screamed at me in what seemed like fury while her arms flew in different directions as she talked. "Who left me all alone in that church to do your work for you?"

"Must've been me."

"Cora, really. Give her a chance to recover before you tear into her."

"Hey, I like the idea of tearing into her. Is that what you've been doing?"

"Cora!"

"Maria! Get over it! You're so damned virginal!"

"I'm not virginal."

"Stop laughing!" she yelled at me. "I wouldn't be laughing if I was shacking up with the Virgin Mary here."

"That's it! Get out!"

"I'm not going anywhere," she snapped in mock fury, snatched my pillow, and hit Maria over the head with it. "Except maybe Brazil when you take off."

"Oh, God, no!" I yelled.

Maria laughed. "Did I forget to tell you that?" Maria asked me, softly, grimacing as if she were about to suffer great pain. I threw my hand, palm up, over my brow and moaned.

"You thought you could leave me behind, eh?" Cora asked.

"I'll give you my car," I offered.

"Keep it. I'm in a traveling mood." Then suddenly she asked, "Which one of you's gonna make the first pass?"

"I hate to tell you, Cora," I said, "but we're way beyond the first pass. We're pregnant."

"¡Ay, Dios mio! How did you guys do that?"

"You'll be traveling with two people fully accomplished in deception," I told her.

"What the hell's she talking about?" Cora asked Maria.

Maria's face was changing colors. "She thinks we'll corrupt you," Maria explained.

"Yeah? I'll be that little woman on the devil's shoulder! This is gonna be some trip!"

"I give up," I told Maria.

"Listen, sweetie, I know you love me, but you're sure you wanna take up with her?" Cora said, cocking her head in Maria's direction.

"I'm sure."

"But she's so damned goody-goody, don't you think?"

"Hey! What about the church?" I had to get Cora off this subject. "Did you finish it?"

"No thanks to you," Cora answered, pleased with herself. "I had to ask Lupita y Conchita to help me clean up your mess, and you are one of the messiest people."

"You asked Lupita and Conchita what?"

"To clean up after you, the day before the mass."

"So the church was ready?"

"¡Claro! We told you already. He had the mass."

"Yeah, but you didn't tell me you'd finished it. I'm really proud of you, Cora...and grateful. Thanks."

"Oh, cut it out!" Cora told me, but she was clearly pleased. She shrugged her shoulders and shook her hair back, which was what she did when she was self-consciously happy, as if she were standing in front of a mirror, admiring herself.

"Let's leave Carole alone," Maria said. "She needs to rest."

"You just want to get on with the move," Cora said, "but I don't blame you."

"I'm going with you," I said.

"Oh, that's great," Cora joked. "You can sit in the house and give orders. You're plenty good at that."

"I can pull my own weight," I informed her.

"But you just got out of the desert," Maria said.

"Keep that woman in bed!" Cora ordered.

"I'm fine," I told Maria. "And besides, I want to see our new home."

"*Our* new home!" Cora exclaimed.

"I told you we were beyond the first pass. You'll just have to get used to the fact that you don't know everything there is to know about us. I mean, we had a major, important, committed relationship in front of your eyes, and you didn't even notice."

"Bull!" Cora argued. "The two of you had zero going for each other until I told this fool to go for it."

"Which fool?" Maria asked indignantly.

"You've had the hots for Carole from day one!" Cora insisted in her loudest, most argumentative voice.

Maria was laughing nervously. "You can't keep a secret for anything," she mumbled, but she wasn't upset. She drew Cora to her side and hugged her warmly. Cora was suspicious.

"From day one?" I asked.

Maria ignored me. "But you're right, Cora. I have you to thank. You pushed me to make a decision, and I'm glad I made it."

"I did?" Cora wondered. Maria laughed again.

"I'm just glad the two of you are friends again," I said.

"What do you know? We've been friends forever," Cora told me.

"Go away," I told her. "I wanna get dressed."

"Don't I get to see you naked?" she asked, feigning excitement.

"Not in this lifetime," Maria answered, and the two of them left the room as Cora joked about how possessive Maria had become.

I lay in bed, the quiet settling over me after all the excitement, laughter, loud voices. It seemed incredible. While I was out in the desert exorcising my demons, Maria had gone through the real task of finding us a home. I had fallen in love with the woman, but the ordinary, mundane part of everyday living hadn't entered my mind.

What did I think would have happened if Maria had said yes from the first? If she had reciprocated my affection and decided to live with me? Where would we have gone? What would we have lived on? Mother's trust fund provided each of her children with $350 a month, which wasn't enough for one person, much less three, and neither Maria nor I was terribly employable. She had no papers, and I wasn't qualified to do very much of anything.

Maria, on the other hand, was as realistic as they come. Having to fend for herself all these years had forced her to be grounded in the reality of everyday living. And that was probably the reason why she accused me of being a romantic. She said it playfully, almost in jest, but to someone like her being a romantic must have seemed archaic, not to mention impractical. She must have wondered how romantics survived the task of living in the real world. I would probably wonder too, now that I'd met her. Surely, life with her would teach me many lessons.

I got up, got dressed, and left the bedroom wondering where Zemi was. I hadn't heard her voice since breakfast.

"Are you sure you're okay?" Maria asked me as soon as she saw me. I nodded, smiling. Maria slipped her arm around my waist and held me. Cora was throwing kisses into the air, acting disgusted to see us in love.

"Get used to it," I told her. She moaned and left the house saying she would wait for the rain to let up before she came back for the rest of the boxes.

"Where's Zemi?" I asked.

"Zemi hasn't stopped riding to the new house since yesterday, when Maria told us we could use it. She wanted to move in immediately. She doesn't know about packing and moving a household."

"And what does Father Arroyo have to say about all this?"

"He's out there fixing the roof."

"Our Father?"

"Not my father," she joked.

"What does he know about roofs?"

"Excuse me, but he just finished building a church. He considers himself handy with a hammer these days."

"I can just hear the sermons from now on," I said and grimaced at the thought.

"Well, dear," Maria said as she slipped her arms around my waist and held me close, "you'll just have to go hear them all alone, because I'm not the church-going type."

We held each other long, easily, comfortable in each other's arms for the first time, and Maria leaned her head on my shoulder to whisper lovingwords into my ear. My body tingled from head to toe, which only made me hold her closer and think of the years to come in the narrow, all-encompassing circumference of her strong, loving arms. It didn't matter where our journey took us, as long as we could make it together.

Outside, the sun was breaking through a line of lavender clouds. In the distance, the rolling deep rumble of thunder could still be heard. Showering a promise of life's renewal, the light fell through breaks in the clouds like magic, like a benediction granted by life-giving sources, over our home, our desert, our little lot of land in our brand-new world.

"If it keeps sprinkling, there'll be a rainbow," Maria told me. We had stepped outside together, our arms still linked behind the other's waist, and headed for the edge of town where Maria Selene's old house leaked rain water through the roof.

"El arco iris," Maria whispered as she gestured to the arch of colors spreading over the sky, over our desert, against the backdrop of clouds struggling to float through it, deliver rain, alter the complacency of the still-life landscape.

Under the spreading colors, we could see Zemi and Clarita riding their bikes, their arms spread out towards the sky, taking in the rain. They would both want to chase the rainbow's end, and they would ride the town in awe of the mystery, the magic, the colors. A few daring birds, scratching on a patch of dirt near the house, stopped and jumped as Zemi and Clarita rode nearby with Miriam's dogs chasing after them. The dogs ran playfully towards the birds, who rose off the ground momentarily like a blue and purple-black cloud. The bikes passed and the dogs gave chase again. The birds resumed their picking at the ground, their meticulous scratching, and their stretching of heads to see if anything else was forthcoming from the woman who not too far away from them was spitting watermelon seeds in their direction.

Sitting on the front steps of the house with her skirt tucked unladylike between her legs, Cora, soaked by the rain, was admiring the crazy alchemy of the sky. She must have seen it a million times through the years, but it had never told her before that anything was possible under the raging glory of such a morning's colors.

Miriam and Maria Selene stepped out onto the porch and spoke to Cora, handing her another slice of watermelon. Maria and I stopped to take in the scene. We were at an angle from both the house and the girls on their bikes, far enough to be unnoticed but close enough to see the playing, happy children, the hungry birds, the dogs, thoughtful Cora sitting at our front steps, Maria and Miriam generously granting us this space and the priest, hammering on the roof, in the rain, at the back of the house.

"There it is…." Maria said.

"Our home," I finished for her.

   She nodded and held my eyes long and deeply with her own, looking perhaps for promises we both had longed to make. "For now."
   I held her close, hugged her, and we walked again towards the house, the angle broken, a circle in its place—a circle about to grow.